Olivier Lafont is a French author, screenplay writer, and actor living in Paris. His fantasy novel *Warrior* was published by Penguin Random House, and was shortlisted for the Tibor Jones South Asia Prize. His other works include *Sweet Revenge*, a contemporary romance novel, *Snowbound*, a fantasy young adult novel, and *Purgatory: The Gun of God*, a fantasy novelette. The first film he wrote, an Indo-French comedy, opened at the Toronto Film Festival and went on to win seven awards at film festivals worldwide. As an actor Lafont has worked in Hollywood and Indian films, in TV serials, and in over eighty television commercials. He has acted in the films *3 Idiots* and *Guzaarish*, amongst others. Lafont graduated with degrees in English Literature and in Theatre from Colgate University, USA, with academic distinction.

THE RISE OF THE
MIDNIGHT KING

{ BOOK 1 IN THE **KUMAON SECRET SOCIETY** SERIES }

OLIVIER LAFONT

An Imprint of Speaking Tiger

TALKING CUB

Published by Speaking Tiger Publishing Pvt. Ltd
4381/4, Ansari Road, Daryaganj

New Delhi 110002

First published in paperback in Talking Cub
by Speaking Tiger in 2019

Copyright © Olivier Lafont 2019

ISBN: 978-93-88874-99-1

eISBN: 978-93-88874-98-4

10 9 8 7 6 5 4 3 2 1

The moral right of the author has been asserted.

For Gina

CONTENTS

1
THE VILLAGE ON THE HILL

Somewhere between rocky Garhwal and green Kumaon lies a strange little village on a hill called Devagarh. In the winter it's not easy to live in because of the snow, but on a summer day like today it's bliss on earth. The village people go about their business with all the purpose of a life guided by the seasons and the rising and setting of the golden sun. For the few visitors who come, however, it can be sheer torture.

Isaac Shroff, for example, could think of few things duller than sitting on the grass of the empty cricket pitch and watching two clouds race each other across a perfect blue sky. He had been there for a good twenty minutes now, ever since his aunt and her friends had ushered him out of the Lodge to search for the strangers they insisted would become his best friends. The next time he looked down from his slow daydreams of immaculate English hedgerows and lawns back home, there they were. Or at least two of them.

They were two girls, one clearly older than the other, both in scuffed jeans and T-shirt. The older one was tall and thin, her hair long and braided into a tight ponytail. She stood with hands on her hips and legs apart, eyeing him critically with large, fierce eyes and spiky eyebrows. The younger one copied the older one, although the ferocious expression she tried to emulate just looked funny on her babyish face. Her hair was shorter and loose, hanging about her plump pink cheeks.

'You must be Isaac,' the older one called out boldly.

Isaac stood up nervously. 'Yes. You're Tal?'

She nodded. 'This is Trikaya—Tri. You're Jyoti Auntie's nephew?'

'Yes.'

They stood there for a moment, Isaac twisting the same blade of grass he had been playing with for the last five minutes.

'Okay,' Tal said, and jerked her head towards the village up the slope. 'Come on.'

And that was that. Isaac joined the two girls, and he had to hustle to keep up with their brisk walk. 'You're eleven, right?' Trikaya asked chirpily, forgetting her harsh demeanour in the excitement of meeting a new person. Isaac bobbed his head, and she nodded solemnly. 'I'm ten,' she said with half a pout. 'I'll always be younger than everyone.'

'How old is… How old are you, Tal?' Isaac asked, since these were obviously the points of conversational interest.

Tal glanced back over the shoulder of her bright yellow T-shirt. 'Eleven.'

By now they were approaching the village, heading towards the main avenue from one of the side streets. The houses in Devagarh were mostly large two-storey rectangles, painted white with grey slate roofs, but there were also a few built of grey-brown bricks. Each house stood on its own terraced expanse, a little away from the next property. Isaac liked the simplicity of the architecture, reminding him of English villages in the country.

They turned onto the main avenue and fell immediately

upon a large square where a church, a temple, a mosque and a Buddhist stupa faced each other. It was the oddest collection, and Isaac had to pause to take it all in. Which was fine since Tal told them to wait before trotting into the temple and disappearing inside, leaving him with Trikaya.

'You're half English, right?' she asked immediately.

'Yes,' he answered. He didn't usually like people inquiring about him and his origins, but there was something sweet about Trikaya's questioning. 'Where is everyone else?'

Trikaya glanced anxiously towards the temple and shushed him with a flap of her hand. 'Don't mention it!' she hissed. 'They've fought and split the Society.'

'The Society?'

Trikaya's face looked distressed. 'The Society? This Society, our Society. Your Society too, now.'

Isaac's head cocked outrageously to the side, as it did when he tried to puzzle things out. 'I'm sorry... My Society?'

'Yes,' Trikaya emphasized as though he were questioning that the sky was blue. 'Our Society. The Kumaon Secret Society.' She rolled her eyes. 'It's okay, you don't know, let me explain...'

But Tal jumped out of the side of the temple just then, a dangerous one-metre drop that had Isaac nearly cry out with fear. Tal brushed her hands in a business-like manner as she strode up to them. 'Right. To Mrs Dangwal's.'

Tal headed back up the avenue, and they had no choice but to follow.

'What's the job?' Trikaya asked.

'Same as last time,' Tal replied.

Trikaya rolled her eyes and sighed.

'Where are we going?' Isaac finally managed to ask.

'Mrs Dangwal's,' Trikaya said.

'Yes, I heard, but why? And, look, can we just stop for a minute!' he cried out, panting.

The two girls stopped, startled.

'I don't know how you do things round here,' Isaac continued, his cheeks heating up, 'But I'm new and I'd think you'd have the courtesy to at least let me know what's going on! I have no idea why we're going to Mrs Dangwal's, what this Kumaon Secret Society is, or why we're walking so fast, and I'd like to know!'

They watched him with wide eyes for another few seconds, as though he was beginning to sprout rabbit ears, and then they exchanged a look that apparently decided something.

Tal put her hands on her hips. It seemed to be her usual stance. 'There's…a bit of a crisis in the KSS.'

'Shari thinks we shouldn't charge for the work we do,' Trikaya explained. 'Tal said we should, and I agree with her. But Iti and Safir sided with Shari.'

'Okay…' Isaac blinked, trying to sort out the names.

'So he broke the KSS,' Tal said huskily.

Isaac suddenly realized that Tal was playing up her anger and fierceness. He could see she was actually upset, and it made him feel sorry for her, that something that meant so much to her was ruined.

Before he could say anything, however, Tal made a fist and shook it before her. 'But I'll show him. We're going to get the job done before him. And then we'll split the money three ways, forget them. Trikaya, you and I, we're making our own Society.' She hesitated, then, her features softened, and Isaac could see what a pretty face she had. 'I'm sorry,' she said, shaking her head. 'I just assumed… Isaac, would you like to join our new Society?'

Isaac looked at Tal, the hidden yearning in her big round eyes, and then at Trikaya, who had just now realized Tal was in her stance, and hurried to stand the same way.

He shrugged, grinned, and said, 'Of course I would. What's it called?'

Tal let out a burst of excited laughter, and Trikaya clapped her hands in joy. 'It's called…' Tal said, drawing it out for drama, 'The *Real* Kumaon Secret Society.'

2

OF CATS AND MEN

Mrs Dangwal's house stood out from the rest of the village, with its bright entrance and balconies of pink wood set against the grey bricks of its walls. It was on the uphill side of town, removed from the main avenue, and had one big apple tree that was blazing with gentle pink flowers.

Tal led Trikaya and the new boy to the house and knocked. While they waited she pretended to scan the sky, and took a look at this Isaac Shroff. He was a slender boy, with unruly hair, good features, and an open demeanour. He would have been just a regular good-looking kid, except there was something about him. A kind of sadness, yes, because he had lost his mother young, and his father had never really been interested in him—but there was something else she couldn't quite put her finger on.

The door opened then, and there stood Mrs Dangwal, an elderly lady in a red and black Kumaoni sari with a welcoming smile on her concerned face. 'Tal!' she exclaimed, opening the door fully to allow them in. 'Only you can help me!'

Tal stepped in politely, the other two following her lead. 'We heard from Pujari Nandan about your case, Auntie.'

Mrs Dangwal nodded distractedly, noticing Isaac. 'Who's this, now?'

'It's Isaac!' Trikaya introduced excitedly. 'He's new, he's part of our Society.'

'Is he?' Mrs Dangwal said, a broad, bright smile crossing her wrinkled face. 'Welcome to Devagarh, Isaac. Where are you from?'

'England,' Isaac replied politely.

Tal winked at Trikaya, and said, 'Isaac, Mrs Dangwal's cat is missing, that's why we're here. Auntie, we know your cat but Isaac has never seen him, do you have a photo you could spare us?'

'Of course!' Mrs Dangwal said, and headed into the next room. Tal followed quickly with Trikaya, and paused so they could see Isaac's expression.

The boy stepped into the adjoining room and froze, eyes wide and face stunned. The walls of the room were lined with posts and pillars, and atop each one was perched a cat, a dozen in all.

A dozen dead cats.

Mrs Dangwal rummaged in the drawer of a cabinet and emerged with a small photo. She saw Isaac's stricken face and laughed merrily. 'Oh, don't be scared, they're all mine. I do some taxidermy.'

Trikaya had both hands over her mouth to stifle her laughter. Isaac glanced at them, and Tal grinned to show it was just for fun.

'You mean you...*stuffed*...and *mounted*...all your cats?' Isaac asked very evenly. Tal was impressed at his composure. The first time she'd brought the others here they had run shrieking, Safir not even bothering with the front door and hurtling out the open window like a rocket!

'Yes,' Mrs Dangwal said. 'I had never really thought about cats before, but when my lovely husband Kumar passed away...' She gestured at a portrait of a nice-looking man that was hanging on the wall. 'The day after we cremated him, this lively fellow showed up.' She pointed fondly at one bright orange feline rearing proudly above all the others. 'I don't know why, but he reminded me of Kumar.' She looked around at her collection, their strangely bright eyes fixed forever on different points in the room. 'And every time one passed away, another would mysteriously turn up in my yard.' She smiled kindly at Isaac. 'You must think I'm crazy. That's fair, but I'm the sweetest crazy person you'll ever meet. Here...' She held the photo to Isaac. 'This is Kumar Fourteen.'

The girls watched Isaac take the photo. His eyes went wide, and his mouth twisted with horror, but he instantly schooled his features and said, with remarkable politeness, 'He's a beautiful cat.'

Tal had had several run-ins with Kumar Fourteen: a balding, one-eared thug of a grey alley cat who was half mange and half scar tissue, with thriving civilizations of lice and copious amounts of hairball hacked up on demand. 'Beautiful' was hardly the word anyone would use.

Mrs Dangwal looked perplexed. 'You're very kind, but he's the ugliest mongrel cat this world's ever had the misfortune to see. Still,' she continued, 'I do love him, and he keeps me company. When he's not off on his misadventures, that is.'

Tal decided it was enough fun, and time for business. 'For how long has he been missing?'

'When he goes off it's usually for half a day or so. And he always comes back for his milky-moo. But it's been two days now!'

There was no need to ask any more questions. Tal knew enough about Kumar Fourteen and his habits and haunts. Every few weeks he'd disappear for a couple of days, and the KSS would track him down to a particularly stinky trash heap, or to a pile of dead fish down by the lake. The filthy feline would look half-guilty, lead them on a merry chase, and finally allow himself to be carried back to his mistress.

'We'll find him, Auntie, don't worry,' she reassured Mrs Dangwal.

'I know you will, dear,' the old lady said, ushering them back out. 'I assume you're charging the same?'

'Yes, five hundred rupees,' Tal confirmed. 'Okay, guys, let's move out. Bye Auntie.' The other two echoed her, and they left.

Mrs Dangwal watched them from the doorway, worry on her face.

Tal looked at Isaac, who was still looking at the photo of the monster with disgust. 'Handsome fellow, huh?'

Isaac looked at them flatly. 'You could have warned me.'

Trikaya laughed and nudged Isaac. 'You should have seen your face!' She made a serious, polite face and mimicked his voice, 'He's a beautiful cat!'

Isaac couldn't help smiling. 'It's just polite.'

'You didn't run when you saw the dead ones, though,' Tal said to cheer him up. She nodded at Trikaya, 'This one flew straight back to the Lodge and hid under her bed until dinner.'

'That...That's not what happened...' Trikaya protested, turning red. 'It's...I was really young! And dead things are scary!'

They all laughed then, and Isaac pocketed the photo. 'Where to now?' he asked.

Tal was pleased at how easily Isaac had joined their new Society. It had almost made her forget her brother's betrayal. She looked at her bright red plastic watch. 'It's almost five. We'll go to Mademoiselle's.'

'Where?' Isaac asked, frowning.

Tal smiled, remembering how much fun it was to introduce Devagarh's unusual delights to new people. 'It's French.'

'Yes, she's French,' Trikaya jumped in excitedly. 'I mean, she's not French, but she was born in France and grew up there, and then came back here and opened up a French bakery, and she loves us because we help her, so when we come here we go there every day because she makes...'

'Let's not get ahead of ourselves,' Tal interrupted before Trikaya gave it away. 'Her name's Ms Fulara, but everyone calls her Mademoiselle.'

'Okay,' Isaac nodded, as they turned onto the main avenue again. 'I'm feeling hungry anyway, so it's good. Is it expensive? I've only got a couple hundred rupees.'

'Oh no,' Tal said, shaking her head emphatically. 'Mademoiselle's from a *really* wealthy family, the bakery's just for fun. And we're her special clients, so we eat for free.'

'Free?' Isaac looked surprised. 'Really?'

'Yes,' Trikaya piped up. 'The KSS always eats for free!' Tal frowned at Trikaya, who corrected herself immediately, 'I mean, the *Real* KSS always eats for free!'

Isaac looked pleased at the thought. 'Maybe Devagarh's not so bad after all.'

'Devagarh's *awesome*!' Tal said brightly, and led them down the avenue to marvellous Mademoiselle's.

3

MADEMOISELLE FULARA

Trikaya all but skipped the last stretch to Mademoiselle's bakery. It was her favourite part of every day, to see what new wonder Mademoiselle came up with. And she was so pretty and vivacious and fun… It almost made Trikaya wonder about having chosen Tal as her hero. She glanced nervously at the older girl. Sometimes it seemed like Tal could read minds.

She could see the wonder on Isaac's face as they rounded that last corner and ended up in front of the establishment. It was the most modern and foreign building in Devagarh, fronted by elegantly crafted French windows. Mademoiselle lived on the floor above, as did most people in the village, but whereas they kept their livestock and other animals on the ground floor, she had turned hers into an artisanal workshop and boutique. A great pink sign in flourishing cursive declared 'Mademoiselle's – Patisserie Boulangerie'.

Already they could see the artful castles of cakes and breads through the glass. A couple were exiting the shop, holding colourful bags full of pastries, their faces lit up with anticipation. As the children stepped in they heard a bell ring, announcing their entrance.

'It's just like Paris,' Isaac whispered in awe, looking around. Trikaya felt a pang of jealousy. She had never been outside the country, and had often imagined Mademoiselle's to be exactly like a real patisserie in a quaint Parisian neighbourhood.

Behind the glass counter, which showed mounds of multi-coloured candies and cakes, was Mademoiselle. She was a young woman, in her thirties, with lovely wavy brown hair, dressed in local Kumaoni woolens, but with a bright pink apron. Glass bangles of a million colours ran up both her forearms. 'Bonjour!' she cried out, 'Tal, Trikaya, you're early. Who's this?'

'Isaac Shroff!' Trikaya blurted. 'He's new, he's in our Society.' She smiled quickly at Tal, who was always patient with her.

Tal gestured with dainty precision. 'This is Mademoiselle Fulara.' Tal always behaved much more lady-like when they were with Mademoiselle, Trikaya had noticed. 'We have a new Society,' she informed Mademoiselle formally, 'us three, we're the *Real* Kumaon Secret Society.'

Mademoiselle's face fell. 'What do you mean? What's happened to the others?'

'They betrayed us!' Trikaya said hotly, knowing it would please Tal to see her passion. 'They've got their own stupid society.'

'Yes,' Tal confirmed. 'We're doing things our way now.'

'Well,' Mademoiselle said with a sad voice, 'I hope you all can get along in future. Do you still do your detective work?'

'Oh yes,' Tal said. 'Why, is there something the matter?'

Mademoiselle hesitated. 'I don't know, I feel a bit silly bringing it up, but...'

Trikaya vibrated with the suspense. 'Tell us!' They'd never gotten a case from Mademoiselle before.

'I...thought I saw a man in town this morning,' Mademoiselle said, leaning over the counter to whisper to them. Trikaya, Tal and Isaac drew closer. 'I followed him to say hello, but he turned a corner and when I reached there he was just…gone. Very tall, very thin, dressed in black. He looked like someone who used to live here. But that person left Devagarh a long time ago, and said he'd never come back here again. I suppose I could have made a mistake, but the resemblance was so… It could just be someone coming for the Festival.'

Trikaya nodded. The next night's Barbarika Festival always attracted a few visitors, some regulars from the villages on the other side of the pass, and sometimes even a few foreigners in search of remote exotica.

'You want us to find out if it's the same guy?' Tal asked.

'Yes,' Mademoiselle said. 'His name was Mer.'

'Just Mer?' Trikaya asked, frowning.

'I forget his first name,' Mademoiselle shrugged. 'It was a long time ago.'

Trikaya saw Tal's eyes narrow slightly, and knew instantly there was something not quite right with Mademoiselle's story. Tal had crazy instinct for things.

'Anyway, shall we discuss your honorariums?' Mademoiselle said, standing up straight with a beautiful smile.

Tal led them to one of the two delicate wrought-iron tables by the French window, and they sat. The patisserie was high up on the end of the village, and the view from the glass wall was breathtaking.

To their left, towards the east, they could see the village road, a beaten dirt track four metres wide, leading down and then up to the high steep pass that was Devagarh's only connection to the outside world. It was a two-hour walk to the top of that pass, and then three hours' climb down the other side to the parking lot where Devagarh's more affluent residents kept their vehicles. Beyond that it was at least an hour's ride on a bumpy path to reach a proper road.

In front of them the picturesque village lay in angular terraces, stretching down the verdant slope to the maidan with its cricket pitch. Lining the lower side of the maidan were a few orchards, which hid the terraced rows of cultivated fields leading down to Akashankh Lake. It was a moody body of water, sometimes happy and bright, other times sombre and impenetrable.

To the right the village ran in a band across the crown of the hill, curling west and then ending in a ravine that had been dug away for centuries by the thick, foaming rapids separating Devagarh from the next hill...

'What's that there?' Isaac asked suddenly.

Trikaya and Tal exchanged looks. They had all been looking to the neighbouring western hill, on the other side of the tumbling streams. From here they could see the eerie summit of that hill, taller and narrower than Devagarh. In the fading afternoon light, black outcrops of old stone could be seen jutting out of the overgrown jungle there.

'That's the Kot,' Tal said softly. 'The Black Kot.'

'No one goes there,' Trikaya warned, her voice thick with dread.

'There's a fort?' Isaac asked, sounding interested.

'Abandoned,' Tal pressed. 'And around the Black Kot there's the old haunted village Yakshagarh.'

Now Isaac seemed to be getting the point, looking nervous. 'Why is everyone living near a haunted village and this Black Kot if it's so creepy?'

'*Because*,' Tal said with an emphasis that indicated it was again the inexplicable illogic of adults at work.

They sat in brooding silence for a moment, staring over the village to that gloomy landscape. As bright and cheery as

Devagarh was, Yakshagarh seemed its extreme opposite: dark and threatening.

'Here you go!' Mademoiselle's voice sang from the kitchen, and the next moment she had brought them a tray full of heaven. Trikaya watched Isaac's eyes pop, and glanced merrily at Tal, who was grinning at the boy's incredulity.

'Nimboo panic.' Mademoiselle presented happily.

They were three impossibly tall glasses filled with a frantically fizzy drink that glowed neon green. Neon green!

'Frozen Jalebi Sandwich,' she added.

On each plate was a marvellous construction: two radiating orange jalebis of intricate pattern squeezing between them a carved disc of golden vanilla ice cream.

'And Dreameringues!'

In the middle she put a basket of multi-coloured meringues, each filled with crème patisserie of delicious flavours: chocolate, strawberry, vanilla, lemon...

Isaac was almost in tears at the vision. 'I'm never leaving Devagarh...' he murmured.

Mademoiselle's eyes shimmered with joy at seeing his awe. 'Enjoy this, I've got to make some more for your friends.'

Trikaya saw Tal's good mood vanish instantly, and they turned to look out the French windows. 'Is that them?' Isaac asked carefully.

Trikaya saw Shari out front, Tal's twin who was also tall and thin, his hair a crew cut. By his side walked Iti, Trikaya's sister and eldest of them all, the only girl of the former KSS who wore a long skirt, with long hair held back by a wide red headband. Trailing sheepishly behind them was Safir, two-thirds of his face covered by those stupendously huge glasses he always hid behind. Trikaya caught Safir's eye through the window, and one corner of his despondent mouth curled up at her.

'That's them all right,' Tal said venomously.

4
REAL VS TRUE

With his twenty-third sigh of the day, Safir followed Iti and Shari into Mademoiselle's, dreading the encounter. There was no avoiding it, they all knew, and for it to happen here and now was inevitable. No one in their right mind missed Ms Fulara's patisserie, especially when she gave away her baked wonders free.

There was a long uncomfortable moment while Shari and Tal exchanged a cold and haughty stare, and then he stepped over nonchalantly and sat at the other wrought-iron table, choosing the chair that put him back to back with his twin sister. Iti's mouth pouted with disapproval at the entire proceedings, but she followed Shari, and Safir had no choice but to do the same.

Mademoiselle swirled into the room a moment later, bearing a tray of the same concoction and inventions she had served the other trio. 'Bonjour! No need to explain, I understand there's a little trouble.' She smiled at each of them as she handed their portions out. 'I'm just curious to know what it's all about.'

'Greed,' Shari replied immediately, spitefully. 'If we help people, we should do it to help them, not for money. That's why we've made our own Society: the *True* Kumaon Secret Society. We help because that's what true friends do.'

Safir could see Tal was fuming, the hairs of her ponytail bristling with outrage. She turned her face to say, over her shoulder, 'We're doing a *job*, not favours. If some people think it's fair to go running up and down the hill for free, they can be my guest.'

'Right,' Shari retorted. 'And that's why our country's going to the dogs. Everyone trying to make money instead of making bonds grow stronger.'

Tal turned in her chair, kneeling. 'God, you sound just like Papa! What do you know about the country?'

Shari also turned, hands on hips, eyes glaring. 'A whole lot more than you. Grow up, Tal! At least I care about something more than myself!'

Mademoiselle stepped in quickly to put a hand on either shoulder. Tal and Shari stopped yelling, knowing how impolite it was to shout under her nose, but still glowered at each other. 'I beg you not to fight in here,' she said softly. 'It makes me so sad to see you fight.'

'Sorry, Mademoiselle,' Tal said, reaching up to hold the lady's hand. 'We'll just finish and go.'

'I'm sorry,' Shari apologized too. 'I'll never do it again.'

The twins turned back to their respective partners, and everyone began to eat. And in spite of all the unpleasantness, everyone forgot everything but the food.

Mademoiselle hovered around them, refilling the glasses with a crystal decanter of shockingly cold Nimboo Panic. The jalebi crackled and leaked glorious juice, the ice cream was just cold enough and thickly vanilla, and the Dreameringues popped and oozed unctuous flavours. They all could do little more than eat and look at each other with awe and giggle. After ten minutes of furious gobbling, everyone slowed down and leaned back, while Mademoiselle hummed a French song and cleared the plates.

Iti and Trikaya had been exchanging some words during the feast, and Safir was just now beginning to catch up on things.

'You're looking for cats too?' Trikaya asked.

'Mr Bisht-by-the-maidan,' Iti said, differentiating this Mr Bisht from the twenty others in Devagarh, 'And Mrs Ahmed, two of her cats.'

'How many cats can disappear?' the new boy, Isaac Shroff, asked. Safir liked the look of him, he seemed nice and smart and polite.

'Do you not know cats?' Tal said ironically. 'They could all move to the moon tomorrow as though it's normal.'

'But what about dogs?' Trikaya asked. 'There could be dogs missing.'

Shari shook his head. 'We checked on the way. All dogs accounted for; only cats are missing, everywhere we asked.'

Everyone mulled over that for a moment. Safir kicked his legs idly, dreaming. Where could the cats have gone? He imagined the entire population of cats of Devagarh convening in a parliament and voting on migrating out of the village. They would each pack a small suitcase with a mouse and a ball of yarn, and then all totter down the hill, build a big boat, and sail away across the lake... Except in his mind, as he ran with the fantasy, something loomed over it all, a brooding presence. He found himself breathing faster and faster, trying to see what it was but also terrified of it. Big and dark, bigger, darker...

'Yakshagarh...' Safir said suddenly.

Iti looked at him, concerned. 'Safir? Are you okay?'

'Yes, what? Why?' He blinked from behind his overlarge glasses, seeing everyone watching him oddly. 'I was just...' Iti reached out to catch his hand. He realized his hands had been trembling for some time. 'I was just thinking of…Yakshagarh.'

Shari reached out to grasp Safir's shoulder. 'Ah, don't think of that place. Anyway, it's probably not so bad, it's just everyone's old stories about it.'

Mademoiselle came back in from the kitchen, smiling kindly. 'All done?'

They got up, Safir last. What had just happened to him? They thanked Mademoiselle, who lightly pinched a few cheeks and ruffled some heads, and a minute later they were all outside.

Now it got awkward. After the scarfing of the majestic meal and the sharing of valuable information, there was uncertainty about how to proceed, and an obvious reluctance from non-twin parties to continue this feud.

What happened next, happened in a flash and cut through the dilly-dallying.

'Cat!' Trikaya shrieked, and everyone whipped around to look.

There it was, startled, a brown tabby frozen only a few metres away. It had been slinking by purposefully, but now watched them with some apprehension.

'Where's he going?' Iti asked softly.

Safir gulped, trying to pretend he didn't know.

'What do we do?' Trikaya muttered as the standoff stretched out.

The cat concluded this group of kids was decidedly shady-looking, and bolted.

'Catch him!' Shari yelled, and they all went off.

Tal and Shari were in the lead immediately, and it was clear they weren't just chasing the cat but also racing each other. Trikaya and the new boy were close behind, while Safir and Iti kept up as best as they could.

They tore down the street, turned onto a lane that ran parallel to Devagarh's main avenue, and from there it was a straight run to the other side of town.

The cat loped ahead leisurely, turning every once in a while to check if they were still pursuing him, only to bolt away again.

A few turns, and Safir saw they were in Dharm Square, where each religion was represented by its own building. The cat zipped across it and onwards. West. They were all out of breath by now. Safir's legs were burning with fatigue. 'I'm not built for this kind of stuff...' he wheezed out to Iti's back.

Beyond Dharm Square was another larger plaza, Bazaar Round, ringed with shops and small restaurants. In the late afternoon light, customers were beginning to find their usual seats, sipping coffee or chai and chatting while they waited for the sun to set.

Safir never failed to feel odd in Bazaar Round, and he knew exactly why. In the middle of the open space stood a statue five metres tall, painted in garish colours, of a fierce warrior king. The warrior king seemed in the middle of a battle, holding out a shield and brandishing a large, round mace. Local lore considered the statue to be of Barbarika, Devagarh's unofficial patron. There were no inscriptions, however, and no mention of when the statue had been built or why. It had just always been there. Which was fine, except that Safir always had the oddest feeling that the statue's stance seemed to be slightly different every time they passed through Bazaar Round...

There was no time to dwell on such things, however, since they had lost sight of the cat. Tal and Shari urged them on fiercely, and under the amused and fond looks of the local populace the children raced through and beyond Bazaar Round.

The village pretty much ended there, the dirt track running straightish past the larger properties of Devagarh. They caught sight of the cat, still running west, passing the Lodge.

As they tumbled past the Lodge, Safir glanced nervously about it, hoping his father hadn't seen him. It was the largest building in Devagarh, a massive wood structure with patios and balconies on three floors, beautiful and ancient. A British officer had built it a long time back, some Colonel Connell Mason whose bust sat in the entrance with a perplexed expression and monstrous mutton chops.

Safir sighed with relief when they left the Lodge behind. Abba didn't mind Safir running with his friends, but was a little suspicious of all this Society activity and their 'jobs'. Better he didn't know they were chasing cats up and down Devagarh…

One by one the children slowed and came to a stop, panting hard. There was nowhere further to go, as far as Devagarh was concerned. Going ahead meant crossing the bridge to Yakshagarh.

They sat and leaned over for a minute until Iti asked the obvious question, 'Did he cross?'

Tal and Shari both nodded.

Safir looked at the bridge. It was an old and solid structure, but it just seemed far too thin and precarious to span the fifty metres that separated the two hills at this height. They could hear the streams cascading below. Beyond the bridge's interconnected beams and rafters they could see the thick forest that hid the empty village. Safir looked further up the hill and saw the broken towers of the Black Kot looming.

'So that's that,' Trikaya said, shrugging. 'We'll have to wait until he comes back.'

But Tal and Shari weren't paying attention. They were

looking across the bridge, frowning. 'Isn't that Mrs Dangwal's cat? The ugly one?' Shari said. Safir saw the new boy root in his pocket and look at what seemed to be a photograph.

'It is,' Tal confirmed. 'And Mr Bisht's too.'

The other children joined Tal and Shari where they stood, a few metres from the bridge. At the other end, where the bridge gave out onto Yakshagarh, were a dozen cats milling about with affectionate nonchalance.

'That's some kitty party,' Safir mumbled, grinning crookedly at Trikaya, who nudged him with a giggle.

'What do we do?' Iti said, always the one to be responsible. 'I don't think it's a good idea to cross.'

'They're right there,' Tal said, putting her hands on her hips. When she did that, everyone knew she was getting ready to be stubborn. 'All of them.'

It was true. There they were, licking themselves and rubbing against each other. Almost taunting them.

'I reckon we can just go across and come back,' Shari mused.

'What if they run?' Iti asked.

Shari replied instantly, 'We turn and come back.'

Iti looked at Tal, who nodded confirmation. She then looked at the others, who were clearly torn between completing the job and the obvious menace of crossing that bridge. 'Safir?'

Safir started. Everyone was looking at him. He felt the sudden pressure of making the decision, realizing that if he said no they would probably call it a day. And feel like failures for not walking just a little more to finish the job. And feel like cowards.

Abba despised cowards.

Safir fiddled with his glasses, trying not to see Yakshagarh's imposing presence. 'I…I guess so,' he croaked, and cleared his throat. 'We could try, at least.'

Tal and Shari's pleased looks made Safir feel immediately braver, but he caught the concern on Iti's face. He suddenly wondered if he hadn't just made a very bad decision. The new boy caught his eye, and they observed each other directly for a moment. Would he be responsible for dragging Isaac Shroff, who had just arrived, into something dangerous?

'Come on,' Tal declared, stiffening her voice and body. 'Let's do it.'

With that, the six children stepped onto the bridge to Yakshagarh for the first time.

5

STRANGER

The bridge was old, but steadfast. It swayed slightly and creaked a lot, but it was solid as rock. That knowledge raised their confidence, and they walked almost normally across it.

Shari kept his eyes on the cats, wondering why they had just happened to congregate on the other end of the bridge like that; strange that only Devagarh's cats had disappeared, heading to Yakshagarh. As if they had been summoned...

'Woah, guys, look,' Trikaya breathed, and they stopped to stare.

The view from the middle of the bridge was one none of them had ever seen. The six children stood suspended between the two high hills of Devagarh and Yakshagarh. Twenty metres below, hissed and churned the many white streams that curled in from behind the hills. The waters were lost within the greying penumbra of forest down below, but they all knew the cascades threw themselves into Akashankh Lake, the Eye of the Sky. There was a small island roughly in the middle of the Lake, but it was said to be low in the water, bare, rocky, and (of course) haunted. No one they knew had ever been there to check, though.

As they stood there for a minute, entranced by the deepening colour of the sky streaked with white clouds, Shari thought he could see that island, winking in and out of sight as the lake's waters lapped over it. Beyond that the far shore was just a line, with the grey and green hills rising abruptly above. Devagarh and Yakshagarh were surrounded by even higher hills, and to the north began the Himalayan range.

'Come on,' Shari croaked, breaking the silence. 'Let's finish this.'

They trudged on. The cats were still frolicking feverishly at the other end. As he approached, Shari realized that most of them were focused on a particular place just out of their line of sight. And then he saw some pieces of biscuits being tossed to a pair of cats, who jumped on them eagerly.

'There's someone,' Tal whispered harshly, and instantly the entire group froze.

There was someone feeding the cats, sitting or standing unseen behind the arched gateway holding up the bridge at this end. The children were quite close to the frenzied felines now, but they stood paralyzed, ready to run back to safety...

'Hsst, come on you scamps, I don't have any more,' a man's voice suddenly broke, and before the children could react, a formidable-looking person stepped into sight, brushing his hands clean of crumbs.

He was ridiculously tall, easily more than two metres in height, and wore a long black coat over a casual black kurta-pyjama. His face was thin, aristocratic and proudly handsome, his dark eyes bordered by crow's feet.

'Mister Mer...' Trikaya muttered to herself in awe.

Shari glanced at her. Mister Mer? Did she know this man?

'Hello,' the thin giant called out, spotting them. 'What are you doing on this side of the bridge? Haven't you heard the stories about ghosts and ghouls?'

'Yes, we have,' Tal shot back. 'We don't care. We're not afraid.'

What was Tal so worked up about? Trikaya, Tal…they both seemed to know this man. Even the new boy Isaac, who had the oddest expression of 'I can't believe it!' on his face. 'We've come for the cats,' Shari said.

'The cats?' the man echoed in an amused tone. 'Good luck catching them! What will you do then, tie them to a sled and go racing up and down the hill?'

Safir snorted, enjoying the image. The man seemed friendly enough, but still the children didn't move closer.

'We haven't seen you in town before,' Shari said casually. 'Are you visiting?'

'No, no,' the man replied. 'I'm from here, but I've been travelling. A long time. I could ask you the same: you're not from Devagarh.' He started towards them, and even though he seemed nice, his height made them draw back. 'But let me guess.'

The children paused, curious. Guess what?

The tall man in black observed them shrewdly for a moment, and pointed at Tal and Shari. 'You are the Kandharis.'

Shari felt electrified. How did he know? He glanced at Tal, who looked equally stunned.

The man then nodded at Iti and Trikaya. 'You are the Pillais.' He gestured to Safir. 'You would be an Idris. And you…' He turned to Isaac, who stood pale and erect, 'You are…' The man paused. Frowned. Stepped closer. 'You…' He knelt down, folding his impossibly long body down to look the new boy in the eye. '*What* are you?'

Everyone stayed frozen in this tableau, with the cats meowing in the background. Until, finally, Isaac squeaked, 'I'm a boy?'

The tall man blinked, and stood up so suddenly that the children almost bolted. 'Yes you are. You're the Shroff boy.'

'How do you know us?' Tal asked in a challenging tone. 'Who are you?'

The man waved a dismissive hand. 'Just a visitor.'

'No, you're not, Mister Mer!' Trikaya cried out, pointing her index finger at him like a weapon, the other hand on her hip.

The man grinned. 'You know my name. Good. I do hope you'll come for my show tomorrow evening.' He held up his index finger, as long as any no.2 pencil they had ever bought. 'For one night only.' He nodded at them. 'I'll see you all later, I'm sure.' With that he strode away back towards Devagarh, each step huge and strong. 'Oh,' he called over his shoulder, 'and the show's on me, my young friends. Tickets in pockets.'

They stared at his back as he walked away quickly. Shari's hand was already searching his pocket, and he pulled out a large ticket that was bright red and printed with gold design and lettering. The tall man's face was set on it, his face haughty and mysterious. In bold letters was written: *The Mesmerizing Mister Mer.*

'No way...' Isaac said with an incredulous voice, huge eyes fixed on the red ticket he had pulled out of his own pocket. 'Do you guys have any idea who that was? The Mesmerizing Mister Mer?'

'He's a magician,' Shari said.

'How did he get all these tickets in our pockets?' Safir asked in a high-pitched tone.

'Uh, he's a magician,' Tal repeated sarcastically.

'Did any of you see him do it?' Iti asked, inspecting her own ticket.

'I suppose that's the point,' Trikaya said. 'Is he famous?'

Isaac almost choked. 'The Mesmerizing Mister Mer is *huge*! He's been touring Europe for the last ten years, he's... he's amazing!'

'We don't know him here,' Tal said half dismissively and half enviously.

'What does he do?' Safir asked excitedly.

'Stuff like this is peanuts for him,' Isaac said, waving his ticket emphatically. 'This one time he made the entire audience queue up and walk out of the entrance of the auditorium, but each person stepping through ended up *on* the stage. It was insane!'

Tal snorted. 'All this won't solve our case. We'll tackle this Mister Mer later.'

The children gathered themselves and looked to the end of the bridge only to see the cats had disappeared.

'Oh great,' Safir groaned. 'They're gone.'

Trikaya, who had boldly ventured right to the edge, peered out into the jungle. 'No, Kumar Fourteen's there!'

Shari stepped up to the end and looked where Trikaya was pointing. The main path from the bridge led straight up into the forest of Yakshagarh, but there was a smaller dirt track to the left that seemed to plunge steeply downhill. There, licking himself up and down indecently, was the abominable Kumar Fourteen, old Mrs Dangwal's current cat. He glanced at the kids ogling him, frowned, meowed, and began trotting down the dirt track.

'Don't let him go!' Tal yelled.

Trikaya charged, always the first to obey Tal's command.

'Stop!' Shari called, but it was too late.

Tal was next, followed by Safir. Iti shot Shari a worried look as she ran to catch her sister. Isaac shrugged and ran ahead.

Just before they disappeared from his sight, Shari huffed, cast one last look across the bridge back to the safety of Devagarh, and sped after his friends.

The dirt track soon broke into an overgrown trekking

path that tumbled haphazardly down the hill, forcing them to climb over dark rocks and huge gnarled roots. The trees had closed overhead instantly, blotting out the sky, and the trunks seemed to lean in towards them. Coming in last, Shari had them all in sight, but could not see if they were still following that infernal cat. 'Tal, stop!' he called out once or twice, but either she was being stubborn stupid or she couldn't hear.

Finally they came to a halt when the land levelled out and the path ended at a small terrace of uneven dirt. The terrace widened to the left to border the rushing water of the many streams that ran between the two hills. The waters here were still mostly separate and wide but beginning to merge into the torrent that cascaded down bigger and bigger falls on their way to Akashankh Lake. The sound the streams made was cacophonous, and they had to nearly yell to be heard.

'Where is he?' Shari cried as he hopped down from the path to the terrace.

'Here!' Trikaya complained as she held out Kumar Fourteen at arm's length. The cat's claws windmilled with pathetic menace as he emitted a warbling roar.

Tal was in the process of tying a thin rope around his neck. She always had that kind of stuff on her. Shari felt an automatic swelling of pride for his sister's smartness, but quelled it, reminding himself that they were playing on different teams now.

'I think we should go back,' Safir piped up nervously, looking around. Not around at the bushes, oddly, but up into the trees. Shari looked up as well, his heart starting to stir strangely.

'Yes,' Iti said, pulling her sister close to her. The group was slowly coming together, everyone back to back, staring out into the jungle. 'Something's not right.'

What had happened? The jungle, which had seemed wild but still fairly normal, now seemed an impenetrable darkness, full of hidden menace. Shari searched for the sun, but realized it must be setting already. Night was falling. Even Kumar Fourteen stopped fighting and stared spookily into the forest.

'Guys…' Safir said, his voice squeaking, 'can…can you hear that?'

The children fell instantly quiet, straining their ears to hear. The silence was painful. Their hearts beat a thunderous frenzy. Shari began to answer no, if only to try to break the unnatural calm…

And then they heard it.

A scratching.

A rustling.

The sound of someone coming through the trees. Some *thing* coming through the trees. They turned now, with popping eyes and open mouths, staring up, and up, and up. For a second they couldn't make sense of what it was. It seemed like the trees themselves were fighting, pushing against each other.

And then they realized the thing that was coming was huge, twenty metres tall, and was pushing two trees aside to step onto the terrace. They glimpsed a flash of eyes up there, of massive crooked hands bending the tree trunks aside like reeds, and then it spoke.

'Caaaat…'

And then the monster rushed straight at them.

6
FEVERS

The shrieks that split the air must have damaged her eardrums, but they were the last thing on Iti's mind as everyone dived in all directions, scampering to get out of the monster's path. The ground shook at each step it took, and as it reached down for them, the children howled and split like the frantic beads of a broken necklace.

There was confusion, noise, and all that Iti could think of was to keep Trikaya safe, to get her away from all this. So she clamped her fingers around Trikaya's arms and dragged her away, while Kumar Fourteen fought against Trikaya's hold on him. All three wailed like churails, stumbling about, and the next moment they were splashing into the streams. Trikaya tripped, and Iti went down with her. The water was so cold it stunned them both, and they sat there blubbering for a moment.

Iti saw Safir also staggering into the water, glasses askew on his face. Behind him that huge, gaunt thing was standing and swivelling this way and that. Around his legs ran the other three, crying out. 'Here!' Iti shouted, straining her voice. 'In the water!'

Shari heard her, and lunged to grab at the new boy. They went down momentarily, but then Tal had joined them and all three sprinted practically arm in arm, hurtling over roots and boulders like in a four-legged race. The trio sloshed into the gushing stream, slipping here and there on the slick rocks.

Iti had pulled Trikaya back to her feet. They were both shaking from the icy cold water, and Kumar Fourteen hung limp in her sister's arms, too wet and miserable to move now. Safir wobbled up to them, righting his glasses. 'Where do we go?' he whimpered.

There was nowhere to go. Iti could only hope and pray...

In vain. The creature turned its huge knobbly head, unnatural eyes fixing on the children in the stream.

The other three were just reaching them when Iti cried, 'He's coming! He's coming!' They turned to see the thing lurch towards them.

Shari and Tal both slipped then, and fell headlong into Safir, who was all arms and legs, and tripped Iti.

And then the water took them all.

The stream spread widely, playing this way and that, but further in the middle the water ran a little deeper, and it was too much for the clumsy, frozen children.

Iti went entirely under water, the cold shocking her horribly, panic shooting to the core of her. Trikaya slipped from her grasp instantly, disappearing even as Iti tried to get a better grip. Iti instinctively called out for her sister, but swallowed a surge of water.

Somehow her body rose, her head breached the surface, and she could take in a miraculous gasp of air, but then she was pulled under again as someone bumped into her. Over and over she tumbled, hitting her leg, her shin, hard against something. She didn't know when to breathe and when not to as the dark water carried her on, flinging her this way and that.

And then she was falling, arms flailing…

She plunged into deep water again, and kicked and pulled herself up. The current had slowed, wasn't tugging so hard, and Iti could see that there were others bobbing around her. 'Tri!' she tried to call out, coughing.

'Iti!' The closest person shouted. The next moment Shari was there, grabbing her, pulling her in.

For a moment Iti allowed herself to go blank with relief, knowing Shari was there, that he would keep her safe. Then she blinked and said to him, 'Where's Trikaya?'

'Here!' her sister twittered, paddling up. 'Where's Kumar Fourteen?'

'Guys, over here, come here!'

They turned to see Safir beckoning from the shore. They had landed by sheer luck in a deep pool where the rapids gathered and slowed momentarily, on the east side. Further to the right, towards Yakshagarh, the waters were thundering down faster and faster. Iti shuddered at the thought of them having gone that way instead, being pulled savagely down that side over the steep rocks…

The new boy was already halfway to them, swimming strongly. 'Where's Tal?' Shari called out to Safir, who stepped aside.

Tal was there on her knees, obviously exhausted, holding on to that infernal cat, trying to keep him warm.

A minute later they all sat shivering on the moist mud of the shore, huddled together.

'We have to get home,' Shari said through chattering teeth.

'Yes,' Iti affirmed, shivering. She discreetly held her shin, hiding the harsh cut on it. It stung viciously, but she tried to ignore the pain, not wanting to bother everyone. At least it wasn't bleeding much. She wished it would just heal and not be any more trouble...

'Where are we?' Safir asked softly.

'Down the hill,' Tal replied surely, still rubbing the cat.

'What was that thing?' Trikaya asked.

They fell silent.

'I don't know,' Shari said.

'It's a monster,' Safir whispered.

'A demon,' Trikaya added, seeming more excited than scared.

'It's our secret,' Tal interrupted. She stood up. 'We can't tell anyone.'

Iti rose unsteadily. 'Are you crazy? We've been attacked by it, we have to tell people! What if it comes to the village?'

It was Safir who replied: 'It can't cross the bridge. It's not allowed. It has to stay on Yakshagarh.'

They all looked at him curiously.

'Safir, how do you know this?' Shari asked.

Safir gulped and looked down at his shoes. 'I don't know...'

'Are you making it up?' Iti asked, perplexed.

'No!' Safir's head jerked up. 'I heard it!'

'Heard what?' Tal asked.

'Heard...something. Someone.' Safir looked uncomfortable, mumbling. 'While we were being attacked, I think.'

Isaac Shroff stood up then. 'First things first. We're going to freeze to death if we don't move now. We need to get back to the Lodge. Who knows the way?'

'I do,' Tal said.

'Let's go, then,' he said, 'and talk on the way.'

As they began to head into the woods of Devagarh, Iti felt some respect for the new boy for getting them on track.

It had always only been Shari or Tal leading, both taking turns where their personality gave them a natural advantage.

None of them spoke once they got walking. All of them were shivering from the cold, staying close together for warmth. As they moved through the sparse forest they felt the familiarity of Devagarh steal over them, comforting them after the terror of Yakshagarh. Safir's words had calmed them somewhat, knowing that that thing wouldn't come chasing them.

Iti hugged Trikaya to her as they went along, but her sister was still the first to sneeze hardly five minutes into their trek. The ground was much more even than Yakshagarh, since Devagarh had been cultivated for so many generations, but still they stumbled a bit as exhaustion set in.

Then they all began sneezing, coughing, and Iti knew they would all be ill tonight.

They crossed out of the woods onto the terraced fields, and minutes later they finally caught a glimpse of the village lights further uphill. They jogged through the orchards, Tal leading them unerringly towards the Lodge, Shari muttering words of encouragement to them all. By now they all knew where they were, except perhaps the new boy.

Iti couldn't quite recall the last ten minutes as they trudged across the cricket field, around the west end of the village, and finally up the wooden steps of the Lodge to tumble into the house.

Their parents were all over them in an instant, swarming like bees, crying out at the state they were in, comforting and bundling them into blankets. By then the fever had set in, and they were shaking uncontrollably as they were carried up to bed.

The last thing Iti remembered that night was looking over to Trikaya's bed to reassure herself that her small sister was there, safe and warm. Tal was in her own bed, mumbling to herself as she tossed and turned.

Iti let herself go then, hoping to rest peacefully, the sting of her cut fading into the welcome numbness of sleep. But there was fever, and with it came dark and strange dreams…

7
VOICES

A little after five in the morning, Isaac Shroff's fever broke and disappeared completely. He took some time to gather his strength, simply lying there in the dark of his new room at the Lodge. He could hear someone rustling around constantly, and when he finally managed to sit up he saw it was Shari, still in the grip of fever.

It was raining lightly outside. The children had been put up in two large rooms at the back of the house, boys and girls separate. When he had arrived with his aunt just after lunch he had seen this room, and it had looked bright and happy in the day. In the night, with the sound of the rain and the corridor light splintering across the furniture in jagged patches, the room seemed far less cheerful.

Safir was missing from his bed, Isaac saw. He must have gotten over the fever faster. Isaac slipped on a light sweater. It had been a strange day, the strangest he had ever lived through. Back in England he had practically grown up in boarding school out in the country, spending the holidays with his aunt in London. He saw his father only once or twice a year. Ishan Shroff was one of England's most respected philosophers, and taught at Oxford. He wasn't an unkind father, really. Isaac sometimes had requests, maybe for a new football kit or a computer. All he had to do was tell his aunt Jyoti, who communicated it to Ishan Shroff, and soon enough Isaac would receive a package in the post. With no personalized letter, of course. It had taken some time for Isaac to understand that this was all it would ever be. A distant, aloof father, no mother. At least there was Jyoti, who loved him and mothered him as best as she could, in spite of having her own life in London.

With a heavy sigh Isaac pushed himself off the bed, felt a momentary dizziness, and then made his way out.

They had kept the lights on at night. Not all of them, but enough to get around. Isaac was grateful for that, since the Lodge was already spooky enough with all the creaking wood and long empty corridors. The children had been kept on the ground floor for years, his aunt had explained. Probably because they made the most ruckus. The adults occupied the entire second floor, as they did every year during the holidays. The Pillais, the Kandharis, the Idrises. The Shroffs too, apparently, before Isaac's mother died. Jyoti said they had brought Isaac to Devagarh before, when he was hardly two years old.

He passed the library on the way, and glanced in. There was nobody inside. The walls were panelled with bookshelves right up to the ceiling. A sitting area with three armchairs indicated this was a room strictly for silent reading. Isaac moved on, searching for the kitchen. He knew it was roughly near the entrance of the house, but he had hardly had any time to look around earlier today, and the fever had disoriented him somewhat.

He finally found it, glimpsing countertops and a corner of an old fridge, but the sound of voices speaking softly made him stop at the door. Isaac peeped around the corner.

Safir, Trikaya and Iti sat at the island counter in the middle of the kitchen eating from a large plate of sandwiches. They looked exhausted, but were still whispering animatedly. Kumar Fourteen seemed to have passed out on the floor on his back, legs splayed out at all odd angles, a squeaky snore coming from him.

'Hi,' Isaac greeted shyly.

They stopped instantly, but when they saw it was him they all smiled. Iti slid off her low-backed stool as she said, 'How are you feeling? You want some fresh apple juice?'

'Sure, thank you,' he said as he climbed up slowly on the stool Trikaya pulled out for him.

'Isaac, you're the new guy,' Trikaya said, getting to business. 'What do you think about the KSS being split?'

Isaac looked at Trikaya, Safir, and then over to Iti who had pulled a jug from the fridge. They were all watching him, waiting for his reaction. 'I...I don't know. You've all been in the Society for years now, I don't feel like it's right for me to say...'

Trikaya waved her hand impatiently. 'Yes, we know, that's okay. Tell us the truth.'

'Well...' he said as he helped himself to a sandwich. 'I think the Real KSS and the True KSS should join up again.' The others nodded vehemently, as if Isaac had revealed some new unassailable truth. 'But it won't fix the problem.'

The others looked confused. 'What problem?' Safir said. 'There's a problem?'

'The problem that led to the split in the first place,' Isaac said. 'Leadership.'

'You mean...we need to elect a leader?' Iti said, looking displeased at the notion.

'Tal will want to be leader,' Safir muttered darkly.

'What's wrong with that?' Trikaya challenged him. 'Tal would make a great leader!'

'Shari would be better,' Iti ruled. 'He's...wiser.'

They began to argue, but Isaac interrupted them, 'No, no! It's exactly the opposite. The problem is that we have leaders. Well, two. We should have no leader.'

The three stared at him as though he were an alien. 'No leader?' Trikaya mouthed. 'But...we *have* to have a leader!'

'Actually Tal and Shari were kind of co-leaders of the KSS,' Iti said.

'A leader makes all the decisions,' Safir insisted. 'Especially the hard ones.'

Isaac shrugged, feeling the resistance from them. 'Maybe I'm wrong, I just...'

'No, you're right,' Iti said, looking thoughtful. 'All along we've just kind of let Tal and Shari be co-leaders. Now they've split us up, and none of us are happy.'

'But if we don't have a leader,' Trikaya mused, 'who leads us?'

'And who do we follow?' Safir asked urgently.

Isaac picked up his glass of juice. 'Nobody, maybe. Everyone, maybe. Maybe we should all be leaders. Maybe we should just follow good decisions, and not any one person.' Again they stared at him with open mouths and wide eyes, so he drank big gulps to try to break the tension.

'I don't know if I can be a leader,' Safir hazarded.

'We could try it,' Trikaya prompted, her eyes twinkling at the amazing idea that she could be a leader in spite of being the youngest.

'Yes, but how?' Iti asked.

'How what?'

All four of them looked at the kitchen doors guiltily. Tal and Shari stood there, arm in arm. Shari looked the worst of them all, leaning heavily on his twin sister.

'How what?' Tal repeated curiously, helping Shari to the table.

'How do we deal with what we saw this evening?' Iti said smoothly, glancing at the others meaningfully to ensure their silence. She got off her seat again to go to the fridge.

'Uh, yes,' Safir joined in.

Tal propped Shari up against her and pulled the plate of sandwiches over to them. 'We'll see,' she said dismissively. 'How are you all feeling?' They all made satisfactory sounds. 'Weird. My fever was really bad, but I'm also okay.'

'All our fevers were horrible,' Trikaya said. 'They called in Dr Negi, don't you remember?' They all shook their heads, surprised. 'He came in and looked at us all. I thought I heard him say we'd be in bed for days, probably a week.'

As the others continued talking about their strangely short bouts of illness, Isaac continued eating. He was ravenous, and asked Iti to please fill his glass again while she was serving Tal and Shari. Should he have volunteered his opinion so freely? It had gotten him into trouble in the past, back in boarding school. The other kids back there liked the order of their world, even if it wasn't comfortable or didn't make sense.

He realized he liked all of them here. Tal with her stubborn righteousness, Shari with his moral strength. The Pillai sisters, Iti clearly mothering everyone in the group, while Tri tried to assert her own personality by copying Tal. Even Safir, who seemed like he could out-timid a turtle, was really kind, and blurted out the oddest, funniest thing at times. He'd like to be part of the reunited Kumaon Secret Society.

But why did Safir look so uncomfortable? Isaac had noticed him glancing at the far corner of the kitchen a few times, and then hurriedly ignoring it. Isaac looked there. It was a section of countertop on the other side of the large communal oven, over which hung shelves with spices and condiments in jars. Had Safir seen a mouse or something? Isaac looked back at Safir, and nearly jumped when he saw the boy staring at him with eyes widened outrageously by the lenses of his glasses.

'Wh...What?' he stammered.

Safir leaned across the table and whispered intensely, 'You see her too?'

A chill ran up Isaac's back, exploding at the back of his neck with a shiver. 'No,' he croaked. 'No, I don't see anything...'

'See what?' Trikaya interrupted, always intrigued by others' whispers. 'What are you looking for?'

Safir whipped back into his spot, playing with his glasses, and stole another quick look to the kitchen corner.

Isaac felt like his fever was returning, but he pushed through his trepidation. 'Safir,' he asked out loud, 'what do you see?'

Everyone shut up, observing the curious drama.

'Nothing,' Safir squeaked, sounding close to tears.

Isaac leaned forward to hold Safir's trembling forearm gently. '*Who* do you see?'

It took Safir a long moment to muster the courage to look up. 'A girl. She...she's been following us since we fell in the water...'

Everyone listened with dread, faces pale and hearts hammering. The rain at the window suddenly seemed to beat harder at the glass.

'What girl?' Tal asked hoarsely. 'Wh...where is she?'

Safir pointed a trembling finger at the kitchen corner. Everyone looked, acutely aware that there was no one sitting there.

'She's there…right now?' Shari whispered.

Safir nodded miserably.

The children sat frozen at the kitchen island, not daring to move.

Dong! The grandfather clock in the dining room next door boomed, making them all shriek. *Ding dong dong ding!*

And then Kumar Fourteen leaped up onto the island counter, stretched his misshapen body out, making his crooked claws pop out and scratch at the tiles. He sat back, whipped his tail back and forth, and said in a shockingly deep voice, 'About time. Let's get to business.'

8

ALLIES AND ENEMIES

'There's not much time,' the cat intoned to the stunned children, 'You're all, *we* are all in grave danger. Mister Mer must be stopped.'

Trikaya held up a hand sharply. 'I'm sorry, I might be a little mad from the fever but...is Kumar Fourteen talking?' Everyone nodded dumbly. She scrutinized the cat. 'How are you talking?'

'Well, I'm not really a cat.' He waved a paw about. 'No, that's not true. I am a cat, but I'm actually human. Was human. I'm Mr Dangwal.'

There was a moment's silence.

'That's it?' The cat blinked, sounding miffed. 'No response?'

Shari mumbled, 'I think we're still getting over the talking cat bit...'

'You're Mr Dangwal?' Tal's words were half statement, half question. 'Mrs Dangwal's husband? Who passed away years ago?'

The cat nodded impatiently, 'That's more like it. Yes, Mrs Dangwal's husband. My spirit's been hopping from cat to cat ever since I died. The thing you need to know...'

Safir's arm shot up as though he were in school, but he

didn't wait to blurt out, 'How is it? I mean, do you like it? Do you, like, share with the cat, or are you completely in control?'

Kumar Fourteen—or Mr Dangwal—took on a philosophical look, cat eyebrows furrowing in an all-too-human way. 'Well, it's all right. I'm not a big fan of mouse, but bird's all r…' He shook his head. 'Look, there'll be time later for all this chit-chat, there's more important things to talk about right now!'

The children waited politely, if still dumbfounded.

'Okay,' Kumar Fourteen began. 'Okay, er…okay.' He pointed at Isaac. 'You're the reason all this is happening.'

The five children turned to look at Isaac, who began to squirm. 'Me? What did I do?'

'You didn't do anything,' the cat continued, 'It's who you are. In fact, who you all are.'

'What do you mean?' Shari asked.

'Yes, I'm confused,' Iti said. 'Is it Isaac or us?'

'It's all of you generally, and Isaac specifically.' Mr Dangwal hissed. 'This was so much easier in my head. Okay, here goes. You all have powers. Super powers. As in, superhuman powers.'

Trikaya waited for the punch line. A quick glance confirmed nobody else was believing what they'd just been told. 'Like what?' she asked with as little sarcasm as she could manage.

Mr Dangwal pointed a paw at Safir. 'This one is called a Listener. He hears things others can't. And you,' he said to Isaac, 'are the ace in the pack. The world hasn't had one of you in a very long time. You're a Catalyst.'

Trikaya eyed Isaac critically. A Catalyst?

'What's a Catalyst?' Tal asked.

The cat rose, stretched out its back languidly. 'A Catalyst makes everyone's powers stronger, better. You were all born with powers, but they were too weak for you to notice. You five might never have discovered your powers if he hadn't come along.'

Tal poked Mr Dangwal's side, making him jump and turn to her angrily. 'Excuse me for being skeptical in the face of a talking cat, but when you say powers, can any of us actually do anything? I mean, except for hear stuff and just hang around making other people better?'

'I don't know yet,' the cat said, licking the spot Tal had prodded. 'That's what you have to find out. And sooner rather than later.'

'How?' Shari asked.

Mr Dangwal bristled with impatience. 'I don't know! Just let me tell you what I do know, then we can *mrrrreeuuuw*!' He sniffed. 'There's not much time left, I have to *mmmmeuuuuuurrrr* what I can!' The cat shook his head furiously, and jabbed a paw urgently towards the corner where Safir's ghost girl supposedly was. 'Talk to he*uuurrrrr*rrr! Find out Mister Me*wwwwwrrrooeew*'s plan! And somebody tell m*yyeoooww meuw meyyyyyrr*!'

And all the sounds that came from the cat now were mewlings and purrings. Mr Dangwal yowled for another few moments, then blinked strangely...and was just Kumar Fourteen again. He hopped off the island and threw himself down in a corner, muttering to himself darkly.

'So...do we listen to the human cat?' Trikaya said, eyeing the others.

'He said to talk to "her",' Shari said.

They turned and scrutinized the kitchen corner.

'Is she still there?' Isaac asked Safir, who nodded.

Trikaya caught Safir's forearm. 'Come on, talk to her.'

Safir turned pale. 'Oh no. No no, I can't.'

'How long have you been hearing things?' Isaac asked Safir.

The boy looked down, hiding his expression. 'A while.' He cleared his throat. 'Cou...couple of years.'

Trikaya's jaw dropped, but she mostly felt hurt. Years? Why had Safir never told her? Didn't he trust her? She'd always thought they were close because they were the youngest two. Trikaya could tell from all the others' faces that they were also wondering why he hadn't told any of them.

Then she thought of what it must have been like for Safir, to be the only one to hear things no one else could hear, to sense things no one else could confirm or would even believe existed. 'Did you think you were...going mad?' she asked him softly, sadly.

Safir looked up at her, and the way he nodded dumbly broke her heart. Trikaya impulsively threw her arms around him. 'You're not mad,' she said gruffly. 'You're just stupid, stupid.' She felt him smiling, and she leaned back, still holding on to his shoulders. 'You're not stupid either. Y'know?'

'Okay,' Safir replied with some strength back in his voice. He looked around the table, sighed, and leaned forward on his elbows. 'I started hearing things when I was seven. Voices, mainly, people speaking. Or whispering, or singing. I wasn't scared then, I just thought it was normal.'

'What voices?' Iti asked.

'People. Dead...people. My grandparents.'

'Like...ghosts?' Tal asked.

Safir shook his head. 'Not really. Most ghostly things are...I don't know, heaps of memories and voices and feelings that tie together and linger. Like something drifting in the sea, not living, not dead, just...there.' He gestured vaguely. 'There's stuff like that everywhere, more or less, but since I kind of instinctively knew what they were, I didn't question it. I mean, like, if you see bushes you don't question whether anyone else sees them or not.'

'What changed?' Isaac asked.

Safir fiddled with his glasses. 'Abba found out,' he said curtly, clearly reluctant to talk about it. 'It's not the kind of thing a Brigadier's son should be doing. Cricket, sports, okay. Not hearing voices and such.'

Tal frowned. 'Is she a ghost?'

'No,' Safir replied. 'It took me a while to realize I…heard other things. People who weren't actually people. That got scary sometimes.' He shuddered, and continued as he looked to the corner. 'She's not…*bad*. She's the one who whispered to me that it couldn't cross the bridge. I've never really paid attention to someone like her, though. But I think she's okay.' Safir drew in a breath, forced himself to look at the corner, and called out, 'Can you show yourself to everyone? Please?'

Trikaya and the others tensed, their imaginations running wild…

Instead what drifted into view was an absolutely normal-looking girl of about their age, sitting on the counter with her legs swinging in and out slowly. Black hair woven into pigtails, brown eyes, slightly sunburnt skin. She wore a pale yellow frock down to her knees. The only odd thing was the soles of her bare feet which were black as though she had been running through coal dust. There was something about her that made one think that she spent her days and nights climbing up and down distant rocks, exploring forgotten gullies and caves, and skipping in meadows no one had ever been.

'Hello,' the apparition said nervously. 'Can you see me now?'

'Yes,' Trikaya said, instinctively liking this mysterious and wild-looking girl. 'How old are you?'

Everyone else smiled at Trikaya's typical introductory interrogation, but the strange little girl in yellow didn't miss a beat. 'About ninety.'

'You're joking,' Trikaya said, mouth hanging open in disbelief.

The girl cocked her head, perplexed. 'No. I was born some time before they built the new bridge. I don't know exactly when, though.' She chuckled. 'Well, that would be the old bridge for you. I've always called it the new bridge even though there's a newer one, the one you crossed today. The old one was narrower.'

'How can you be ninety?' Shari wondered.

'I'm not human,' the little girl replied. 'I'm a rakshasi.'

Iti's hands flew up to her mouth in alarm. The others just stared.

'What?' the girl said defensively.

'Don't rakshas hurt humans?' Tal observed.

'And eat them?' Trikaya added with morbid fascination.

'Hurt?' The girl cried out. '*Eat*? No! Not us. Not me, not my family! Those are the bad rakshas.'

Safir nodded quickly. 'She's okay, she's not bad. I'd know, I know the bad ones too. She's not one of them.'

Trikaya boldly slid off her chair to approach the girl cautiously. She held out her hand. 'Are you real?' The little girl stilled her swinging legs so Trikaya could touch her. She felt totally real, Trikaya realized. 'What's your name?'

'Kariba,' she piped, and proudly added, 'Great-granddaughter of Barbarika the Blessed!'

'Barbarika?' Shari nearly jumped out of his chair. 'Not… Barbarika from the *Mahabharata*?'

'Patron of Devagarh?' Trikaya queried with rising eyebrows.

'Whose festival will be celebrated tonight?' Safir squeaked.

Kariba the rakshasi grinned widely. 'Yes.'

Tal threw out her arms to get everyone's attention. 'Okay, this is fun and all, but we've got a crisis. Kumar Fourteen said we have to stop Mister Mer. But why? What does he want? And who is he?'

The look on Kariba's face went from cheerful to cold. 'Mer has been preparing Devagarh for a dangerous ritual since yesterday,' she said, her voice dropping. 'Wherever he's been travelling, he's learned a lot.'

'Mister Mer is from here, though,' Isaac pointed out.

'Yes,' Kariba confirmed. 'He lived here fifty years ago.'

Iti exclaimed, 'What? He doesn't look that old.'

'That's because he's not entirely human,' the rakshasi said. She paused and looked at them sharply. 'And neither are any of you.'

Trikaya felt the shiver run through them all at the same time.

Kariba's head suddenly whipped around. 'Someone's coming!' she whispered, and instantly began to fade from sight.

'Wait, what...What are we supposed to do?' Tal said frantically.

'Nothing for now,' Kariba murmured. 'I have to go anyway. Just stay here. I'll be back by noon...' And with that the rakshasi was gone.

'What if she's not back by noon?' Safir intoned, speaking everyone's thought.

'Hey, what are you all doing up?' a voice cried out, startling them.

9

GIFTS

Mrs Zoon Kandhari stood at the kitchen door, angry concern on her face. 'Get back into bed!' She was a tall woman with unruly black hair, and though she seemed stern just now, there was too much kindness in her to keep it up. They all protested for a good five minutes, and finally Mrs Kandhari relented, allowing them to troop into the Lodge's large living room to hang out. They would have had to vacate the kitchen anyway, since Auntie Sophie the housekeeper would be coming to prepare food for the day.

Shari put on the old music system loud enough to cover their conversation, and they all lay on the thick rug in a circle, heads together. Kumar Fourteen plodded up alongside, scaled an armchair, and rammed his head between the pillows to get some sleep. Satisfied that the cat wasn't going anywhere, the children focused on themselves.

'Right,' Shari said as he eyed them all in turn. They all seemed as perturbed as he, their foreheads wrinkling with thought. 'What do we do?'

'Kariba said we should stay,' Safir piped up first, just as Shari expected. Safir always preferred to play it safe. Although now, knowing how he had spent years of his life hearing voices that no one else could hear…Shari felt guilty that he had always judged Safir to be a little less than brave.

'We have a job to finish,' Tal countered, but not with the same cutting tone she usually had when she spoke to Safir. 'We still need to get Kumar Fourteen back to Mrs Dangwal.'

'We shouldn't leave,' Iti insisted. 'And not just because Kariba said so. The fact is we were all terribly sick last night. Just because we feel better doesn't mean we can just run around like normal.'

Trikaya's impatience was clear. 'We can easily go and come back in thirty minutes. It's only across town. And Mrs Dangwal must be worried sick!'

Shari figured Trikaya would only agree with Tal. 'I think we should stay,' he said. 'We don't know what's going on. Kariba still has a lot to tell us. And this Mister Mer…'

'Mr Dangwal said we have to stop him,' Tal interrupted. 'And we can't do this sitting around here. He's getting something ready for tonight; I bet it's that magic show he's set up.'

'Yes, of course!' Trikaya exclaimed, punching the carpet in excitement. 'Everyone in town will be there. And it's the Barbarika Festival too.'

'You think this ritual involves Kariba?' Isaac said suddenly. The way he asked that made them all stare at him with apprehension.

'What do you mean?' Iti asked.

Shari watched Isaac hesitate before saying, 'I don't think this Barbarika Festival and Mister Mer's show is a coincidence. And Kariba is Barbarika's—what did she say? His great-granddaughter? Maybe he needs her or something.'

Shari felt the unease passing through them all. 'You think she's heading into a trap?'

Isaac shrugged. 'I don't know anything that's going on in this place. I don't even know who Barbarika is!'

'I'll tell you in a bit,' Shari promised, feeling bad for Isaac. Shari himself was starting to feel overwhelmed by everything he didn't know—he couldn't imagine how much more clueless the new boy would be feeling. 'First we've got to decide if we're staying or not.'

'Correction.' Tal cut in drily. 'First *you've* got to decide for *yourselves*. *We*, the Real Kumaon Secret Society, will decide for *ourselves* what *we* will do.' She scrambled up to her knees. 'In fact, we need a Society meeting right now.'

Shari could only hold back his anger as Tal bustled Trikaya and the new boy Isaac Shroff into the sofa in front of the fireplace. They started whispering amongst themselves, with not a few sidelong glances at the three who remained behind. So Shari gestured, and Iti and Safir closed the circle.

'We all agree that we should stay, right?' Shari asked. Iti and Safir nodded. 'They're probably going to go out just to bug us,' he muttered angrily. 'She doesn't get that this isn't a game. This is dangerous!'

'Maybe I can convince Trikaya to stay,' Iti said, looking uncertain. 'I can say I'll tell Amma if she leaves…'

'Society rule,' Shari reminded her. 'We don't use parents over each other.'

'I know,' Iti said glumly, turning nervous rings in her hair with her fingers.

Safir, in the meantime, was watching the others whisper away. 'I think Isaac's convinced them to stay…'

'What?' Shari said, surprised. He craned his head up to steal a quick look. Tal and Trikaya were nodding slightly as they listened to Isaac. Shari frowned. Tal never listened to *anybody*.

They seemed to come to a consensus because they

rose from the sofa and returned, with Tal leading the way. 'We decided we're staying, *for a while*,' she said, her tone challenging. 'What are you guys doing?'

'We're staying too,' Iti said quickly, smiling with relief.

'What do you mean, a while?' Safir asked. 'Aren't you going to wait until Kariba comes back?'

'We'll see,' Tal said mysteriously, and beckoned Trikaya as she turned to go. 'We'll get the Box.' It was house rules that all the children kept their belongings in the Boxes, one in each bedroom. It meant unpacking and packing their stuff every day, but it seemed to be a parent's job to complicate their kids' lives unnecessarily.

Iti and Safir shuffled apart to make space for Isaac, who dropped between them. 'Now?' he asked Shari.

'Barbarika,' Shari began, 'is the patron god of Devagarh. He's the son of Ghatotkacha, whose father is Bheema from the *Mahabharata*.'

'He's a rakshas?' Isaac asked.

'No, he's a yaksha.'

Isaac cocked his head to the side. 'But wasn't Ghatotkacha a rakshas?'

'Half,' Shari agreed, nodding. Isaac scrunched his eyebrows, trying to figure, but Shari and Iti just shrugged.

'Okay. How did he become the patron god of Devagarh? And if he's a yaksha, shouldn't he be the patron god of Yakshagarh?'

Iti fussed with her hair, tracing loops with her fingers. 'That makes sense, but we don't know. It's all old legends and stories.'

All three jumped when they heard a bang and a loud yowl, and they scrambled up to see Tal hobbling in angrily, holding one end of a large wooden box painted red, followed by a concerned Trikaya hauling the other end.

'What happened?' Iti cried out, rushing to help. Tal dropped the Box on the floor, sank into the sofa, and gingerly began rolling up her jeans.

'Too much furniture in this stupid old place!' Tal hissed, eyebrows bristling with fury.

'She knocked her shin,' Trikaya added.

Shari felt a pang of pity and compassion for his sister, but held back from expressing his sympathy. He could see the knock from there, a red mark that would bruise fast. For a second a guilty thought flashed in his mind: it was better like this, if she was hurt she wouldn't go running to endanger herself.

Iti began ministering the bruise, rubbing and pressing it lightly while she murmured caring words to Tal. She had always been like this, nurturing and even mothering them all. She was the eldest of them anyway, so they deferred to her that way, but in fact they all kind of liked it. Iti always said and did the right thing, soothing their pain away with her kind words and touches.

'I don't think you can go out with this,' Iti ruled warily, knowing Tal wouldn't like it.

Shari took Iti's hint and said, 'It's not a good idea for you to go limping everywhere.'

'That makes two of us injured,' Isaac agreed.

'Really?' Safir piped up. 'Who else?'

'Iti,' Isaac said.

They all looked at Iti, who seemed uncomfortable with the attention. 'It's okay, I just got a cut in the river.'

'Iti!' Tal cried out, appalled and upset not just because Iti hadn't told them but because it was typical of her to downplay her own injuries.

Iti began to blush, waving her hands. 'It's okay, really, I can barely feel it!'

'Show me,' Trikaya said sternly, half-thrilled to have a chance to reciprocate her elder sister's medical authority.

Everyone began to press Iti, who clicked her tongue and flicked the hem of her skirt to show them the cut on her right leg. 'See, there, it's tiny!' she said, then paused, seeming confused. She put her left leg forward. 'Here, see?' Again she stopped, astonished.

They all stared at the perfectly unblemished skin of her shins. 'Where?' Tal asked.

Iti sat down, flipping her skirt around her legs, turning her calves this way and that. 'It was there... Last night, it was right there!' She looked up at them with wide eyes. 'I'm not making it up...'

'I remember it,' Isaac jumped in, reassuring her. 'I saw it, it was on your right leg.'

They all eyed each other in silence, coming to the same conclusion instantly. 'It's your gift,' Shari breathed.

'You can heal super fast,' Safir said with awe.

'Look!' Tal yelled excitedly, showing everyone her own leg, where hardly a minute ago the red mark was beginning to bruise. The mark faded as they watched, the redness turning to healthy brown. She looked at Iti and grabbed her hand tight. 'Iti, this is amazing! Nothing will ever hurt us with you around!' She paused, and declared, 'Which is why we're going to go now.'

Shari's heart sank. 'It's only seven, there's still hours until Kariba comes back.'

'Exactly,' Tal retorted. 'We'll go and come back in half an hour.' She jumped up and pumped her fist. 'Real KSS, let's go!'

Trikaya pumped both fists in the air, adding a little hop. 'Real KSS, *yeah*!'

Shari and Iti exchanged a quick look. 'Tri, can you stay?' Iti asked gently.

That took the enthusiasm out of them. 'What for?' Trikaya asked.

'I'm...worried,' Iti said, looking at her own hands. Shari suddenly realized she wasn't just lying to keep Trikaya back. 'I don't know what this...power means.'

Trikaya hesitated, torn between Tal and her sister's appeal, but Tal saved the moment. 'You stay, Tri. Iti needs you. The Real KSS goes where it's needed. Or stays, actually, in your case.' Shari blinked. Did Tal wink quickly at Trikaya just now? 'Isaac, are you ready?'

Isaac got up assuredly, straightening his T-shirt. 'Sure.'

Without another word Tal grabbed Kumar Fourteen and marched off. The new boy followed, but not before he glanced at Shari and nodded. Shari nodded back, and they were gone, but he somehow felt reassured. There was something in the new boy that inspired trust and capability, and he had all but told Shari he would take care of Tal and keep her out of trouble. Well, as much trouble as one could ever keep her out of, Shari thought wryly.

Their absence made the remaining four look at each other. 'And now?' Safir asked out loud.

Trikaya took her sister's hand and began stroking it the way she had always seen Iti do it to others. 'Now,' she declared, 'we find out the rest of our powers!'

10
POLES APART

Tal dropped Kumar Fourteen on the grass outside the Lodge and scolded him as she tied a leash to his collar. 'Don't run away, now! Understand? I'm not carrying you, or chasing you anymore! Got it?'

'How much of him is cat and how much Mr Dangwal?' the new boy asked as he joined her in the driveway, stuffing his arms through the sleeves of his very British-looking blue jacket, with an impressive golden crest on the breast pocket.

'Seems mostly cat,' Tal adjudged from the feral, sly look of the beast's eyes. 'I think Mr Dangwal can only come out every once in a while.'

They started off towards the village. 'So he's just along for the ride?'

'I guess.' She kicked her leg in wonder. 'I can't believe my shin's fine!'

Isaac smiled at her delight. He suspected she'd gotten her share of bruises and knocks over the years, seeing how spunky she was. 'So Safir can hear ghosts and things,' he mused. 'And Iti can heal.'

Tal waited for him to continue, then added, 'And you're the one making all this possible, Kumar Fourteen said.' She made a face. 'Should we be calling him Kumar Fourteen or Mr Dangwal?'

He shrugged. 'I never knew either of them.'

'I think Kumar Fourteen fits better for now, at least until Mr Dangwal shows up again.' Tal squinted up at the sky. It was just past seven or so and still slightly murky, but she could tell there was serious cloud cover. She shivered. Mornings were cool, but this was borderline cold, and she realized she should have taken her...

'Here, your jacket,' Isaac said, holding it out to her.

Tal took it, grateful. 'Thanks.' The new boy was something else. He seemed to see things which escaped everyone else's notice, and on top of that was nicer than anyone she had ever met. He held out his hand for the leash, and wrangled Kumar Fourteen while Tal slipped into her jacket. 'Much better...' she said brightly. He handed the leash back to her, but she shook her head as she pulled triumphantly from her back pocket a small yellow walkie-talkie. She took the leash back and they started walking, stepping out onto the thickly packed dirt road.

'Does it work? Isaac asked curiously.

'Of course! Tri and I changed the batteries and checked it.' She shoved it into the pocket of her jacket. 'Our parents bought it for us a couple years ago. We used it one summer and then just left it.'

Isaac blinked. 'This is what you went to get from the Box.'

'Yes!' Tal crowed, 'And Shari doesn't even know we've got it!'

'Why didn't you tell me?'

Tal paused. 'What?'

'When we huddled, you didn't tell me. You and Trikaya went off and did this on your own.'

'Well, yes...' she started, getting flustered.

'You let me in the Real KSS, but you don't really trust me,' he pronounced.

'What? No, that's not it!'

'It's okay,' Isaac said. 'I think I've proved I can be trustworthy. You made your own decision not to trust me, not because of something I did.'

The way he said that only made it sting worse. It was true. He had proved to be worthy of trust, and worthy to be a member of the Real KSS. Why hadn't she told him in the huddle? Was she really a distrusting person? She didn't think she was...except what had happened seemed to prove otherwise.

Walking in silence, they saw a couple of people already heading to work down the hill, dressed in Kumaoni colours with scarves bundled around their heads. Tal risked a look back at Yakshagarh and the Black Kot poking up darkly from the forest. Had they actually been there in that brooding jungle last night? It seemed like a disturbing nightmare, the kind you didn't even mention because you preferred to forget it.

'What's that?' Isaac said suddenly, grabbing Tal's arm, making her look up with alarm.

There, right in the middle of the street, was an arcane and elaborately constructed pole looming over them, about five metres tall, which had definitely not been there the day before. It was like some kind of abstract, metallic tree, thin enough at the bottom for Tal to wrap her hand around, but then branching out frantically at the top into odd clusters of thin filaments that drooped down to the street. It was black iron, hard and tough, but strangely organic and smooth.

And it felt very, very...odd.

As Tal and Isaac approached the pole cautiously, she could feel something emanating from it. A sort of vibration, or a sound so low she couldn't hear it but felt it in her bones. It was a creepy thing. And if that wasn't enough, Tal looked down the street and saw another one a short distance away, and another one after that... A whole row of these weird poles bisecting the village.

'I don't like it,' Isaac muttered. 'Do you feel that?'

'It's Mister Mer's,' Tal replied instinctively, 'for his show tonight.' Isaac nodded in agreement. She reached out to it.

'Don't touch it!' Isaac nearly yelled, snatching her hand away. He seemed embarrassed by his own reaction, stammering, 'It's...I just...I don't know, it *feels* dangerous.'

'I know,' she said, spooked by the intensity of his voice.

'Let's go,' Isaac said.

'Wait,' Tal said, seeing something else further down. 'Quick, this way!' He hesitated, turning to see where she was looking. Instead of letting him slow them, she grabbed his hand and pulled him after her into one of the side alleys that branched off from the main road. They climbed up the slight slope swiftly, quietly, then turned into one of the parallel roads and crouched down behind the wall of a house.

'Was it Mister Mer?' Isaac asked urgently.

Tal shook her head, ponytail flying. 'No, it's worse. They call themselves R2R. Local kids, a couple years older than us.' She crooked her index at him, and they both peeked over the edge of the wall.

There were three older children standing around the pole down the street, examining it idly. Two girls and a tall, mean-looking boy. 'Rudra,' Tal whispered in introduction, 'and the girls are Ruma and Reva. One of them is his cousin, I think. They're kind of our enemies.' Everyone in the KSS had been bullied and teased by R2R at least once, which was why they never went out alone anymore. 'I don't think they saw us. Come on.'

They snuck off down the street, rejoined the main road, and walked down the entire row of metal posts. The

Devagarhis curiously peered up at the poles, touching and prodding the metal. A small boy tried to climb one but just kept sliding down.

Mrs Dangwal opened the door as soon as they knocked and made a small fuss about Kumar Fourteen, scolding and kissing him at the same time. The cat closed his eyes and rubbed his head against the old woman's neck, letting out a throaty purr like a tiny buzzsaw. 'Thank you Tal, and Isaac, isn't it? Here...' She pressed the money into Tal's hand. 'Milky-moo!' she crooned to the cat, hurrying to her fridge to get him a drink.

When they stepped out of the door, however, Kumar Fourteen zipped out to catch up to them. Tal looked at Mrs Dangwal with concern, but the old lady sighed and waved her hand as she said, 'It's okay, I just wanted to know he's fine. He seems to like you, I'm sure he's safe with you.'

So they left Mrs Dangwal's with the capricious cat in tow. Kumar Fourteen was visibly thrilled to have the leash off, and he leaped here and there as he followed.

Tal took them back to the main road, and when they turned onto it she saw a familiar face. 'There's Mademoiselle.'

There indeed was Mademoiselle Fulara, in a bright yellow salwar-kameez and sky-blue dupatta, standing with arms crossed under one of those metal poles, frowning up at it. Her hair seemed especially unruly today, a thick brown river.

'Mademoiselle!' Tal called out, and the beautiful pâtissière greeted them with a radiant smile.

'Hi guys,' she said, reaching out to squeeze both their shoulders affectionately. 'What're you doing out here so early?'

Tal nodded solemnly. 'We're on the job. We brought back Mrs Dangwal's cat.'

Mademoiselle knelt down to exchange a comical look

with the cat, who appeared entranced by her. 'Oh yes, Mrs Dangwal's cat. Kumar X, fill in the number.'

Tal laughed, liking Mademoiselle's cleverness. 'Oh by the way, you wanted to know about Mer. It is him, like you thought. We met him yesterday.'

Mademoiselle turned on her haunches to face them both, suddenly serious. 'You met him?'

'Yes.' Tal hesitated, then added, 'On Yakshagarh.'

'Yakshagarh?' Mademoiselle said, her expression alarmed. 'What were you doing there? It's…not safe!'

'Getting Kumar Fourteen back,' Tal explained.

'What did Mer say?'

'Nothing, really,' she lied, feeling instantly guilty about it. 'He gave us tickets to his show.'

'Do you know what these poles are for, Mademoiselle Fulara?' Isaac asked abruptly.

The lady stood up and brushed her kameez straight. 'I don't know. But if they're for his show, they must be important.' She smiled. 'I have to go now, but I'll see you later tonight, I suppose.'

'You're coming for the show?' Tal asked.

'I think so,' Mademoiselle said. 'I made something special for the Festival.'

'What did you make?' Tal pressed eagerly.

Mademoiselle laughed brightly. 'It's a surprise! But since it's you, I'll tell you. It's in honour of Barbarika's father, Ghatotkacha. I made this pot entirely out of chocolate, and layered it with chocolate cake, chocolate mousse, nougat, and Kumaoni strawberry compote. Can you guess the name?'

Tal thought furiously for a second, but it was Isaac who suggested the answer first: 'Gateau-tkacha?'

'Wow!' Mademoiselle exclaimed. 'You must be a mind-reader.'

'Gateau-tkacha!' Tal repeated, loving it.

'Keep the secret!' Mademoiselle sang at them conspiratorially, and walked away in her gracefully brisk gait.

Tal watched Mademoiselle glide away, and then turned back towards the Lodge. Isaac fell into step. 'Mademoiselle Fulara knew Mister Mer well,' he murmured to her, although they were out of earshot.

'I know,' she said back quietly. 'I saw her blink.'

'Do you think she knows he has real magic?'

Tal glanced sideways at Isaac, who looked back with that open expression of his. 'I think she does.'

They walked on in silence.

Then Isaac said, in a tone that told her this was serious, 'I wanted to be a magician. Because of Mister Mer.' He put his hands in his jacket pockets and squinted at the road ahead as they moved through the village. 'Auntie Jyoti took me to his show once, at the Royal Albert Hall. He was making things appear and disappear, and become huge and then tiny, he just seemed so...so powerful. Like he could do anything, and it was easy. I remember feeling that if I had power like that, maybe I could also change...some things in my life.' He hesitated, staring at his shoes. 'Or maybe change myself.'

Tal looked sharply at Isaac. 'You do have power. And you're pretty great. Everyone thinks so.' He squinted at her uncertainly. 'They do.'

'They do what?' a voice called out, startling them.

Tal grabbed Isaac's sleeve. 'It's them.'

Ruma stood there in the middle of the street, in a brick-red salwar-kameez with a black cardigan, arms crossed, a nasty look on her face. 'Who's the new boy?'

Isaac glanced over his shoulder. 'Behind too.' Tal turned to see.

Reva was there, in a sky-blue salwar-kameez and a black

sweater. She held a long stick casually, the end dragging behind her.

Before they could say anything more Tal took off up a side street, tugging Isaac until he got up to speed. They tore up the slight slope, Ruma and Reva at their heels. If it was just the girls, Tal thought, they'd be okay, just so long as it wasn't...

Just as they reached the next juncture, Rudra stepped out from the corner, in dark jeans and a black T-shirt. He was tough and tall, and Tal had no illusions about both of them taking him on. Especially with the other two goonettes with him. 'Where are you running to, little rat?' Rudra called out as Ruma and Reva closed the circle.

Tal looked at Isaac, feeling angry and sorry for him. She had led him into this trap, without even thinking.

They were done.

11
TO THE RESCUE

Half-unpacked, the Box had still managed to litter half the living room. Iti sat with the box between her legs while she shoved old toys, puzzles and board games back in. Was this really all theirs? Some of it must belong to the older ones: her brother Abhra, and Safir's siblings. She picked up a wooden horse that looked like it had (barely) survived a nuclear war. There was probably also stuff here from when their parents were kids, holidaying at the Lodge very much like they were today...

'Flight mode on!' Trikaya yelled, launching herself from the sofa into the air, one fist aimed up at the ceiling. When she landed on her two bare feet, her disappointment was palpable. She sighed and muttered, 'I give up... Take it off the list.'

Safir, sitting deep in an armchair, raised the notepad in his lap. They had worked out a chart on paper, with each of their names at the top, and down the left were the thirty or so superpowers they had come up with. He carefully drew an X where Trikaya and 'flying' intersected, secretly relieved. After twenty different leaps and loud commands to activate her power of flight, it was probably time to move on to quieter investigations.

Iti glanced at Shari, who stood concentrating in front of

the large framed mirror by the door. While he focused his thoughts, his face made small grimaces, eyebrows twitching, mouth twisting... Iti clapped a hand over her own mouth, stifling giggles. Shari heard, caught sight of her in the reflection, and began grinning with embarrassment and amusement. 'Yes, okay, take invisibility off the list, Safir.'

Safir obliged, repeating, 'Shari, invisibility, X.'

'Here,' Trikaya said, climbing down to sit on the other side of the Box from Iti. She lightly pressed two fingers to each temple and glared at her sister. 'What am I thinking?'

'That...you need a bath?' Iti guessed.

Trikaya squealed, 'Seriously, I'm transmitting my thoughts! It's, what is it, Safir?'

'Telepathic,' he enunciated.

'Telly pathetic,' Trikaya repeated, focusing on Iti's long, wavy hair. How did Iti always look so groomed, even the morning after such momentous events? 'Okay, I'm projecting my thoughts into your mind... What am I thinking now?'

Iti put down the ragged teddy bear she had picked up. What should she do? Clear her mind or something? She tried to make her mind blank and focus on only one thing at a time. 'I'm thinking of...the Box. Now of Kariba, what she's going to tell us. Of...of Kumar Fourteen talking... Anything?'

Trikaya grunted with frustration and grabbed a handful of the blocks that were strewn around the carpet. 'No, I was thinking of the apple pie in the fridge. Take it off the list, Safir.' She stopped suddenly, and stared intently at the three blocks in her hand. 'Wait, wait...'

Everyone sat up, Iti in the middle of packing a deck of Uno cards away. The silence stretched as Trikaya's brow furrowed further and further, they could hear everyone's excited breathing...

Then her shoulders slumped. 'I thought they moved. I guess you can take the other telly off.' She tossed the blocks aside and rolled over despondently onto her side.

'Telekinetic,' Safir specified, and added another X in the box. He cleared his throat. 'Actually maybe apple pie doesn't sound too bad...'

'Did you see something?' Shari asked out loud, jumping to bring his hands close to Iti. She watched as he snapped his fingers a couple of times. 'I thought I saw a spark...'

'No,' Iti said, sorry to disappoint him. 'Can't make fire, I guess.'

Safir declared, 'Shari, fire, X.' He slithered off the armchair and joined the other three around the box. 'Maybe we've got weird powers. I mean, unusual ones, not super strength and stuff. I hear things, and Isaac makes our powers stronger. Iti's power is standard, though; healing's in all the video games.'

'Yes, healing's awesome,' Shari said. Iti's toes curled with delight at the admiration in his voice. 'And her power totally makes sense for her. She's always taking care of everyone.'

Trikaya curled herself back up onto one elbow. 'I just keep going over Kariba's words. That Mister Mer is not entirely human and...neither are we. Do you think she meant all of us? Maybe only some of us have powers?'

The others didn't reply, gloomily reminded. What did it mean to not be human? Were they...monsters? And what were monsters? Kariba seemed human enough, and not too different from them. But that thing in the forest that had attacked them yesterday? That was a monster, without a doubt. Could they possibly become like that one day?

'SOS!'

A crackling cry made them all jump and look around, spooked. Trikaya dived into the sofa, flinging pillows aside to pull out a yellow walkie-talkie. Iti recognized it instantly, the old one from several years ago. When did they start using it? And…did Trikaya actually hide it from them?

'Come in, over!' Trikaya called into the walkie-talkie. The others gathered.

Strange sounds came through the walkie-talkie from the other end, thumps and grunts and yells… And then came Tal's frantic voice, 'R2R ambush, intersection at Mr Bisht-who-burps, they're…!' Another bump, grunt, and a muffled, 'Let go!' Then Tal again, her voice strained, 'SOS KSS, SOS K…'

The walkie-talkie went dead.

The silence was deafening.

Then they all leaped up instantly, in emergency mode. Trikaya didn't even bother with socks, punching her bare feet into her shoes. They all ran to gather their jackets. Two seconds later they were at the door ready to run when Iti remembered in a flash. 'Kariba!' The others stopped, looked back at her. 'We're supposed to be waiting for her!'

'Someone has to stay back,' Shari said.

Trikaya clapped a hand on Safir's forearm, 'Safir, you'll hold the fort?'

Safir nodded, looking a little pale. They couldn't know it, but the moment he had stepped out of the door his mind had done a double take. To his eyes, the colour of the sky, the grass, the trees had warped slightly, and gone a little hazy, as if waves of heat were rising up between him and them. A sudden disharmonious blend of sounds assailed his ears, a susurration that buzzed incessantly as though a nest of wasps had taken up lodging behind his ears. His heart was thundering with panic, he could feel his palms slick with sweat. 'Sure,' he said, light-headed, 'I'll stay.'

Iti thought Safir looked a little odd, but the urgency of Tal and Isaac's situation made it imperative to go. She squeezed his shoulder for comfort, and then all three took off at top speed.

It took hardly ten minutes to reach the intersection, a dirt crossroad between tall stone houses with traditionally carved windows. They inspected the area, but there were no signs whatsoever of Tal or Isaac or even R2R. Trikaya and Shari were close to desperate after a couple of minutes, and Iti racked her brains trying to come up with a plan...until she spotted Kumar Fourteen.

The hideous feline was sunbathing on a porch a ways down, as if nothing had happened, tail jumping every few seconds.

'There!' Iti called out, pointing. She was still out of breath from the run, Trikaya and Shari had always been far more athletic than her. Those two set off at a dead sprint, but Iti had to take a couple of breaths, gathering herself, before following.

The moment they ran, Kumar Fourteen's eyes twitched open and he scampered off, determined to give them a run for their money. Down the lane he went, then up two streets, through someone's yard, while Shari and Trikaya mustered their strength.

By then, Iti was left far behind, and knew it was hopeless to try to catch up. She gritted her teeth against the guilt and shame. Safir should have gone with them. Even he, young and timid as he was, would have been more useful. She was the oldest of them all, she should have been looking out for them. And here in a crisis she couldn't even be there to help. What would she do against R2R anyway? Just stand around and pretend to be willing to fight.

She had to sit for a minute, on a stone wall between houses, her breathing ragged. How strangely peaceful it was out here, while the KSS was struggling to stay together, and now to protect its members. The sun had finally shown itself, scattering the early morning clouds and blessing the Devagarhis with its interstellar hugs. She wiped the sweat from her brow, and with nothing better to do began gathering her hair back together, dishevelled by the running. From here she could see some villagers ambling back and forth in the main avenue: Dr Negi, always hauling his black doctor's bag dutifully around, walking with a foreigner, probably some tourist here for the Barbarika Festival; the staff of Bintu's, one of the more popular food joints in Bazaar Round; and there was Rudra, skulking down the street in his usual...

Rudra!

Iti sat up, electrified. Instinctively she thought of the walkie-talkie, but it was with Trikaya. Where were they? Still chasing that less-than-attractive cat, presumably.

Rudra was taller than everyone in the KSS, with floppy hair and a perpetual surly expression, as though someone had spoilt his entire life. What was he doing? Hadn't they just abducted Tal and Isaac? Why was he hurrying up and down the streets, looking around? Iti frowned. That was it: he was looking for someone.

Not wanting to attract his attention unduly, Iti sat peacefully, but the moment he had passed out of sight she bolted down the lane and peered around the corner. There he was, heading east from Bazaar Round and Dharm Square, looking frustrated. Since the avenue was long Iti had a clear line of sight. She could keep him in view while running to the next crossroad, and hide around the corner.

Finally he seemed to give up, and took the next turn left, up the hill. Iti followed him on the parallel street up, running to each next intersection. After a couple of streets the village just ran out, the houses giving way to wild brush and tangles of low trees and bushes. She kept herself low, now, as she trailed him, keeping a considerable distance between them. As they went up, the trees thickened, beginning to tower, becoming imposing pines and oaks. The air cooled slightly, and the wild sounds of the forest replaced the stillness of the hills.

They were now in proper jungle, further than she had ever been. What was up here, above the village? The cemeteries, she knew. Some people had plots of land, but they were generally left barren, most of the cultivation was down below in the village. Where was Rudra going?

At the next turn Iti dropped down low, heart thumping. Rudra was standing in the middle of the path, staring up into the trees to the side. She hadn't seen him turn around, so he couldn't have seen her, but had he perhaps heard someone following? No, he slowly lowered himself and picked up a stone from the path, sized and weighted for throwing.

Iti shifted, climbing up the grass carefully to see what he had seen off the path… She saw it immediately, a golden flash that instantly attracted the eye, and her jaw dropped open.

It lay asleep on its back, nonchalant, one black front paw behind its black head, the other draped on its yellow belly, and one black hind leg crossed over the other. She had never seen a yellow-throated marten before, only heard about them with words of warning from the locals. They were small, savage hunters, unafraid of anything, and despite being half a metre long were known to bring down deer. What was it doing in Devagarh, so close to the village? And lying on a tree branch like this, in such an unexpectedly human pose, blissfully aloof to the danger?

Before she had the time to do or say anything Rudra had shot off the rock, and it hit home with a sharp crack. The marten fell from the tree, stricken by the stone, and lay still. Rudra snickered, but didn't dare go up to check the state of the animal. If by any chance it recovered, it would come for him, and nothing short of an armed-and-armoured soldier would approach an angered yellow-throated marten. In fact he hastened his pace, trotting up the hill, still chuckling to himself.

Iti got up to follow, glancing at the marten a couple of times as she went up the path...and couldn't bear going any further. The poor thing, lying there peacefully, until Rudra's cruel throw knocked it from its perch. But what could she do? It was a wild animal, and as cute as it was she had no illusions about its ferocity.

A soft whimper reached her ears then, a sad, moaning warble. That was it for her. She turned and approached the poor creature with measured steps, but it lay unmoving at the base of the young Himalayan yew. Finally she was close enough to see it, prone on its side, facing her, its bright black eyes lidded with what she thought was pain. 'Oh,' she sighed, 'you poor thing...' It didn't respond, but its breathing quickened, its little chest heaving faster and faster. Iti crouched down at a short distance. 'I'm not going to hurt you,' she whispered, and extended her hand close enough for it to get a scent of her. It sniffed the air nervously with its black nose, and seemed to relax slightly.

How beautiful it was, with its silky black head and golden-white body and black tail. It opened its pink mouth, small sharp teeth showing, and emitted a querying cry. 'Yes,' she replied, inching closer until her hand was close enough for it to place its moist nose to. 'I'll try,' she said, and timidly touched its black paw. But what could she try to do? How exactly had she healed Tal, and her own leg? There wasn't any magic formula or gesture, she had just wanted her friend and herself to get better.

The marten whirled around in a blinding flash of black

and gold, and suddenly it was standing to its full bristling height before her, eye to eye with Iti, hardly ten centimetres from her face. Her breath caught in her throat. But all he did, for it was a he, was cock his head to one side and extend a paw and press the clawless pads to her forehead.

Then he casually turned and leaped away sinuously, his long black tail bobbing, scampering into the bushes. His black-and-gold head popped out for one last look...and then he was gone.

It took Iti a moment to gather her wits again. 'Right,' she finally muttered, dazed. 'Rudra.'

She ran, now, both to catch up with the bully but also to put a little distance from that dangerous scamp she had just saved. It thrilled and warmed her heart to have been able to heal him. He had seemed quite seriously injured. Yet all she had done was touch him and wish in her heart that he was well, and...there, miraculously, he was fine! To think that she could do something so lovely as heal with a touch.

Well, she figured as she caught sight of some movement ahead, now was as good a time as any to prove what more she could do. She slowed down and moved from tree trunk to tree trunk, since the path had faded to practically nothing. There was Reva, she saw, hanging outside a small, shabby stone-and-wood cabin. Some people owned these shacks on their plots of land, here where no one ever really came. So R2R had commandeered someone's cabin. Iti prayed that Tal and Isaac were there, and that they were safe.

It took her a few minutes of creeping to scout around the cabin area from a secure distance. There were windows on both the front and the back, and from the tangle of bushes it was clear no one went behind the cabin. She crawled and rolled her way to the back wall, carefully slid up it, and peered at the glass of the window. It was dusty and dirty, but she could see inside clear enough.

Tal and Isaac were there.

12

OLD FAMILIES

Once Safir had calmed down from the lurid vision of the world outside, with a little help from Auntie Sophie's chunky apple pie, he sat alone in the middle of the sofa in the living room and thought about everything that had happened. He couldn't quite understand how they had all ended up in this situation, with rakshas and Mister Mer and talking cats. Holidays in Devagarh had always been easy, the worst of it being R2R's taunts and bullying, which they had managed to mostly neutralize. It was frustrating to be stuck in the Lodge when Tal and the new boy were in trouble. Surely they were living through a legendary time of the KSS, they would talk about it for months, maybe years, and what would they all remember? That Safir sat at home while everyone was out on the front line. Not that he didn't feel slightly relieved to be sitting there with his feet up and apple pie in hand.

With a sigh Safir finished off the slice and put the plate down on a wooden side table. Time to work. He began trudging around the room picking up the stuff from the Box. Cards and pieces from board games, colouring books, the most mismatched collection of crayons, pencils and chalks on earth… Did they really unpack *all* this in the name of superpower experimentation?

He trod on something hard and looked down: the three blocks that Tri had tried to move with her mind, multi-coloured and with large letters on each face. But…were they stuck together? Safir picked them up and frowned. What was with these? They were attached in an imperfect row, as though they had been glued to each other. He tried to pry them apart, but after thirty seconds of repeated effort he gave up. Weird… He peered at them up close. No solidified gobs of glue squished out the sides. Twisting them didn't work, they had no give. How strange, how really very…strange…

'Woah…' he crooned as it dawned on him. Tri had done it. This was her superpower! Whatever it was. What was it? Fusing things, or joining things? He looked at the cleanly attached blocks with newfound attention, awed. How excited she would be! Or, well, not. He recalled the raucous zeal she showed when they were drawing up the list of superpowers. Flight had thrilled her, super strength too. He could imagine how this would make her react: 'What's my superpower? Joining blocks together? Yay, I'll be a magical carpenter, and work with Chacko Uncle when he comes to fix the locks…'

He put the blocks on top of the cupboard, so it wouldn't get packed up with the rest of the stuff as he cleaned up. 'Better than hearing stuff that doesn't exist,' he murmured to no one.

It took him ten minutes to finish tidying up, which was faster than he had anticipated. The news of Tri's superpower was making him feel more energized than usual. Was this what people called 'enthusiasm'? What an unusual sensation it was.

'Safir!'

His name called out in that way brought out the automatic response: stand up, spine straight, hands down by the sides, chin up, feet together! 'Yes Abba, coming!' Safir squeaked, and trotted out of the living room.

Brigadier Safdar Idris loomed at the entrance of the Lodge, framed by the morning light. Tall and dashing, with steel-grey wings of hair on the sides of his close-cropped hair, and two moulded blades of moustache on his upper lip, the soldier stood almost two metres tall, the epitome of an Indian Army officer. He had donned a cream-coloured sweater vest over his rugged khakis, and flipped a cricket bat this way and that. 'How about a little cricket with us old folk?' he called cheerily as Safir trudged out to meet him.

'Are the others gone?' Dwijesh Pillai asked, rolling up with a bunch of white gloves. He was roly-poly and chuckling about something or other as he looked around. 'Where are they? Trikaya! Iti!'

'They've gone out on an errand,' Safir mumbled.

'An errand?' Zoon Kandhari, Tal and Shari's mother, shook her head knowingly as she whirled a colourful scarf around her neck. 'They're off on some misadventure again, aren't they?'

'So long as they're not misbehaving,' Mr Idris shrugged, and looked down approvingly at Safir. 'I'm glad you're here, at least, instead of bothering the people in town again.'

Safir gave him a tight smile which he knew must look fake.

'Who's misbehaving?' Avalok Kandhari pretended to shout, brandishing his own worn cricket bat threateningly. 'There will be punishments! Heads will be spanked and bottoms will roll!' Mr Kandhari attacked Safir, poking him with a long finger and making him chuckle. His shiny, balding head always seemed freshly waxed and polished, and the round glasses he wore gave him a look like from old Indian movies. 'Fifty pushups! Rations will be halved! Transferred to the Chinese border where your snot will freeze right up your nose and tickle your brain!'

'Oh God, the rubbish you all speak!' Urmi Pillai chided as she entered, beautiful and elegant in her sari. She pointed the three stumps she carried at the three men. 'Always going on about the children misbehaving. Look at the example you set!' She patted Safir's head affectionately. 'We're going to play cricket on the maidan, dear, do you want to come?'

'No thank you,' Safir responded sweetly, feeling his father's gaze on him.

'Why not?' Mr Idris demanded. 'The other kids are out, you're here all alone. It's just cricket.'

'I…I have things to do,' the boy explained in a faltering voice.

'Things, what things? Read comics? Play with toys?' Mr Idris scowled. 'Come on, cricket is a man's game, don't you want to be a man? You're always inside, and reading nonsense, and growing your hair out like a gi—like some kind of hippie.' The other parents stayed quiet, shifting slowly. This was the point when Safir's mother Tahfeem usually scolded her husband, but she was resting upstairs, and the other adults hesitated to interfere between father and son. For Safir it only made everything worse: his father standing over him, humiliating him in front of his friends' parents, and him not being able to say a word. He felt hot tears rising and a thick rock of tension in his throat.

'Okay, okay,' Mr Pillai said, rubbing his belly, 'If the boy's got plans, who are we to keep him? Who knows, Safir may save the world one day? Cure the common cold, or become prime minister!'

'Exactly!' Mr Kandhari exclaimed. 'We shouldn't disturb the track of his destiny.' He tossed a bright red ball in the air. 'But *you*, Safdar…your destiny is to go down this morning, for all to witness!'

Mr Idris hefted the bat and pointed it out the door. 'Like the last time I hit that six and you dropped your pants?'

The others howled while Mr Kandhari blushed and protested, 'My belt broke! I bowled really hard!' Mrs Kandhari and Mrs Pillai had to hold each other to keep from keeling over with laughter. 'It was an old belt.'

Mr Pillai took Mr Idris by the shoulder and guided him out, saying over his shoulder, 'But your boxers were brand new, weren't they? With purple giraffes all over them, weren't they?'

Everyone but Safir followed. Mrs Pillai stopped to plant a kiss on top of the boy's head, and Mrs Kandhari gave him what she hoped was a comforting smile before closing the front door.

Safir adjusted his huge glasses, and took that opportunity to rub his eyes quickly with his index finger. 'I do have things to do,' he muttered. 'Like saving Devagarh.' He sniffed and went to the kitchen. That apple pie needed some saving too.

He was shovelling another piece onto a new plate when he heard someone coming down the stairs. Didn't sound like Ammi. Should be Auntie Jyoti.

'Hello Safir!' Jyoti said when she spotted him, bringing a couple of empty mugs to the sink. 'No cricket for you?'

'Hi, no,' he said around a mouthful.

She was a good-looking lady, with streaks of white in her carefully groomed hair. Safir thought he had heard that she was in newspapers or something... 'Is that apple pie? How many slices have you had?' She smiled as she shook her head. 'Let me make you a sandwich, it's healthier than that.'

Things were looking up! 'Sure,' Safir piped, and quickly added, 'thank you please.' Jyoti laughed, and began to gather the ingredients while he slid onto a stool at the island table. 'Auntie Jyoti, you write newspapers, in London?'

'Yes, all of them.' She grinned at his expression. 'No, I edit one. Meaning I decide what kind of pieces we feature in the newspaper. We have writers who write the stories, and I correct and make some changes if need be. I also write some pieces. Why, do you want to be a journalist?'

He shrugged. 'No, not really. Does Isaac live with you?'

Jyoti's face changed as she cut slices of the bread Auntie Sophie had baked yesterday, and Safir was alarmed. Had he said something he shouldn't have? 'No, he doesn't. He goes to Seamarch School, a boarding school in the west of England, in Somerset. It's very nice, and very old.'

Safir's two brothers and sister were in boarding school, had been for years because of their frequent change in postings due to Abba's job with the Army. Abba and Ammi had quarrelled now and then about Safir staying at home but she had won in the end, arguing that as Abba became more senior they could more comfortably keep a child with them now. Ammi had always felt sad at missing so much of her older children's growing up, and mothered Safir more than Abba liked. 'So...' he began cautiously, 'How are you and Isaac related to Devagarh?'

She looked up with a smile. 'That's a long story, it's so nice you're interested.' Jyoti began building the sandwich, with red pepper mayonnaise covering slices of local cheese and fresh vegetables. 'I'll try to give you the short version. I don't think you know Isaac's father, Ishan?' Safir shook his head. 'Ishan's grandmother was from Devagarh, and left the village with her marriage to a Shroff. And actually, if I remember correctly, *her* mother's first cousin married a girl from Kerala, and their daughter is Iti and Trikaya's great-grandmother. They moved to Kerala and stayed there.'

Safir let out an ooh. 'So Isaac is related to Iti and Trikaya? Like a distant cousin?'

'Yes.'

'Am I related to Isaac or anyone?'

Jyoti thought. 'Not that I know of. I think your family is an old Devagarh Muslim family. Even before the British time. I think Idrises served under the officer who built this Lodge, Connell's Lodge. What was his last name again? Mason? Your great-grandfather was in the famous Kumaon Regiment, in the Indian Army before and after Partition. Did you know that?'

'Yes, he was a naik and was awarded the Victoria Cross in the Second World War, for outstanding bravery in combat,' the boy declared automatically. Brigadier Idris had drilled the family's ranks and achievements into all his children's heads from a young age. And he still popped out quizzes to test Safir... 'What about Tal and Shari?'

'Their great-grandmother left Devagarh on her own to join Mahatma Gandhi on the Salt March.'

'Alone?' he asked, surprised.

'Yes!' Jyoti exclaimed. 'In 1930, that too! Some poor chap had to run in from outside, climb the pass, and tell Devagarh what was going on in the world. She just dropped everything and left when she heard about Mahatma Gandhi, using some money she had saved from working at the Lodge. Her parents forbade her to go, but she still went. And stayed outside, and married and settled in Bombay—that's what it was called then.'

'Even their great-grandmother was cool,' Safir murmured in awe and envy.

'Here,' she said affectionately as she dropped the sandwich in front of him.

'Thank you,' he intoned, and reverentially grabbed the huge chunky treat.

Jyoti pulled a stool up to join Safir and observed his

focused scarfings with a smile. 'So how's Isaac doing with you guys? I hope you're all getting along.'

'Oh yes,' Safir said, struggling to eat, breathe and talk at the same time. 'Yes, everyone likes him. He's really smart. I like how he pays attention to people and things. This is really delicious, thank you! And I think he's a nice guy.' He paused, seeing her hiding her smile. 'What?'

She got up to go to the fridge. 'Let me get you some juice, Safir. I'm afraid for you, I don't know when you get time to breathe!'

The boy grinned, embarrassed. 'Sorry, I get hungry when I get nervous.'

'Nervous?' Jyoti repeated as she poured him some fresh apple juice. 'What are you feeling nervous about?'

Safir froze, coughed, and cleared his throat. 'Nothing, just... We, uh...we were all sick last night, you know... And... It's all a bit... Y'know?' He gratefully took the glass and drank it all down to shut himself up.

'Yes, we were all really worried,' Jyoti said. 'I was terrified!'

'Hello,' a sweet voice called out. Auntie Sophie entered the kitchen, holding a large bag of groceries. She was old and small and quick, and often sang Kumaoni folk songs to herself while she worked, just like a mountain songbird.

'Hello Sophie,' Jyoti said. 'Would you like some help?'

'Oh no, no, don't mind it... Safir, are you all right?'

The two ladies looked at the boy curiously.

'Yes,' he croaked, sweat beginning to form on his forehead. 'Excuse me, I'll just go finish in my room.' He hardly waited for their approval before he was out of the kitchen, plate of sandwich in hand.

'He's a little nervous,' he heard Jyoti explain to Sophie as he ran.

Safir ran to the boys' room, slammed the door closed,

smashed the plate down on the old wooden desk by the wall, and stood shivering in the middle of the room. The moment Auntie Sophie had walked in he had heard a separate voice, as clearly as if it had been spoken in his ear: 'Safir, help me...'

It was Kariba's voice.

The boy adjusted his overlarge round glasses with shaky fingers. He had always heard whispers, soft singing or humming, sometimes angry mutterings. The sounds of beings and things he should not normally perceive, but they were usually muffled or remote. Never had the voices been this strong, this clear. It was as though Kariba had been standing at his elbow, although she was clearly elsewhere. Was this going to be his life now?

He sighed and shook his head. There were more important things going on than his own fears. Whatever his life would be, it would be, and he would have to face it. Right now Kariba needed him. Where was everyone else? Still out, evidently. Should he wait for them, and go in force? Or should he go alone, knowing full well he had very little to provide in terms of help?

While these thoughts ran through his head Safir realized he had gone to the closet and was pulling out his blue jacket and getting his sports shoes. Did he really have a choice? he mulled sarcastically. Abba always said brave men are brave because they choose to do the right thing. Safir wasn't so sure. It didn't feel like he had a choice here but to do the right thing. Kariba was in danger, and that was that. As inadequate as he may be, he was all she had.

'Safir...'

He jumped at the sound again, his heart beating hard. 'Kariba,' he said softly, then louder, 'Kariba, can you hear me?'

'Safir...' the rakshasi's voice came again, plaintive and heavy. 'Please come, help me...' Was she hurt?

The jacket and shoes came on in a flash, and Safir was out of the door with the sandwich plate. He darted into the kitchen, where Auntie Sophie was tying an apron on while she chatted with Jyoti. 'I'm going out,' he announced as he grabbed some paper napkins from a drawer. He was gone before they could say anything.

The sandwich was rolled up in the napkins and jammed deep into his pocket as he jumped down the stairs of the porch and hit the ground running. Maybe she'd be hungry, he justified. Or maybe he'd get scared and need a quick bite to calm himself down. Whichever, the sandwich gave him some sense of comfort. Because he knew exactly where he was heading.

Somewhere in his mind he noted that something must be different about him, as he crossed the bridge to Yakshagarh at a purposeful trot. Yesterday he had been dying all over the place at the thought of that bridge and the sinister things that lay on the other side. No one in their right mind would be unaffected by the creepiness of that jungle, or the hint of those wrecked buildings, or the uncomfortable shadow of the fort overhead. And yet, knowing all this, Safir's step didn't falter. Well, at least until he reached the other side and tried to figure where to go next.

His new vision was strange, making him feel slightly dizzy. It was like he saw everything in two layers, he realized. He could see the normal world as it always had been. And at the same time he could see some kind of other intangible layer over it all. Or under. The trees of the jungle, for example. On one level they were just regular trees, but they were also moving, writhing, twisting, rising up and down, shaking. Their colours melted and swirled, the trunks seething with motion, the leaves blurring red then yellow and black, before turning a sickening purple and on to orange... On and on, everything changing, turning into something other than what it was. It was strange, but after a couple of minutes he decided it wasn't quite so dangerous. The sky, which was on the surface blue with some few clouds drifting across it, was also an ocean of churning acid shifting dark colours... but it wasn't going to just crash down and drown him. Nothing like that. Safir realized he wasn't seeing strange, menacing things. They just seemed so because they were unfamiliar. No, he was just seeing more of the world than most people did. He could feel the trees moving, the earth's slow pulses of natural life, the rocks' slow, slow erosion by wind and water and plant. Listening was his power. Safir nodded, feeling a stirring of excitement in his heart. What else could it be but that he could Listen and hear the universe itself?

'Safir...'

When Kariba's voice came to his ears, he turned in its direction. She was downhill, in the jungle, deeper than they had gone yesterday. Well, at least it wasn't up into the village. That might have been a little more than he could handle alone.

The gloom and cool of Yakshagarh's forest closed in on him quickly, and within thirty seconds he was lost in its heart. Of course he had been in a jungle before—but it hadn't been this alien and watchful then. Once again he came to the conclusion that it wasn't dangerous, it wasn't threatening him, it was just forbidding. Of course, if that monster they met the day before was here, it would be a different story. Safir knew, however, with a certainty he couldn't explain, that he would know if that monster was coming for him. The jungle would tell him in some manner, he felt.

No, what he needed to do now was find Kariba, instead of thinking of Yakshagarh and its uncanny dwellers. And that was easy enough, with her voice chiming in his ear every moment or so. She was leading him through the forest straight to her. What was the matter with her, though? She sounded like she was in danger, but she didn't say anything more than his name, and plead for his help. Was she unconscious and somehow unable to send out thoughts more coherently?

Whatever it was, he was on the trail. It felt like he was getting closer, he knew it, just a few more steps—there! There was an outline of someone, through the trees, at a distance. Safir quickened his pace, running as fast as he could over the rocks and between the tree trunks. 'Kariba!' he called out. He had done it. He had found her. 'Kariba, I'm here! It's Safir!' Him, Safir, all alone. What a triumphant return he would have, back at the Lodge. While they were out rescuing Tal and Isaac from R2R, he had crossed the bridge to rescue Kariba on Yakshagarh. Alone! Just beyond this large oak, now, and there was Kari...

Safir skidded to a halt, nearly tumbling into a thornbush.

It was not Kariba.

'Hello Safir. Fancy meeting you out here.'

Rising up to his height of more than two metres, his dark face a mask of friendliness, Mister Mer looked down at the boy. 'And all alone, too...'

13
INTO THE TEMPLE

Five minutes after Kumar Fourteen had effectively disappeared, Shari pulled up short and waited for Trikaya to catch up. They were both out of breath, sweating and hot, and frustrated to boot.

'Did you see him?' Trikaya asked, knowing the answer.

'He's long gone,' Shari replied, and sat down on the bottom step of a house. Behind them, to the side, two goats scrutinized them while chewing grass, sheltered in their ground-floor stall, 'Did you see Iti?'

Trikaya collapsed on the step next to him with a shuddering moan. 'No,' she gasped, too tired to say anything more. If Safir had been around he'd have had something to snack on and keep their energy going.

Shari grunted. He figured Iti would be able to take care of herself. She would find them either here or back at the Lodge, but he still felt bad about losing her. He had known she wouldn't be able to keep up, but the urgency of saving Tal and Isaac had taken precedence.

The yellow door above opened, and they turned to see an older Kumaoni lady come down the stairs with two copper glasses of water. 'Hello, hello!' she sang to them, smiling around the wrinkles that were beginning to form on her sun-browned face. 'You're the little ones from the Lodge here for the holidays, right?' They began to shift to stand up and say hello, but she hopped down to them nimbly. 'Don't move, I've seen you running all up and down. Here, have a drink, poor little drongos!'

Poor little drongos? They controlled their smiles, thinking of the ruffled, indignant looks all drongos seemed to have. 'Thank you,' they chirped and drank the water gratefully under her kind eye.

'Do you know what's going on tonight,' she asked, 'at that Mister Mer's show?' They shook their heads. 'I wonder what he's really doing back here. What a funny fellow he was…'

Shari and Tal shared an electrified look. 'Did you know him?' he asked as casually as he could.

'Well, you kind of know everyone in the village. But then you wonder if you *really* know everyone. You know what I mean?' She adjusted the folds of her green sari to sit by them. 'Mahipati is the only child of the Mer family, which I was told is one of the oldest in Devagarh.'

'His name is Mahipati?' Trikaya asked instantly, her too-straight expression making it hard for Shari to keep a smile down. 'Mahipati Mer?'

'Yes. The Mers fell on hard times a few generations ago. The story they told was that they were of royal blood, although no one is sure how. There used to be an old royal dynasty in Devagarh, but I don't think the Mers were related to them. Anyway, Mahipati's grandfather was trying to regain the family's presumed old standing, and was desperate to buy out the Lodge. But he was also a gambler, and lost everything they had. Mahipati's father Kshithiraj was forced to rent land and farm it, which was impossible for Mahipati to face. It was clear he was ashamed of his father, although everyone else in the village respected Kshithiraj for doing whatever he could to provide for his family. Mahipati refused to work the land, and spent most of his days out in the hills, or studying those old books in the houses of worship.' She paused, sighing at the tragedy of those lives.

'His father's name was Kshithiraj?' Trikaya interjected, letting a little smile show. Shari poked her to make her stop.

The lady looked slightly perplexed by the same kind of question coming from the little girl. 'Yes, dear. Everything seemed all right, really, until that dreadful monsoon. Poor Kshithiraj and his farm were washed away in the rain in the dead of night. Mahipati was travelling outside, and missed the funeral by a day. He scattered Kshithiraj's ashes in Akashankh Lake and then…disappeared.'

'Disappeared?' Trikaya whispered throatily. 'With magic?'

'Magic?' the lady frowned. 'No, it's a figure of speech. He packed a suitcase and rode a mule up to the pass. He disappeared, meaning he left, for, I don't know thirty or forty years? Until yesterday, when he reappeared out of the blue. Not with magic. Or, well, I don't know, maybe with magic now. He's a magician, isn't he? So…maybe.' She plucked the copper glasses from their hands. 'I need to get back to my cooking. Would you like some more?'

'No thank you,' they both chimed. Trikaya grabbed the lady's forearm and leaned forward to kiss her on the cheek. The lady chuckled and returned the favour with delight before climbing the steps up to the first floor and closing the door.

Shari grabbed Trikaya, and hustled her down the lane back to the main avenue. 'So Mister Mer is old royalty,' he summarized as they trotted past a group of men in turbans carrying rolled-up carpets, one of Devagarh's few exports.

'Yes. And his name is Mahipati, Mahipati Mer,' she reminded him emphatically, grinning.

'Yes it is,' Shari chuckled. 'I think we should head back to the Lodge. We didn't find the walkie-talkie, so maybe they still have it. We give it a little time. Tal is scrappy, and Isaac is a smart guy. I'm sure they'll find some way to communicate with us.'

'Okay,' the girl nodded, but it was clear she didn't like it. There was nothing else they could do now, however, and she knew it just as much as Shari did. He hoped that Iti had reached the same conclusion and would be back home already.

They reached Dharm Square in a couple of minutes, keeping away from those strange black poles with the thin filament branches hanging down. Shari had figured it was Mister Mer's work because of the weird feeling Trikaya and he both got about them.

At this time of day Dharm Square was mostly deserted, a thoroughfare for people going from town to Bazaar Round or the Lodge. It was a large clear space about twenty metres across with each house of worship on one side.

To their right, on the north side and uphill, was the Hindu Barbarika temple, the oldest and most impressive of the four buildings, made of the grey-brown granite of the Kumaon hills. Through the entrance pillars and a cluster of brass bells, they could catch a glimpse of the Barbarika idol within, his large crowned head smiling out to the valley.

To the immediate left, on the east of Dharm Square, was the mosque, painted brilliant white with a beautifully carved minaret at one corner, its inner courtyard made of pristine white marble.

On the south side, facing the Barbarika temple, was an old Buddhist stupa, a plain yellow sandstone dome with a simple entrance and a cavernous appearance.

Opposite them, on the west, was the church, a wood-and-stone building with a triangular slate roof and large wooden doors kept open all day to welcome visitors.

A round of benches sat in the middle of the square, and on one of them sat two persons they knew, who watched them approaching with big smiles.

'Good morning, Bhante,' Shari called out to the Buddhist priest, and then to the Hindu priest, 'Good morning, Pujari.' Trikaya followed his lead, echoing his greetings.

Bhante Rinzen jumped up to give them affectionate hugs, wrapping them up in the bright orange robes she always wore. 'Hello Shari, Trikaya!' She was in the middle of her twenties, an exceptionally young age to be the Bhante of such an ancient stupa, which was how everyone knew she must be very accomplished. With her round bald head and stylish red glasses, she was beloved of everyone at Devagarh.

Tall and stately, old Pujari Nandan was more restrained but equally friendly from a distance, doing a namaste at the children, who reciprocated.

'What's the business these days?' Bhante Rinzen asked them with twinkling eyes.

'Same old,' Shari replied quickly, before Trikaya's usual eagerness made her reveal anything. 'Doing our jobs and stuff.'

'Jobs,' Trikaya stated emphatically, picking up on his discretion. 'Nothing weird or unusual at all. What's up with you?'

Bhante Rinzen made a face. 'Just a bit worried. Father Ewan and Imam Azlan have been sick all morning.'

'Are they okay?' Shari asked, concerned. The four spiritual leaders were often seen together, talking animatedly about their congregations, trying to find ways to help and support each other. The Kandharis weren't as religiously active as the

Pillais, who went to the Barbarika temple a couple times a week, but they knew Pujari Nandan fairly well, and knowing one of the four meant knowing all the others.

'Not really,' Pujari Nandan said, scratching his head ruefully. 'It's a strange ailment. They don't actually have fever or anything, but they say they feel tremendously weak.' He paused, breathed deeply, and blinked. 'I went to see Imam Azlan this morning, he could barely stand. I helped him back into bed, and he just lay there, he couldn't even speak.' The other three watched him carefully as he cleared his throat, and raised a trembling hand to his forehead. 'He just...' Again he blinked, slowly and deliberately, and then started slumping sideways.

Shari quickly caught the old man before he could hurt himself. Bhante Rinzen called his name anxiously as she helped him lie down on the bench.

'What's going on?' Trikaya squeaked nervously as she hopped here and there.

'Let's get him in the stupa,' Bhante Rinzen grunted as she put her effort into helping him stand. Pujari Nandan's eyes were open, they could see, and he was trying to stand by himself, in vain. Shari took handfuls of the priest's brick-red kurta to get a good grip, and together they helped the old man hobble across to the closest temple, the stupa.

They entered the stupa, a tunnel that dug deep into the thick walls that made the old dome. Shari had never entered the stupa before, and was awed by the cool and solid presence of the yellow sandstone arching overhead. He felt Trikaya press up against him, and glanced at her. 'I've never been inside,' she confessed softly, clearly intimidated.

The tunnel emerged into a round chamber, with a ceiling that was covered in faded paintings. It was surprisingly warm, Shari thought, probably because of the numerous light bulbs that had been set up here and there. There was a stone pillar about a metre tall in the middle of the chamber, with a Buddha sitting cross-legged carved into it. The room was otherwise mostly bare, but there were some cushions laid out against the walls for worshippers to sit and meditate. Trikaya ran to gather those, and they laid Pujari Nandan down on them. He was very still and quiet, but his eyes watched them intently. Bhante Rinzen quickly went to get a blanket from a large chest near the door, and in that moment the priest's eyebrows moved. Shari put a hand on Pujari Nandan's hand, wondering what to do. The priest's lips moved. Shari quickly put his ear to hear if he had anything to say.

'My spirit…' was the slightest whisper that came. 'Help it…' There was nothing more.

Shari leaned back, feeling an emptiness in the pit of his stomach. Help Pujari Nandan's spirit? What could it mean? The priest's eyes were fixed on him a moment more, and then drifted away. Pujari Nandan relaxed, and didn't respond when Bhante Rinzen came to cover him with a blanket.

The boy stood up, seeing Bhante Rinzen was checking the old man for fever or other things. He looked around, seeing Trikaya wasn't there. She was wandering around, inspecting the stupa with her typical innocent curiosity. On the opposite side, not far from the entrance, was a desk with two simple chairs. A bookcase next to the desk contained forty or fifty thick ancient tomes, which Trikaya peered at.

'Don't touch them,' Shari warned as he approached, making her stick her tongue out at him. 'We don't want to offend Bhante.' She rolled her eyes, and nodded. He stood nearby a moment, then stepped up to the desk himself. He had to admit he was curious. There were long and wide clay jars on the other side of the table, old and dusty with stoppers still in them. On the desk were a dozen modern notebooks stacked on top of each other, and a long piece of paper with ancient illustrations on it. He frowned, looking closer at it. It was a black-and-white copy, he saw, a printout on modern paper of some old scroll or something. The writing on it was completely foreign to him, they looked like lines of stick figures.

'That's Brahmi script,' Bhante Rinzen said, suddenly appearing behind them. She looked worried and tired, but was still enthusiastic. 'Do you know it?' Trikaya made an exaggerated I-don't-know face, and Shari shrugged. 'It's one of the oldest scripts known in India. The writing on the Ashoka Pillar is in Brahmi. It's the origin of the Devanagari script, and all the other scripts in India. This is Devagarh's oldest historical document,' Bhante Rinzen pointed at the long scroll copy, then at a stretch of writing separate from the rest. 'Here, you can read its title: Origin Scroll. It talks about the origins of Devagarh and Yakshagarh. The script is Brahmi, but you must understand there's a difference between script and language. Sanskrit is a language. You know it today in one script form, but it used to be written in different scripts.'

'Different scripts?' Trikaya exclaimed. 'Like...if I wrote Hindi with English letters?'

'Exactly!' Bhante Rinzen cried out, delighted that the little girl understood. She guided them back to the scroll copy. 'So I originally thought this was Sanskrit written in Brahmi, but it wasn't working. Then I realized it was Prakrit written in Brahmi, and it all made sense.'

Shari frowned. 'What's Prakrit?'

'Sanskrit was actually the language of the elite: the educated, the aristocracy, and the priests. But the majority of people spoke Prakrit of their own region, a vernacular language. Prakrits were sort of the local version of Sanskrit.'

'Oh yes,' Shari said, 'Like Mumbaiya is for Hindi.'

'Yes,' Bhante Rinzen said, and chuckled, 'Ooh, this much excitement, it's…it's a bit…' She turned and sat down on one of the chairs suddenly.

Shari glanced at Trikaya, who made a face of concern. Was the same illness striking Bhante Rinzen? 'Bhante, maybe you should lie down?'

The priest nodded. 'Yes, I understand. It's safer.' She tried to get up once, twice, and then with the children's help managed to stand. 'I'm so sorry,' Bhante Rinzen murmured, shuffling her legs.

Trikaya grabbed some extra cushions from near Pujari Nandan and made a small bed, then went to get another blanket. Shari helped Bhante Rinzen down, saying, 'Should I get Dr Negi?'

The priest shook her head. 'No need. It's not an illness, there are no symptoms. It's just…exhaustion.' They drew the blanket over her, tucking the sides and corners in around Bhante Rinzen's small form and pulling the red plastic glasses off her face. 'No need to bother Dr Negi. We'll…just…sleep it off.'

They stood looking down at the priest for a moment. 'What do we do?' Trikaya asked.

'I say we check in on them later,' Shari suggested. He knelt by Bhante Rinzen and cupped her hand. 'We'll come back, Bhante.'

The priest blinked to show she understood, and then closed her eyes.

Shari stood up, gestured for them to exit, and jogged out of the stupa with Trikaya. The moment they exited, blinking in the sunlight, he stepped close to her and whispered, 'Did you hear what she said about that scroll? It's about the origins of Devagarh and Yakshagarh!'

'Yes!' Trikaya whispered back intently. 'Maybe there are clues to figure this whole thing out.'

'Let's head back for now. When Kariba comes we'll know what the new plan is, and when we go out next we'll drop by the stupa. We can check in on Bhante and Pujari, and get Dr Negi if they seem worse. It'll also give us a chance to get another look at the Origin Scroll.' Trikaya nodded, and they hurried away.

Things were getting spookier by the minute, Shari thought. The demon on Yakshagarh, Mister Mer's creepy black poles, and now all four spiritual leaders taken out by some mysterious ailment... And through this all, he kept failing. Tal and Isaac Shroff were captured by R2R, and it made him sick to imagine what those bullies were doing to his twin and the new boy. Shari knew that Tal was a fireball, which is why he had always been the patient and calm one, the one they could all rely on. Even with the KSS's split. It hurt him, and them all, and Tal too, he knew. But he had thought they would all turn to him eventually, and Tal would have no choice but to follow the democratic flow.

How foolish he seemed to himself now, and weak and helpless. He, dependable? What had he done when the demon attacked? Iti had shouted at them to get into the water, which had gotten them away from it. And then after they were swept away, Isaac Shroff was the one who had gotten them heading back to the Lodge. And Shari had just run around, and been terrified, and been useless. Some leader he was.

For a while now he had felt Tal thought about things differently than him. And sure enough the KSS had broken. How could he not have seen it coming? Tal was always doing dangerous, impetuous things, jumping into things before thinking them through rationally. And where Tal jumped,

Trikaya leaped screaming. And with Trikaya went Iti and Safir. Shari sighed. He was losing the KSS. And if he wasn't leading the KSS on the right path...who was he?

'Hey,' Trikaya called out, tapping his arm. 'What's with the sad face?'

'Just,' he said quickly. 'Tal, and the KSS and stuff. Come on.' Shari turned up the speed, and Trikaya followed. Even here, he thought bitterly. Trikaya had her mind on what mattered, while he was dreaming about being the leader of the KSS. 'Come on,' he muttered again through gritted teeth, this time at himself, at Shari. Come on, Shari, back to take things head on.

Back to the Lodge.

14

PRISONERS

No matter how much she twisted and turned her arms, Tal could just not loosen the thick strings that had been double-looped around her wrists.

'Leave it,' Isaac advised softly, 'You'll hurt yourself.'

'Iti will heal it,' she retorted, but stopped with a sigh. It's true her shoulders were aching from the effort. When had R2R learned to tie real knots? And behind their backs too. The only comfortable position was lying on their bellies, and she would never do that before those thugs.

She shifted around to sit with her back to the wall, next to Isaac, and studied the cabin they were imprisoned in for the eighteenth time. It was a simple enough affair of stone walls and wood roof, with a cot and no other furnishings. Bundles of dry twigs took up the entire cot, however, stacked up almost to the ceiling. Which genius had decided to stack wood on the only piece of furniture? Not that they could really use it, Tal fumed, trussed up like this.

The door shifted slightly with the wind, giving them wider and narrower glimpses of Reva and Ruma standing guard outside. Well, standing guard was probably too sophisticated a term. They were walking around bored, kicking at things, while gossiping about school, sports, and clothes. If only they could cut these bonds… Tal was sure that Isaac and she could take on the girls, with Rudra absent. He had left so long ago, it felt like an hour.

'What's their plan?' Isaac asked suddenly.

Their plan? What was R2R's plan, ever? To humiliate and torment the KSS, what else? 'I don't know, lure out the others?'

'And then what?' the boy continued.

'They have the IQ of a rubber chicken,' Tal replied. 'There is no plan. It's just to mess around with us.'

Isaac didn't look convinced. 'Have they ever tied you guys up and brought you to this cabin?'

'No, that's new,' she had to confess. 'Usually it's just a bit of roughing up and some insults.' It was true, this was a far more elaborate plan than any she remembered from R2R. Was Isaac Shroff right? Was there something more to the thug patrol this time than usual?

'Can I ask you a personal question?' the new boy asked, interrupting her thought.

'Sure.'

'Why did the KSS split?'

Tal looked at Isaac for a moment, not sure what to make of it. 'Tri must have told you already,' she said, letting him know she knew that he knew.

He nodded, 'Yes, but I wanted to hear your reason.'

Tal didn't answer for a few seconds. Why did the KSS split? There was no question it saddened her deeply. When their parents had first brought Tal and Shari here on holiday years ago, there had been no end to their fury. Devagarh seemed like the dullest, horriblest place on Earth. Then they had met Iti and Tri and Safir. They had formed the Kumaon Secret Society, and the KSS became the be-all and end-all of her life, at least here. Year after year the KSS had been the saving grace of Devagarh, a place without mobiles, Wi-Fi, television or automobiles. It was a wonder they even had electricity…

So why did the KSS break?

'I think…' she began, unsure about her thought. 'I think it's because we're growing up.' And with that admission came relief and worry—relief that she had finally put her finger on it, but worry that saying it out loud would only precipitate the demise of the one thing that defined Devagarh for her. 'I think the others were happy with Shari and I leading because we were all kids, it wasn't such a big deal. But now they're all questioning our decisions. Even Shari and I…' She had to pause a moment, realizing how much it hurt that there was such a divide between her and her twin brother. Sure, they had always seemed to disagree on some small things, like toys and TV, but those things hadn't really mattered. Not like the KSS. 'Well, Shari and I are literally on different teams right now,' she concluded bitterly.

'Is it really that bad a thing?' Isaac asked gently. 'That everyone's growing up?'

No, Tal figured. It wasn't, in and of itself. And furthermore… Tal felt a new stirring of determination. She realized everyone growing up would make the KSS stronger, especially with these new powers. If only she could find a way to keep them all together. She hadn't been particularly spectacular at doing that recently. And she had to admit to herself that Shari's argument about the KSS doing the right thing did make her wonder. Wonder if she really was that good after all. Wasn't she the one that had pushed for them to cross the bridge yesterday? To go after the cats, which made them meet Mister Mer, and then come face to face with that demon on Yakshagarh? Even now she and Isaac Shroff were in danger because she had insisted on going to return Kumar Fourteen to Mrs Dangwal. What was the need to do that? Just her need to be a hero.

'I'm sorry,' she said suddenly.

He looked over his shoulder at her, puzzled. 'For what?'

'About the walkie-talkie. I should have told you.'

Isaac grinned, a little embarrassed. 'It's okay, forget it. I mean, we're on the same team, right? And that means we don't let things like that get in the way.'

Tal smiled, 'That's right. You're in the Real KSS.'

'Shouldn't we have code names or something, now that we're getting superpowers?' he joked.

'We should,' she laughed, lying back down and looking out the dirty window to the sky. 'Safir's pretty easy, we'll call him the Ear.'

'He'd hate that! Iti should be—Witch Doctor.'

'Nice! She'd pretend to be shy about the witch part, but she'd actually like it. And you, what would you be? I know!' She sat up, wriggling to get cross-legged so she could see his reaction. She made a hard face and growled, 'The Maximizer.'

Isaac groaned. 'That's terrible. And good. But I get to fix your name when we know your power!'

'Deal,' she said, and automatically tried to reach out to shake his hand. They both started laughing.

'What's so funny?' Rudra called from outside, kicking the door open. He leaned in and scowled at them, Ruma and Reva peering around him. 'You're going to be spending the next few hours like this, is that cause for amusement?' There was sweat on his face, and his eyes seemed unable to focus on any one thing for too long.

'Why are we here?' Isaac asked him casually.

'Because I say so,' Rudra replied, stepping into the cabin. Tal hadn't noticed at first, but in his hand was a long wooden stick ten centimetres thick. Not the kind you poke around in bushes with. She felt something stirring uneasily inside as she watched him tap that stick on the ground. Ruma and Reva came in and closed the door.

'Who are you keeping us here for?' Isaac pressed.

Rudra began to answer, stopped himself, and became inexplicably furious. 'You shouldn't talk!' he yelled, pointing the stick at Isaac. 'You're new here, you don't know anyone, and you join up with them?'

Tal knew she should say something, anything. She could see Rudra was acting strange, but her jaw couldn't move to speak. Isaac was talking, and drawing all of Rudra's mad attention, but he didn't know Rudra, didn't know that there was something wrong with him, something off...

'There is someone, isn't there?' Isaac continued, nervously eyeing the stick. Why did he keep talking? 'Is it Mister Mer?'

Ruma and Reva stood frozen near the door, as frozen as Tal felt. She wanted to yell at them to stop Rudra, but the girls looked strange too, their eyes glazed and their thought slow. Well, slower than usual.

'Mister Mer!' Rudra screamed. Tal and Isaac recoiled from the boy's howl. Ten different expressions played on Rudra's face at the same time. His free right hand reached up to rub his forehead above his eye, hard. 'Mister Mer! I'm sorry, I couldn't find him!' He hefted his stick, winding up for a swing at Isaac. 'I couldn't find him,' he mumbled, and stepped forward...

Tal let out a sharp scream and lunged to the side, trying to cover Isaac...

Isaac put up his legs to try to fend off the stick with his sneakers...

The door flew open again, cracking against the wall loud enough to make R2R jump.

Iti stood in the doorway.

'Er... I'm here,' she said. Then she took a deep breath, put her right hand on her hip, and pointed her left index at Rudra. 'You stop that right now, or I'm going to take care of you!'

15

IN THE DARKNESS, A STAR

There was a moment of silence, and then Rudra turned slowly, letting the stick rest on his shoulder. 'What was that?'

Iti waited a moment for inspiration to strike...but nothing came. 'Umm...' she started, trying to think of what to do next. 'I said stop, Rudra. Put that down. Nobody should get hurt.'

'Everybody gets hurt,' Rudra drawled. 'All you can do is try to get hurt less than before.'

Ruma and Reva smirked at Iti, who just now realized that as necessary as her intervention had been, her plan beyond the interruption of Rudra's assault was kind of lacking. She had thought that with her there the odds would have evened to three on three, but hadn't considered that Tal and Isaac were still tied up, which effectively made it three on one.

The two girls advanced on Iti, who put her hands out instinctively, and they grabbed her arms. 'No, stop!' she cried out, and pulled back. The girls were stronger and tougher, however, and they began shoving her further into the cabin while Rudra watched and snickered.

Finally Iti had to move or get dragged bodily, so she skipped forward, and found herself standing over Tal and Isaac. Between her and the door now were Ruma, Reva and dark Rudra with his stick. 'Iti, goodie goodie perfect girl,' he mocked, his eyes becoming strange again. 'You're not really needed, are you?' His teeth began to chatter, clicking together madly for twenty seconds, so long that even Ruma and Reva stared at him warily. 'You first, then.'

'Stop!' Tal shouted, unable to stand any harm coming to Iti.

'Or what?' Rudra taunted, glancing at Tal.

Tal shook with anger, furious at her helplessness, at the situation. She felt oddly focused, at the same time, and had the strangest sensation in her hands, as though they were becoming heavy, but not. 'Or else...or else...' She didn't know what to say, but the sensation in her hands was becoming unbearable, she had to release whatever it was or burst. Tied behind her back, Tal's hands snapped open involuntarily, fingers spread, and she let go of that heaviness.

A flash of light, bright as a camera's flash, burst from behind her, illuminating the wall for an instant and startling everyone.

Iti saw Tal blink in shock, looking around. Then their eyes met and they both knew. This was Tal's power. 'You did it!' Iti breathed, smiling with excitement.

'You did,' Rudra told Tal, 'whatever useless trick that was. And it made me do this.' He moved towards Iti, swung the stick back, ready to hit...

The strangest sound stopped him this time, a small inquiring yowl. Everyone turned to look at the open door. No one was there. They looked down. Something was there.

He stood on his two hind paws, all thirty centimetres of shiny fur and bristle, sleek black, white, and yellow, a hunter and warrior of the forest, peering at the scene with bright black eyes: the yellow-throated marten.

'What's that?' Isaac shot off spontaneously, having never

seen one before. No one else answered, because they all knew what exactly had stepped into the cabin with them.

The marten eyed Ruma, studied Reva, then looked further to focus on Iti. His tiny pink mouth opened and a small fuzzy sound came out. Then his glossy eyes shifted to Rudra and narrowed. This was the one who had knocked him off the branch. Through the confusion of falling, of his pain, he had sniffed out the smell of that nasty human boy who had attacked him. This was the same smell, no doubt. His small hackles rose, and he showed his teeth to the human boy.

Rudra shakily held the stick out between himself and the marten, cold terror rising in his spine.

The marten let out a marten laugh, held out his front paws. The human boy had a stick? He had claws. *Shikt* Twenty of them.

Iti's mouth popped open as she saw the marten dart forward in a blur of colour, sinuous tail flowing behind him. He ignored Ruma and Reva and made straight for Rudra. Everyone in the cabin began yelling and whooping, but Iti threw out a hand and shouted, 'He's with us!' and Tal and Isaac somehow understood and managed to stay calm. As calm as one could be with a marten on a rampage two metres away.

R2R began a maniacal dance, all of them jogging frantically, knees high, hopping to get away from the marten's teeth and claws. Rudra was running circles around Ruma and Reva, trying to keep them between him and the marten, while the marten gleefully slashed and grabbed at whatever was nearest.

It was Reva who tripped up first, alas, and the marten grabbed on to her leg and gave it a neat little gnawing. In the meantime Ruma and Rudra took off as fast as they had ever run in their young lives, bawling all the way down to the village. The marten let Reva go and sped after the other two, but after a few dozen metres outside decided to let them go, and returned at a measured trot.

Reva had collapsed to the floor, holding her wounded leg, crying and shrieking, shaking her hands and calling for her mother. The marten sat down near the door and watched her with an amused expression, sleek black tail twitching.

It took two minutes for Iti to untie Tal and Isaac, and the first thing the girls did was hug each other.

'You were amazing!' Tal panted.

'You got your power!' Iti giggled. 'What did you do?'

'I don't know!' Tal squealed, rubbing her wrists.

Iti saw there were red lines where her friend had been tied up. 'Let me see that.' She ran her fingers over the chafed skin, praying that it would heal, and sure enough it did.

'You're doing it, you're controlling it!' Isaac remarked, eyebrows arched in wonder.

'I am,' Iti smiled. 'Here, let me see you.' She took Isaac's hands, which were less marked than Tal's.

'Thanks,' the boy said. 'You should fix the girl, she's hurt.'

They looked at Reva, who was still curled up on the floor, but watched them through her tears.

'You don't deserve it,' Tal spat out. 'But we're the good guys. Do it, Iti.'

Iti knelt on the floor by Reva. 'I'm going to heal it, don't move.' She carefully pulled aside the strips of salwar from the girl's shin, awed by how the marten had so expertly shredded the sky blue cloth. The wound on Reva's leg was bad and messy. Iti looked Reva in the eye, 'Are you ready?' The injured girl nodded, pressing her lips together. 'On three, okay? One, it's done.' Iti sat back, and looked down at Reva's leg.

Every single scratch and bite that had been on the girl's leg a few seconds ago was gone. Reva's jaw was wide open as she gingerly poked and rubbed the smooth unmarked skin. 'How did you…? Thank you! Thank you!'

'Okay, enough grovelling,' Tal snapped, standing over Reva with her arms crossed. 'Why did you kidnap us?'

The girl thought, and thought, and frowned, and thought, before saying, 'I don't know… I can't remember. Did someone tell us to do this? I don't know. And we brought you here, then Rudra left to go get…someone, but…I don't remember who.'

Tal leaned over to look her in the eye. 'You expect us to believe this?'

Iti and Isaac exchanged a look. 'Tal, I think she's telling the truth,' Iti said. Reva seemed too traumatized by the marten's attack to lie.

'I am!' Reva squeaked.

The three moved off to huddle together. Tal whispered, 'I think so too, I was just hustling her to check. It's Mister Mer, isn't it?'

'Probably,' Isaac nodded. 'Almost certainly.'

'What do we do with her?' Iti wondered.

'Feed her to your little friend,' Tal gloated, making an evil face. She sighed at the concern on Iti's face. 'Or let her go home to mummy, so she can come back and plot against us another day.'

'That sounds more KSS, doesn't it?' Isaac declared cheerfully.

They turned back to Reva. 'Okay you can go,' Tal said, 'Where's our walkie-talkie?'

'Outside,' Reva said, getting up and brushing dirt off her clothes. She timidly stepped out for a moment and returned with the yellow walkie-talkie. 'It's fine, we didn't do anything to it. We were probably going to keep it.'

'"Steal it" is the right expression,' Tal corrected. 'Say you're sorry to us, and thank you to Iti, and say sir and ma'am.'

Annoyance flashed in Reva's eyes, some of her old spirit, but she swallowed it and said, 'I'm sorry sir, ma'am. Thank you, Iti ma'am.' Tal nodded, and she turned to go, but Iti tugged at her sleeve.

'I know you didn't really want to do it,' she told the thug. 'You, and Ruma, even Rudra. We're not your enemies. I'm not your enemy.' She smiled at Reva. The bully looked embarrassed, wagged her head, and left, giving the marten a wide berth. He ignored her. Iti turned back and saw Tal rolling her eyes. 'What?'

'You're too nice,' she said, pulling her tight black ponytail to the front to see how badly it had got disordered and if it needed redoing.

'I just think you're nice,' Isaac shrugged. 'There's no such thing as too nice.'

Tal rolled her eyes again. 'Yes, of course there's no such thing as too nice. I think you're nice, Iti, not too nice.' She tucked the walkie-talkie into her jacket pocket. 'Now let's get home. What's the deal with your friend?'

They looked at the marten, who uncurled himself, stretched his lithe body, and waited expectantly.

'I don't know,' Iti said. 'I think he does his own thing.'

They left the cabin a moment later, and the marten pranced alongside them, a black and yellow ruffian running smoothly through the grass.

'So what's the plan now?' Isaac threw out.

'Back to the Lodge,' Tal ruled. 'Meet Kariba, and then see.'

'But what did Mister Mer want with this kidnapping?' Iti thought out loud.

They exchanged looks as they started down the slope back to Devagarh. 'We don't know,' Tal judged, holding their eyes, 'But one thing's certain: he wants something from us.'

16
A TANGLE OF ROOTS

'Well, this is rather fortuitous,' a cheerful Mister Mer said, producing a cup of hot chocolate from the air and holding it out to Safir.

'Thank you,' Safir mumbled as he accepted the cup, sweating profusely.

They sat side by side on a tree trunk that had fallen ages ago, staring out into the jungle. Well, Safir stared out, while Mister Mer smiled and studied him.

'I understand, it's a bit unnerving,' the magician said, pulling some enticing-looking thing from his sleeve, drawing Safir's eyes back. 'Cannoli?' he offered.

'Yes please,' Safir said, trying to keep his voice from trembling. He plucked the cannoli from the older man's hand and began munching on it. 'Oh,' he said, eyes widening. It was just as good as Mademoiselle's cannoli! He blinked, inspected it. In fact, it looked exactly like Mademoiselle's cannoli.

'Don't tell her,' Mister Mer whispered conspiratorially. 'There may be a couple more missing from her tray this afternoon. Now, the question is: what exactly are you doing wandering around Yakshagarh in the middle of the morning?'

'Me?' Safir piped. He cleared his throat and brought his voice down to a less humiliating pitch. 'I come here all the time.'

Mister Mer laughed out loud. 'Well done! But, come on, look at you. You're terrified! When you saw me you were shaking so much I could see the calories melting off you. You're shaking less now, but I dare say you're generally in a constant state of trembling.' He gestured grandly at the deep forest around them, the dark trees towering overhead, the tangle of bushes and tall weeds. 'Don't get me wrong, this is a pretty frightening place. I'm scared. Yes, right now, at this very moment, I'm scared. Who knows what kinds of things lurk on this gloomy hill? Ghosts. Dead things. Things that should be dead. Rakshsas of all sorts...'

Safir glanced from the corner of his eye, but Mister Mer was still gazing dreamily into the jungle. Good. He had to find a way to ditch the magician and find Kariba. In a way that wasn't suspicious. And yet, when he focused on the forest, on Kariba's voice, when he tried to Listen, he couldn't hear or feel anything anymore. As though Kariba wasn't there anymore.

Or never had been in the first place.

The shiver that convulsed him nearly made him spill his hot chocolate. 'Oh, careful!' the magician exclaimed, and pulled from a pocket a narrow but sturdy wrought-iron coffee table for Safir to put down his drink. 'My, you're all sorts of jumpy. I don't understand it. Aren't you Safir Idris? I thought Idrises were all hulking heroes. And with a name like Safir, too...'

The boy looked at the magician. 'My name? What do you mean?'

'You don't know the meaning of your name?' Mister Mer huffed in indignation. 'Criminal negligence! With a name like yours?' He stood up, appearing to Safir's eye almost as tall as the trees around them. 'Safir, son of Esclabor, who was a high lord of Babylon? Safir was one of the premier knights of King Arthur, one of Lancelot du Lac's great allies and friends, and a Saracen from Arabia! He was made Duke of Languedoc. Do you know where that is? The southwest of France today, a powerful and magical region back in King Arthur's day. That's who you're named after!'

Safir sipped his hot chocolate. 'That's cool.'

'Yes, it is cool!' Mister Mer declared grandly. 'But you're young, I know. And when you're young, things loom large, and the unknown has terrifying dimensions. That's normal. You'd be mad if you weren't a little scared. But you're an Idris! The blood of Fierabras!'

'Who?' the boy asked meekly.

The magician looked gobsmacked. 'Wha...hu...who? Who, you ask? Who is Fierabras?' He squatted, in a daze. 'I mean, I can understand not knowing the meaning of your name, but not knowing your own ancestors? You *have* to know your ancestors, otherwise how can you know yourself? Well, at least some of yourself. I know all my ancestors, the good ones, the best ones, the not-so-good ones.' He saw Safir had finished his cannoli, so he pulled one more out of the breast pocket of his black coat, and flipped it at the boy, who caught it awkwardly.

'Fierabras,' Mister Mer began, standing again to declaim, 'was one of the greatest knights of Charlemagne, the first Holy Roman Emperor of Europe, who founded all the nations that we know today as France, Germany, Italy and so on. Fierabras was also a Saracen knight, and became King of Spain. He was a giant, more than four metres tall!'

'Four metres!' Safir cooed, stunned.

'The Idrises have shrunk somewhat over time, but isn't your father huge by modern standards? And your brothers, and all your relatives?'

That was true, the boy thought. The Idrises were all really

tall. Qahir, Zaad, even his sister Adara. Except for him, of course, who always overachieved in underachieving.

'So you see, you have no cause for fear, Safir Idris. Descendant of a great knight and king, named after another great knight and duke!' Mister Mer pulled back his sleeve to inspect his watch, a particularly humongous timepiece. 'Oh my, look at the time soar. I'm sure you have things to take care of, since you come here all the time. I have to go meet a bear before she hibernates.' He beamed at Safir. 'Well, this was fun and all. Have a good day, Mr Idris.' With that he turned and walked away humming to himself, his long legs carrying him swiftly into the jungle.

For a whole minute Safir sat there sipping his hot chocolate and eating his cannoli, wondering what in the world had just happened. He put the cup back down on the coffee table. Should he just leave that there, in the middle of nowhere? He guessed so. The boy stood and peered around, trying to judge where he was so that he could head back to the Lodge. There was no doubt in his mind that Mister Mer had lured him out here, sending out a false Kariba's voice. Just to talk about his name and his ancestor? They were cool as beans, sure, but did that warrant a summons of this nature?

He began to move in the direction he thought was uphill and sideways towards the bridge. It was a tricky geography. Head uphill and he'd wind up at the haunted village. Head sideways east and he'd end up near the waterfalls where the demon had attacked them. It was one thing to be able to sense its approach, but to venture towards its last known position? So uphill and sideways, carefully.

As he went he continued trying to figure out Mister Mer's intention for drawing him out here. Was it in fact to get him away from the Lodge? No, nothing stopped him from entering that house, and if he was such a great magician Safir was sure he could put everyone to sleep, or make himself invisible, or some such thing.

Then he was struck by a thought: Kariba might in fact actually be here somewhere! Where else would she have gone to investigate stuff? Didn't all this hullabaloo have something to do with Yakshagarh? Maybe he could look for her while he was out here? No, he could hardly go traipsing around shouting out her name. Unless...could he use his Listening power now to actually find Kariba?

It was a novel and frankly exciting thought. Safir looked around for a clear spot and found an outcrop of rock to climb that would afford him a clearer vision of the surroundings. At its top he realized he could see a little further up the slope and along the hill, but it was only trees, trees, trees.

Not knowing what else to do, the boy closed his eyes, took a deep breath and put his arms out. Listen, he told himself hard in his mind. Listen. After a minute his arms got tired so he put them down. Another minute and he blinked his eyes open and sat down on the outcrop. Well, that was disappointing. How was he to activate his power?

Almost in response, he felt his senses pulled to the right, downhill. Someone was coming up. A trill of alarm went through him, and his immediate thought was to flee. But he controlled himself, and stared in that direction, trying to focus. Yes, there it was, he could do it! Someone was coming, but it wasn't the demon, nowhere near as big. The presence was smaller, more intense. A rakshas. Not Kariba, but another young rakshas. And...more than one. Two, four, no seven, seven rakshas, all travelling up towards him. It didn't even occur to him to run now. They could all catch him in a flash, and they didn't feel hostile anyway. He felt them slow down as they come closer, had they seen him? Yes, it felt like that, because they now moved away, circling around him.

Not once did he actually see anyone, though he tried to peer through the foliage and catch sight of them. They faded out of sense within moments, on their journey to elsewhere.

Safir got up and started off again; but now that he had somehow awakened his Listening, things became weird again. The colours and shapes of things became a little hazy, that strange perspective superimposed on the reality he was familiar with. With that came all the usual sounds again: whispers on the wind, indecipherable but unthreatening. It was all still a little bit much, and he felt slightly dizzy as he made his way through the jungle.

Until he stepped out into a small, clear area. And there, sprawled out comfortably against a shelf of brown rock, sunning and rubbing himself down with a boulder bigger than Safir himself, was yesterday's demon.

They both froze, startled. The creature put down the boulder and said in a voice like a British stage actor, 'How the devil did you find me?'

'Find you?' Safir said, desperately trying not to make any sudden moves. 'I've been trying to avoid you since yesterday.' Were they actually conversing? This thing was hu-u-uge, twenty metres tall, five metres wide. He was dark. His skin— or hide?—a murky green-brown, rough and calloused. He seemed humanoid, with two legs and two arms, but they were nothing like human limbs. His legs didn't end in feet, they spread out thicker at the bottom, like bell-bottoms, and were like mossy pads with small tendrils that undulated of their own will. His hands, so to speak, were just two extensions at the end of his arms, like two large flat opposable thumbs. He had eyes, two of them that were recessed from his flat noseless face; a face that transitioned seamlessly to body without neck or shoulders. The top of his head tapered to an uneven hump fringed with the same moss that was to be found everywhere on his body. All in all, he looked like some kind of gigantic mossy log that had decided to get up and go.

'Oh yes,' he said, articulating his words so well it might have been comical on television. 'You're one of those little chaps from yesterday, the ones with the cat. Terrible thing you did, bringing it here and then taking it away. One shouldn't taunt people, one shouldn't.' His eyes narrowed slightly. 'Unless you brought a cat. Did you? Did you bring one? Where is it? Show it to me.'

The boy showed his palms to the demon. 'No, no cat, sorry.'

'That's disappointing, but not entirely unexpected,' he sighed. 'Still, it doesn't explain how you're here.'

'Well,' Safir began, 'I walked from the Lodge and crossed the bridge...'

'No, no, not how you're here on Yakshagarh. How you managed to get *here*, inside my chateau. Close to me.' The demon leaned over, and doing so cast a long shadow over Safir. 'I wove a spell, is what I'm saying. To make you stay away. Not you personally, of course.'

'Sure,' the boy said, his knees rubbing together in fright. 'I don't know, then. I was just looking for Kariba...'

'Kariba!' the creature yelped, and tossed the rock aside. 'That rascal! Always running around getting up to no good. She needs to learn to respect her uncle, it's a shameful time when one's own family is...'

'Uncle?' Safir interrupted. 'You mean...you? You're her uncle?'

'Last I checked,' he chuckled, leaning back into his reclining position. 'Rabakak the Treeborn, the Rakshas Lord, Guardian of Yakshagarh, at your service. Not at *your* service, really, that's just an expression. I serve my duty to Yakshagarh, of course.' He glanced at the little human with the glasses. 'Are you all right?'

Safir was not all right. The moment Rabakak had spoken his own name, the boy felt like he had fallen, or slid sideways, slipping aside in his own mind. His mouth opened wide, and a voice that did not come from him fluted out: 'Rabakak, old friend, is that you?'

'That voice,' the rakshas said, sitting up. 'I know you…'

'You can hide from me and my magic with your rakshas spells, but you can't hide from a Listener. Anywhere you go, he can hear you. Not that he would want to, which is why he needed a little nudge. Anyway,' he noted cheerfully, and immediately what followed was gibberish, some long and unintelligible sequence of the most absurd and slightly frightening sounds.

'Stop!' Rabakak roared, slamming one hand down to try to get up. But it was too late.

A hundred roots tore out of the hillside around him, dirt and stones and debris tearing out in a maelstrom of sound and fury. The roots whipped around him, thick and strong, burying him almost instantly. Rabakak strained against the roots, and for a moment it seemed like he would be able to burst free. Then he fell back, the roots pulling him to the earth, cracking dirt and stone underneath. More roots dug out from below, crumbling the hill face. The rakshas sank into the ground in a series of jerks, lower and lower, while the roots snaked around, covered him. Buried him. Loose dirt and gravel slid back into the place where, moments ago, Rabakak the Treeborn had been lying.

He was gone.

Safir stood ten metres away, unharmed and expressionless. His eyes those of a magician watching from a distance. Then he blinked, and the boy's eyes returned, wandering and unfocussed. The boy began walking away nonchalantly, taking off his glasses to rub his eyes. Where was he? The forest...but how? Hadn't he been at the Lodge just now? His mind sharpened, trying to understand, but a soothing voice murmured at him inside, and he let go, settling into a dreaming slumber while his body mechanically traced an unerring path back to the Lodge.

17

RUMPUS REUNION REST

It was a few minutes' walk and jog to cross Bazaar Round and then the open expanse to reach the Lodge. The day had bloomed beautifully, Trikaya noted, the hill not too cool and the sun not too hot. A gentle breeze played down on them, lulling them with its fragrant touch. Every sign was pointing to harmony and joy, she thought, when in fact things were getting weirder by the hour. She hoped Iti was back at the Lodge. Iti was always so grounded and collected, nothing ever seemed so bad when she was around.

Shari was looking a bit off, though, like he was mulling particularly unpleasant thoughts. He was probably missing Tal. The twins put up brave fronts, and had been fighting a lot lately, but no one doubted the fierceness of their bond. Or maybe he was thinking about the split KSS. She wished there was something she could do to mend the group, to put it back together…

She also wished Shari would slow down a jot. It was a tiring day, she huffed. They had been sick all night, and then had woken up early, and then they had met Kariba, and then they went to rescue Tal and Isaac. It was fine and all, but they were kids. They needed a break sometime!

The Lodge was only about thirty metres away when they

heard some noises fluting in the wind from behind them. They both turned to see what or who it was.

'Iti!' Trikaya cried, 'It's them!'

There they were indeed. Iti and Tal and Isaac walking towards them from Bazaar Round, hands waving.

Shari was off at a dead sprint, and Trikaya followed grinning. She didn't mind a quick run for this kind of occasion!

Given how things stood in the KSS, Shari and Tal didn't jump into each other's arms, stopping instead to shake hands emphatically. There was a great deal of back-patting and hand-grabbing, with Trikaya hopping up and down in the middle of everyone, and after the excitement died down they got to exchanging stories.

Then Trikaya screamed, 'Look at that!' and everyone bubbled with the thrill of seeing the yellow-throated marten. He was in a state of excitement as well, seeing so many children, and all of them overjoyed to see him. He prowled back and forth at a safe distance, not sure how to react. The children didn't come any closer, however, except for Iti who was the only one who dared put her hand close to that triangular head.

'I want to give him a name,' Iti said wistfully.

'Martin!' Trikaya cried, hand in the air.

'Martin the marten?' Tal questioned flatly.

'It's ironic!' Trikaya defended. She shook her head, 'Okay, okay...Mahipati!' The others groaned. 'No, Steve!'

'How about Galahad?' Isaac suggested.

They all considered it with slow smiles.

'A knight of King Arthur,' Shari mused.

'The one who found the Holy Grail,' Isaac specified, 'by definition the bravest and best knight in the world.'

Iti crouched down by the marten. 'Galahad,' she said.

The marten blinked his shiny black eyes slowly and bobbed his head. 'It suits you.' The marten nibbled gently at her knuckle, glanced at the others, and flowed away through the grass into the forest behind the Lodge.

'Galahad's not bad,' Trikaya conceded through her pout.

Shari was quick to get back to the subject. 'So it was Mister Mer who kidnapped you,' he concluded grimly.

'We don't know for a fact,' Isaac said, 'but we're all pretty certain it was.'

'Reva didn't remember anything,' Tal said, 'and she looked more shocked than us about that. He messed their minds up.'

'How do we stop him from doing that to us?' Trikaya asked, anxious.

'We'll ask Kariba,' Shari said, and pointed at Tal's watch. 'What's the time?'

'Ten to twelve,' Tal replied. 'We should head, then.'

They moved towards the Lodge again, and Trikaya wormed her way next to Tal. 'Show me now, show me now!'

Tal grinned and cupped her hands. 'I've been trying all the way back, it's a bit tricky but I think I'm getting the hang of it.' Trikaya watched Tal's palms began to brighten, as though someone were turning up a halogen lamp on them, but then she realized that the light was coming from *inside* her hands! 'My hands are easiest, but I got my forearms to light up a bit. Isaac thinks I can light up my entire body!'

'That's awesome!' Trikaya shrieked, not knowing how to contain her zeal. 'That's A-grade stuff, Tal!' She poked Tal's palms gingerly. 'Wow, it's warm too!'

'It makes sense,' Isaac said. 'Light makes heat.'

Trikaya clenched her fists in glee and thrust them out in front of her, imagining having Tal's power. 'Maybe you can make heat rays and melt cars and stuff!'

They reached the Lodge stairs, and as they started to climb up, the fatigue of the day beginning to pull at them. A groggy weariness seemed to settle on them, and they trooped through the entrance and into the living room with a great sense of relief. They all collapsed on sofas and armchairs, and were quiet for a moment.

'Who has the other walkie-talkie?' Tal asked suddenly.

'It's here,' Iti said, pointing at the yellow piece on a side table.

'Wait, where's Safir?' Trikaya asked. 'We left it with him.'

'He must be in the fridge,' Shari reasoned, and everyone agreed, not wanting to budge to go look for him.

'So when do we go check out Bhante's scrolls?' Tal mumbled.

'Later,' Shari said.

'Hey, good job on the scrolls,' Tal threw out.

Trikaya sat up beaming. 'Thanks! It was both me and Shari though. Like the good old days, both KSSes working together...' Her voice died away as she saw Tal's eyes light up with hostility. 'I mean...just nice to be figuring things out together...' She saw Iti gesture frantically to drop it, so she clamped her mouth shut and sank back into the pillows.

The quiet deepened, and small rumblings rose from the five children as they napped for a good forty minutes.

In the meantime sounds stirred in the kitchen, the clatter of cutlery on plates and dishes. The soft creaks of footsteps upstairs, the distant buzz of voices exchanging words. And then Auntie Sophie popped her head in, white hair done up in a bun. 'Hello, hello, sleepy children! Time for a little belly-filling!' She moved on to the dining room down the hall with her usual bustle.

Trikaya's head popped up and she chirped, 'Come on, everyone, it's lunch!'

One by one the children stirred, taking stock of where they were. The upstairs sounds intensified, and became sets of footsteps on the stairs coming down to the ground floor.

'Where's Safir?' Shari yawned. 'Still in the fridge?'

'I'm here,' Safir called out. They turned around and over sofas to see him sitting in the separate armchairs set in the corner of the living room, feet up, comic book in hand. 'I've been here all along.'

Tal came around, wisps of hair sticking out of her head and ponytail. 'All along? I thought you weren't here when we came back.'

'No, I was here,' he said, sitting up and adjusting his glasses. 'Where else would I be? Even Kumar Fourteen's been here a while,' he added, jerking his chin to the other chair. Underneath it was the monstrous feline, purring and caressing himself.

'So what happened while we were out?' Trikaya said, bouncing up to Safir.

'Nothing,' he said glumly, then blinked. 'No, nothing.' He frowned. 'There was something I was going to tell you, Tri.'

'What's that?' she asked.

'I don't remember.' He put the comic down, shrugging, and stood up. 'What I want to know is what happened to all you guys, because you came back and slept like hibernating bears!' He paused, frowning. 'Hibernating bears...'

'Okay,' Trikaya said, grabbing his hand and pulling him to sit with the others in the middle of the room. 'So, see, basically Iti saved Tal and Isaac, and Shari and I saved Bhante Rinzen and Pujari Nandan...'

'Kids!' They stopped as Mr Kandhari looked in. 'Time for lunch.' He pointed towards the bathroom. 'Hands, everyone. I can see you've all been outside. We'll inspect each and every finger before you sit down.' He left, already talking to someone else down the hall.

The children dutifully trooped out of the living room and down the hall towards the bathroom. Trikaya tugged Safir back to whisper loudly in his ear, 'I'll tell you later!'

18

GROWING UP, LEFT, AND SIDEWAYS

Lunch at the Lodge totally reminded Isaac of meals at Seamarch School back in England. All thirteen of them sat in tall chairs at a long oak table, adults at one end, children at the other. The dining room was a long and wide wooden hall with one end done in high glass windows overlooking the fields between the Lodge and Devagarh. Cupboards brimming with memorabilia from British times lined the walls, separated by portraits and photographs of various important people of the community's history.

The table was laid meticulously, with fine and highly polished dinnerware, sterling silver cutlery, and crystal glasses. The six children all sat facing each other, the foot of the table left empty. Isaac saw that they were still Real KSS on his side—him and Tal and Trikaya—and True KSS opposite—Iti, Shari, and Safir. Auntie Sophie bustled back and forth from the kitchen, carrying pots and serving plates with some help from the parents, while the children buzzed with excitement about the meal. The food was passed around with alacrity, and soon everyone was happily into their meal.

'How are you kids doing?' Mr Idris called out from his usual seat at the head of the table. 'You gave us all a scare last night. And today we found out you're running all over town! I don't think that's very smart.'

'Come on, Safdar,' Mr Kandhari chided, 'Don't you remember when we were kids running up and down Devagarh? You used to go jumping into the lake from that giant boulder down there, what was it called, some unusual name?'

'Hanuman's Toe,' Mr Pillai answered. 'I don't think anyone ever found out why it was called that.'

'You used to swim there?' Shari made a face. 'Isn't it all mucky?'

'Nature is not mucky,' Mr Kandhari clarified. 'But yes it was gross, and that's what made it so glorious.'

'It was a sight,' Jyoti laughed. 'These three skinny monkeys jumping in the lake.'

'Four,' Mr Idris corrected. 'Ishan was there too. Well, for a while.' Some glances went Isaac's way.

'Yes, four,' Jyoti said evenly, smiling at Isaac. 'Your father couldn't swim across a puddle to save his life. He barely dipped his toes in.'

'That's why you need friends,' Mr Idris declared. 'To help you take those jumps into life's decisions!'

Mr Pillai stabbed a cut of meat on his plate and held it up high. 'Like: chicken or mutton?'

'What about Mister Mer?' Isaac asked.

The children stared at him. The adults looked a little thoughtful. 'Mister Mer?' Mr Kandhari said, fingering his bald head. 'Funny he's back in town. Wasn't he gone forever?'

'He's a famous magician now, isn't he?' Mrs Idris remarked. Tahfeem Idris was herself a poet and classical singer of international renown, a striking-looking woman with long black hair and a proud and elegant nose. She was one of the few of them that Isaac remembered since she travelled regularly to England to perform, and Jyoti had taken him to watch her sing a few times at prestigious London venues. 'I wonder what he's going to do tonight, back home for the first time.'

'Did you all know him well?' Tal threw out from her end of the table.

The men and Jyoti exchanged concurring looks. 'No, none of us really,' Mr Kandhari replied for them all. 'We knew of him, of course, because he was one of the eccentrics of the village. But he didn't socialize much. Or at all, in fact, as far as I can remember.'

'He was strange,' Mr Pillai announced around a mouthful of lunch. 'I saw him more than once walking around alone, talking to himself. And not just thinking out loud. Like he was having conversations.'

'Was he into magic back then?' Trikaya called out.

'I remember one time,' Jyoti said, puckering her brow with the effort. 'I went with Mama to the temple to see the old books they had there. Pujari Nandan was already here back then. I remember this Mer was at the temple when I went, reading the books. I mean, he could actually read the Sanskrit fluently! Pujari Nandan showed me some of the books, but Mer gave us such a hostile vibe I only glanced at them for a minute and left.'

'Mer, Mer is his family name, what was his first name again?' Mr Kandhari wondered out loud.

The children's smiling heads whipped around to Trikaya, who gathered herself and yelped, 'Mahipati!' They burst into peals of laughter, and the parents also joined in with the mirth, although they looked uncertain.

'Why are we all laughing, though?' Mr Idris asked.

'His name is Mahipati!' Trikaya repeated emphatically.

'What's with Mahipati?' Mr Idris insisted. 'Does it mean something, is it a joke?'

'No, Abba!' Safir exclaimed excitedly, 'It's just an old name no one uses anymore, it just sounds funny. Mahipati Mer. Mahipati Mer.'

Mr Idris fixed his son seriously. 'I don't get it, what's the joke?'

Safir wilted under that gaze. 'Just… No joke, just… Mahi… It sounds funny…'

'Didn't this Mahipati have the most awful haircut?' Jyoti jumped in, changing the subject. 'And the same hair for *ages*, like one of those village mullets, long in the back…'

'And short and wispy in front, yes, yes!' Mr Pillai roared, smacking the table. 'Does he still have it? Is he still loyal to the old look?'

'No,' Shari said, 'it's all medium and styled and stuff.'

'We all had tragic haircuts back then,' Jyoti shrugged.

Mrs Kandhari sweetly rubbed her husband's bald forehead. 'Things have certainly improved since then!'

Everyone laughed, but he protested, 'It's gone now, but when I had it I always had the best!'

'That's true,' Mr Pillai nodded. 'You always used to set the trend.' He made a forlorn face. 'I wish I had never grown mine out long in school.'

'You should have done like me,' Mr Idris scolded. 'Short and blunt. Like Shari.' He pointed at the boy's crew cut admiringly. 'Look at that hair! Avalok, your son has some soldier in him, I tell you. Safir, take a look at Shari, learn from him.'

Mrs Idris sighed, 'Safdar…'

'Okay, okay, I'll stop being the tough dad,' Mr Idris grumbled. 'Forgive me for wanting my son to grow up a bit.'

Isaac saw Shari put a sympathetic hand on Safir's shoulder as the parents' conversation moved into other subjects.

'I think your hair's great,' Tal told Safir from across the table.

'Me too!' Trikaya added.

'Modern, but not flashy,' Iti judged.

Safir grinned and poked his glasses back up his nose. 'I don't know, maybe it is a bit long…'

'No way,' Shari said, reaching up to put his hand on Safir's head. 'I wish your hair were way longer, it would look…' He moved his hand dramatically away to show how long it should be…and that entire tuft of Safir's hair went with his hand, lengthening so suddenly and smoothly that the children's mouths dropped open.

For a second the boys stared at each other, Shari holding the end of Safir's newly sprouted half-a-metre lock of hair. Trikaya covered her mouth with her hands to stop herself from screaming.

'Hey, we're done!' Tal declared suddenly, jumping up and grabbing her plate, which had last bits of her lunch. She made eyes at everyone, and they immediately leaped to action, taking their own plates. Shari hustled Safir around so his new growth of hair was facing the wall, and he marched the bewildered boy carefully to the door of the dining room.

'But…dessert?' Mrs Pillai asked, crestfallen.

The other children made a big noise, shoving chairs, clattering cutlery, anything to divert attention from Safir and Shari's escape. 'No thank you!' Trikaya retorted. 'Maybe later!'

Within seconds they had cleared out of the dining room, and the last they heard from there was Mr Idris commenting pointedly, 'They've left before dessert! I'm telling you something's up with them, they're still sick from last night's fever…'

Isaac followed the pack as they hurtled down the hallway, past the kitchen where Auntie Sophie let out a whoop at the sight of them, and straight into the bathroom. Iti locked the door tight. Trikaya jumped up to slam the small window shut. They all turned to stare at Safir, huddled shoulder to shoulder in the cramped space.

Safir stood there holding the long wisp of hair, staring at it in disbelief. Then he looked at Shari, smiled, and said, 'You did it. This is it. This is you!'

Everyone's eyes went from Safir to Shari. He held up his hands and frowned at them. 'What, grow hair? Like, the anti-barber or something?'

'Good name,' Tal pronounced, winking at Isaac.

'Can we cut my hair now?' Safir said nervously.

'I've got it,' Iti volunteered, and looked into the cupboard under the sink for a pair of scissors.

'Maybe you can grow Mister Mer's hair so much he can't stand anymore,' Trikaya suggested. 'Like it's too heavy or something.'

'He's a magician,' Shari pointed out. 'I'm sure he cuts his own hair with a flick of his hand.'

'But is it just hair?' Isaac wondered. They looked at him. He stepped to the side and made way for Shari to the small flower that sat on the windowsill.

Auntie Sophie was an orchid aficionado, and had been replanting a boat orchid here every year for as long as they could remember. It flowered once in winter, which they never came here for, so right now it was just a bunch of green stalks sticking out of a flat ceramic pot.

Shari stepped up to the windowsill, surprised at how anxious he felt. What was it he had done? Just touched Safir's hair, barely, and...what? Was it the movement? He put his hands out tentatively, and the children hushed all around him. The plant just sat there, still as a statue. Shari waited a few seconds. It didn't just happen, then. He moved his hands around a bit. It wasn't the movement either. What was it? He had just been moving his hands around, and wishing that... *Wishing*. Shari knew with a certainty now. He reached out a finger and touched the smooth, plasticky stem. Then he wished for it to grow.

It happened so fast they all jumped back.

The stalks expanded, growing leaves, then bulbs, and then the bulbs popped open soundlessly, a firework of bright-red flowers that made them oooh in chorus.

Shari moved back from what he had done, awed. He felt slightly drained, but within a moment was back to normal. 'I grew a plant,' he said out loud, realizing how funny it sounded, but also how profound it really was.

'You grew a plant,' Tal repeated intensely, and hugged him. For a second they stayed there, heads together, and then they settled back, still on separate teams.

'We're all almost there,' Iti said, putting arms around as many of them as she could.

'Except me,' Trikaya murmured meekly. She was always the last one...

'Don't worry,' Safir said, nudging her arm. 'You're probably going to have the biggest, most wicked power of all, and save all of us.'

Trikaya pouted another second, then grinned. 'Yes, probably.'

'So we've got a Listener,' Isaac said, pointing at Safir. Then at Iti, 'And a Healer.'

'A Catalyst,' Tal continued, nodding at Isaac, then at her brother. 'The new kid on the power block, Dr Green Thumb.'

'Hey!' Shari said, smiling. 'Better than you, Lady Flash in the Pan.'

The other children groaned and laughed, giggling...

A sharp knock at the window made them scream and jump into each other's arms. They stared at the window, shocked. Who—or what—would be knocking at the bathroom window?

Another smaller knock, but more persistent, and a voice whispered from outside so softly they couldn't make out the words.

'Do we open?' Safir breathed.

Tal puffed up her chest. 'This is our home base.' Before she could move, Isaac had already stepped forward and reached for the lock. He pulled it, jerked the window open, and hurriedly backed away.

Two seconds of silence.

Then a pair of hands grabbed the lower edge of the window, and Kariba's wild and pretty face peeked up from the edge. 'What are you all doing in here?' she asked suspiciously, frowning.

Since Kariba was supposed to meet them at noon, shouldn't the kids have been wondering where she is?

19
STUDY TEAM,
ACTION TEAM, GO!

The minute they closed the door of the boys' room, with all six of them gathered and Kumar Fourteen on the windowsill, Kariba winked into sight, sitting on one of the beds. Trikaya saw her face was tight with distress. 'My uncle has disappeared,' she told them quickly, 'I've been looking for him for hours. I mean, he's usually difficult to find, but today he's actually gone. Can you help me find him?'

They passed confused looks around. 'Your uncle?' Tal said, 'Of course we'll help. But what do we do about Mister Mer and his show?'

'I don't know,' the girl said, pigtails bobbing. 'But Mister Mer is messing around with my uncle, and he's the Guardian of Yakshagarh, so it's all tied in somehow. I think finding my uncle will help us with Mister Mer.'

'Okay,' Shari said. 'Where is he, where did you see him last?'

'On Yakshagarh, yesterday in the evening.'

'What does he look like?' Isaac asked.

Kariba looked puzzled. 'You know what he looks like.'

The children didn't know what to say. Iti played with her

hands nervously as she said, 'Um, Kariba…we've never met your uncle. We don't know what you're talking about.'

'Yes you did,' the rakshasi replied quickly. 'Yesterday, in the jungle. We were together when he smelled the cat, Kumar Fourteen, with you. He's a little out of control with cats, I guess you noticed. I know he gave you a big scare, but he's really harmless. That's when I saw you all, and followed you down the wat…'

'Your uncle is the monster?!' Trikaya squealed. The others looked aghast.

'Monster?' Kariba exclaimed, then frowned. 'Oh, of course, I thought I had told you this morning, but we were interrupted, and then… Yes, he's my uncle, the great rakshas Rabakak the Treeborn, the Rakshas Lord. He's the Guardian of Yakshagarh.'

As Kariba continued talking, Trikaya saw Safir shift oddly, and glanced at him. His face looked absolutely normal, but two fat teardrops coursed from his eyes as she watched. 'Safir…' she said, grabbing his arm, startling him.

'Wh—what?'

Trikaya's heart felt sick at the sight. 'You're crying… Why are you crying?'

It was so strange, he genuinely looked surprised as he reached up and wiped away the tears, that now poured out unobstructed, making a mess of his cheeks. 'Why am I crying? Tri, what's going on?'

Everyone else crowded around, stunned and concerned, and even Kumar Fourteen wormed his way around their legs, seeming solicitous. Trikaya ignored them, catching Safir's face with her little hands. 'What is it, tell me!'

'I don't know,' he responded honestly, and she could see he was bewildered. 'I'm sad… I don't know why, I'm just feeling so sad…'

Trikaya pulled Safir to a bed and sat him down, keeping an arm around his shoulders. He sniffed for a minute or so, then chuckled shyly. 'I'm sorry, this is so weird. I don't know why this happened.'

Shari put a hand on his arm. 'There's a lot going on. Don't worry, we're all with you.'

'Okay,' Safir replied sheepishly, drying his tears with a tissue Iti had brought. 'Sorry, let's continue.'

They all climbed up on two of the beds and sat in a huddle, legs dangling.

'Mister Mer has been sending cats to Yakshagarh since he arrived yesterday, hordes of them,' Kariba started again. 'My uncle is a great and proud warrior, but cats have always been his weakness.'

'He keeps them as pets?' Iti asked.

Kariba gave her a pointed look. 'Pets? He eats them. A lot of rakshas do. Like…a *lot*.' She noticed the horror on their faces and immediately started flapping her hands. 'But I don't! A lot of the young rakshas don't. It's more of an older generation thing. I just find them a bit…fiddly, you know? They bite and claw, they don't go down easy.' She cleared her throat, realizing this course of conversation was alienating her new friends. 'Anyway, I don't eat cats. But Rabakak does, he goes unhinged for them.'

'That's why the cats have been missing all over town!' Tal said punching her fist into the palm of her other hand.

'And they were all going to Yakshagarh,' Trikaya added.

'But that failed,' Kariba said. 'I think my uncle figured out it was Mister Mer, or at least someone trying to do something fishy. He spelled himself into hiding yesterday, so cats and Mister Mer wouldn't be able to find him, but I still should be able to.'

'Wait, wait,' Isaac interrupted. 'If Mister Mer is going after

your uncle, and your uncle is the Guardian of Yakshagarh...
then is Mister Mer actually going after something in
Yakshagarh?'

'Yes!' Tal hissed, giving Isaac a small push of approval.
'That's what he's after! Kariba: what is he after in Yakshagarh?'

The rakshasi was silent for a moment, then took a deep
breath. 'The Rakshas Lord guards the hill and town of
Yakshagarh, yes, but what he really does is stop people from
getting to the Black Kot.' Again she was silent, and the look
on her face made them all feel a little dread.

'Kariba,' Iti asked in a low voice, 'What's in the Black Kot?'

She shrugged helplessly. 'I don't know. No one knows.
That's the whole point. It's a secret, and Rabakak does not
tell. Whatever it is, though...I know it makes him very
uneasy. I have asked him a couple of times over the decades.
The only thing he ever mentioned, one time, was that the
Black Kot almost fell a long, long time ago, and that if it had
it would have been disastrous. Like, disastrous for the world.
"Cataclysmic" is the word he used.'

They were all quiet for a moment, considering that word.

'But you're all here,' Kariba continued, eyeing the six
friends. 'These things don't happen by coincidence. Isaac
Shroff comes to Devagarh, and all of your powers come to
life? I told you earlier you weren't exactly human. It's true.
You're all descendants of the yakshas. Your powers are proof
of it.'

The children didn't know what to make of that. 'What
are yakshas?' Isaac asked directly.

'Yakshas are great and powerful spirits that also have
human form,' Kariba explained. 'They're forces of nature,
beings in whom a massive amount of umm, how do I say
it? It's like the universe has focused on them, and endowed
them with vast amounts of spirit and power. They're different

from devas, who are gods. And of course asuras, who are the enemies of the gods.'

'So…Devagarh and Yakshagarh,' Safir reasoned out loud. 'Devas and yakshas lived here together?'

'Defending the Black Kot,' Kariba confirmed, 'In the old stories. And by old I mean thousands and thousands of years old. They're legends that have survived with us because we're longer-lived, but you humans have completely forgotten them.'

'Our families too,' Safir continued, 'we're all tied to Devagarh, Auntie Jyoti told me. And I guess Yakshagarh. We're all from old families.' He looked at the others one by one. 'Idris. Pillai. Kandhari. Shroff. Our ancestors all moved out from Devagarh, and now we live in Delhi, and Mumbai, and Cochin, and London, but…we come back here. We always have.'

Trikaya looked around at the others, seeing their bemusement, but also the realization dawning in them, the realization of something they felt very strongly but couldn't quite put their fingers on. She felt it too. Like she was about to understand something so important, but so simple, and knowing it would then change everything in her life.

'You called me a Catalyst,' Isaac said suddenly. 'And Safir a Listener. Are there names for what the others can do? Iti can heal people, Shari can make things grow and Tal can make light with her hands.'

'Yes,' Kariba nodded, 'These are great powers that have been known and named.' She looked at Iti. 'You're a Cure. You do far more than heal bruises. You can cure the deadliest poisons, bodily, mental, and spiritual ailments, and other diseases even more complex.' To Shari she said, 'Yours is praised as a blessing from the gods: you're a Gardener. If it's alive, it grows, and if it grows you can affect it with your power.' She took Tal's hand and examined it. 'There are a couple different kinds of powers that have similar effects, but it's clear what you are. You're a Star. You can radiate light and heat, that's the easy stuff. The stronger you get, the more you become like an actual star. You'll be able to affect gravity, radiate all sorts of things other than light. But be careful. Stars that go out of control can become black holes and destroy everything. That's not a figure of speech.' In the end she hugged Trikaya, who looked glum, and said, 'You'll find your power soon enough. There's no question. I can feel you have it.' She addressed everyone again, 'Just know this: for yakshas your power is your nature. All your powers are expressions of who you truly are on the inside. The better you know yourself, the stronger your power will be.'

The children leaned back, eyes shining and satisfied. At least, and at last, some questions were answered!

'So now we need to find Rabakak,' Shari put forward, with resolve.

'Yes,' Tal said.

Trikaya punched both fists into the air. 'Let's go!'

'Can I suggest something?' Isaac interjected, one hand hesitantly rising. 'Bhante Rinzen has this scroll that explains the origin of Devagarh and Yakshagarh. I know finding Rabakak is critical, but if he remains missing, then we don't have a clue. Could someone go to the stupa and at least try to read the scroll? Or ask Bhante, maybe she's translated it already?'

They turned to Kariba, who was clearly anxious about her uncle but could also see the sense in the situation. 'Okay,' she nodded. 'But who?'

'The studious ones,' Trikaya shot out immediately. 'And the active ones go with you.' Tal and Shari both chortled, making Trikaya frown. 'What?'

'Nothing, you're absolutely right,' Tal said. 'So who's studious and who's active?'

There was a pause, and then all six smiled. They all knew the answer. Iti leaned over, put her hands out to Isaac and Safir, and declared, 'Study team!'

Trikaya leaped into the gap between the beds and pointed at the twins. 'Action team, go!'

'Thank you,' Kariba said suddenly, hugging her hands to her chest. 'I'm sorry for putting this on you. I do have other friends on the hill, but they're forbidden by law to interact with the Guardian of Yakshagarh. Rabakak is my uncle, so I can get involved because I may be a candidate to replace him one day, but otherwise I had no one else to turn to. So thank you.'

Tal jumped up and pulled Kariba to stand too. 'Come on, enough chit-chat, let's go find your uncle.'

In a flurry of excitement and activity they got ready: Trikaya grabbing the walkie-talkies, Safir pocketing some cookies from a jar in the kitchen. They reunited at the entrance, with Kariba out of sight, and were about to step out...

'Safir, where are you going?' They stopped and saw Mr Idris's tall frame coming from the dining room. 'Out again? No, no, I think you should stay in. You were terribly ill last night, and then you skipped dessert. I don't want you running around like this.'

'Uncle, we're all fine,' Shari said, smiling politely. 'And we need Safir, he's...'

'That's good and all,' Mr Idris interrupted. 'But Safir will stay. I don't know what all your parents think. If they're fine with you running around like this, it's up to them. If you relapse, Safir, then it'll be your mother looking after you for days. You can skip your playing for one day, and if you're all right tomorrow then we'll see.'

The six children looked around, not knowing what to do. 'It's okay,' Safir said, 'I'll hold the fort again. Keep both walkie-talkies, you may need them.'

With Mr Idris still watching they began to leave, Trikaya last. She gave Safir a quick hug, whispering, 'We'll be back soon, don't worry!'

The door closed. Through the tall, narrow windows lining the front door Safir saw his friends hurry down the steps, Kumar Fourteen at their heels. He sighed and turned to head back, feet dragging despondently. He was almost in the boys' room when someone cleared their throat behind him. Safir turned and realized his father had followed him halfway down the hall, and was standing there in a funny way.

'Safir, you know...' Mr Idris began, then stopped. The boy didn't know what to think. He had never seen the Brigadier hesitate to say or do anything. It was like discovering his father secretly put on yellow sweatpants and went breakdancing on Saturday nights. 'You know I'm not *trying* to be mean to you. Right?'

Now Safir was the one who didn't know quite how to stand, or talk, or anything really.

'I have ideas about how things should be,' Mr Idris said slowly. Safir looked at his father's military face, half-lit in light, and knew he would remember this moment, and his father's expression, forever. 'But I know that everyone is different. I want you to grow up to be a great man, but I only know my way to do it. If you have your own way...I'll try to understand, okay?'

They stood there for another awkward moment.

'Does that mean I can go out?' Safir ventured.

Did a smile actually twitch on Mr Idris's face? 'In your dreams, boy. At ease.' He turned and walked away briskly.

Safir headed into the boys' room with a wry smile. Well, it had been worth a try…

20
THE ORIGIN SCROLL

'Poor Safir,' Iti bemoaned as she and Isaac walked down the path towards Dharm Square. 'His father's always bullying him, and he can't do anything but take it.' Behind them Kumar Fourteen ferreted around all over place, but generally kept up with them.

'I think Safir's really strong,' Isaac opined, 'Stronger than most credit him for. He's been hearing voices and seeing things for so many years. I think most people would go nuts with the kinds of things he's experienced. If I saw some young girl following us that no one else could see, my skeleton might climb out of my skin and run off screaming.' Iti giggled at the image in spite of herself. 'I see how my Catalyst power affected all of you, but he was already a Listener from way before.'

'That's true,' Iti said as they entered Bazaar Round.

The place was bustling now, the several food joints packed with people. The Barbarika Festival really only started in the evening, but that never stopped the Devagarhis from getting a head start. A hundred or so people were milling about already, holding paper plates and glasses, dressed in their colourful holiday regalia. Somewhere a gang of musicians were taunting the crowd with notes of twangy string and hard drum.

Iti saw Isaac looking around curiously as they made their way through. The rest of them knew the Barbarika Festival, since they were here every year at the same time. She guessed Isaac Shroff didn't often see an Indian festival like this. She liked him. He seemed very open and honest, but also intelligent. What he had just said about Safir and his father was insightful and so… Iti shrivelled on the inside, suddenly remembering that the boy had lost his own mother and, for all practical purposes, his father. He was at that boarding school in England because he was pretty much an orphan. And here she was talking about Safir and his father so carelessly. She hoped Isaac hadn't taken what she said badly.

They left Bazaar Round behind and jogged towards the stupa. Kumar Fourteen emerged from the crowd a moment later and hurried to catch up. Iti wondered how much of Mr Dangwal controlled that cat. Kumar Fourteen seemed surprisingly focused, given the kind of hoodlum he generally was.

'Have you ever been inside a stupa?' Iti asked as they reached the entrance to the stone dome. She thought it would be dark inside, but she could see light in the tunnel.

'No, they don't have many of them in England,' Isaac replied, flashing her a grin.

They went in, feeling the weight of that dark yellow stone above them. Iti had never been in the stupa before. She found it intimidating at first, but actually surprisingly homely. The inner chamber was lit with many light bulbs strung up on the curving walls, and it was only slightly cooler than the outside. They saw the two priests lying near the wall, and hurried to kneel by them.

'Bhante,' Iti murmured, prodding her lightly. The priest's eyelids fluttered, but her eyes didn't open.

'Is she okay?' Isaac asked in a hushed voice.

She put a respectful hand on the priest's forehead. Her temperature was normal, she wasn't feverish or sweaty. Every time Iti had healed so far she had vaguely sensed, in her mind, what was wrong: Reva's wound had felt sharp and rough, while the bruise on Tal's shin felt like a thickening lump. Now she was going to consciously focus on Bhante Rinzen, and was a bit scared of what she would perceive.

The first thing Iti sensed as a whole was that the priest was fine, absolutely healthy. Shari and Trikaya had reported that there were no symptoms, that this was not actually an illness. Iti had to agree. So what was it? As she sat there she felt as though she was getting closer and closer…and then suddenly fell into Bhante Rinzen, even though she was still sitting there. Iti knew instinctively and instantly that the priest had had jaundice as a child, had broken her left forearm when she was thirteen, was vegetarian since fourteen, had a sweet tooth she felt guilty about… As Iti fell deeper and further into the priest, she felt the peppering of tiny knocks, bruises, discomforts, cuts, stings, every single injury Bhante's body had ever experienced. Through it all, however, a general impression formed, one that overwhelmed the Cure: Bhante Rinzen's body, brain and mind appeared to her like a universe, an entire cosmos wrapped up into a small Tibetan woman. The priests's nerves and neurons and thoughts all stretched out about Iti like endless constellations of connected stars.

And then she felt it.

There *was* something wrong, but it was not physical. Bhante was being drained of something, something essential and pure, that was the actual energy of living, not the body's mechanical energy. It was leaving her from everywhere, slowly slipping out from every pore, in every breath. Iti wondered why her energy hadn't run out yet, but then she saw that the energy was being replenished, constantly, churning out of the priest's body, her mind, her very being… She realized immediately. This energy being drained of her, it was…

'Her spirit,' Iti mouthed, opening her eyes and removing her hand from Bhante's forehead. 'Something is draining their spirit,' she began, wanting to tell Isaac, but all of a sudden her mind went blank, and the next thing she knew she was lying down staring at the ceiling of the stupa, the light bulbs shining strangely. Isaac Shroff was bent over her, his mouth moving frantically, but she couldn't hear anything. He seemed in a panic. 'I'm okay,' Iti whispered. 'What happened?' She tried to sit up and managed, with a little help from the boy.

'You passed out,' he said, settling back, panting. 'I freaked out, I didn't know what was going on! Are you okay?'

She felt unduly tired, as though she had run a quick sprint, but then after a few seconds felt completely fine. 'Yes, I'm okay.'

'I think we're too new to these powers,' Isaac said with concern. 'We don't know anything about how to use them. It's like expecting a newborn to walk.'

'We have to do it, though,' Iti said, shifting closer to Bhante Rinzen. 'I don't think I can do this alone. Do you know how to make me stronger?'

'I have no clue but I'll try,' Isaac said.

'For me there's no hocus-pocus, no spell or anything. I just wish for the hurt to be healed. If it's slow or too big I push it a little more. With my mind. And it happens, somehow.' The boy nodded and moved next to her. He put one hand on her arm, and she put her hand on Bhante's forehead again.

Iti looked at the priest's face, focused deeper into her, and… She was inside instantly, and everything was different. The last time, minutes before, she thought she could see Bhante Rinzen's entire being like a cosmos. Now, with Isaac boosting her, it was like everything was richer, more intense. She could see every detail of Bhante's being from the tips of her hairs to the nails on her toes. More than that, she could see the spirit escaping from the priest, and knew exactly what she needed to do even though she didn't know how she would do it.

Whatever it was sucking the spirit from Bhante Rinzen, it was external to her and couldn't be controlled. What Iti could influence, however, were the paths the spirit took to leave. With just a touch of her mind she altered all the spirit channels, guiding larger flows, turning smaller flows. Soon the entire flow of spirit energy was moving in a single circuitous direction around and through the priest's body. There was still spirit leaking here and there, but most of it was shored up.

The girl opened her eyes and collapsed back, exhausted. She managed a weak thumbs up to Isaac to show she was okay. He nodded and shifted his attention to the priest.

After a few seconds Bhante Rinzen exhaled, blinked once or twice, and asked softly, 'What did you do?'

Iti rolled onto her side and replied, 'I don't know. Your spirit was draining out everywhere, I just made it flow in a circle inside you.'

The priest smiled. 'You did good, very good. Do you think you can help Pujari Nandan?'

'I'm sorry, it'll take some time…'

'No, no!' Bhante Rinzen said, trying to lift a hand, but only her finger twitched. 'He'll be alright, I was only asking. You rest. Whatever is doing this is taking just enough to keep us down.'

'What is it?' Isaac said. 'Who's doing this?'

'Finding out who is a big task, more than I can do,' the priest shook her head. 'What it is is simple enough: some kind of spell or mechanism that's spinning spirit out from us and collecting it somewhere else like yarn.'

'But what for?' Iti asked.

'For one big, powerful spell.' The priest's expression was the most serious they had ever seen on her usually peachy-cute face. 'How did you get caught up in all this?'

Iti put a hand on the little Tibetan's shoulders. 'That's a question for later, we need to get to work. Did you translate the Origin Scroll? Can we see it?'

'Well, yes, of course. I'm translating it for everyone,' Bhante said, taken aback by Iti's decisiveness. 'Although we've barely started, Pujari Nandan and I. The translation is there on the desk, the red notebook.'

'Is the original here?' Isaac asked, trotting over to the desk and carefully beginning to look through the notebooks there.

'Yes, in the bookcase. Please be gentle!'

Iti had joined Isaac by the time he picked up a large and heavy plank of clear plastic from the bookcase. She cleared the desk, and he carefully placed it on the flat surface. 'What is it?' she asked in an awed voice.

It was a solid plastic case. Encased inside was a collage of twelve strips of what looked like a nut-brown paper that was written on and illustrated. The strips were lined up together in six rows and two columns, and like an ancient puzzle created a whole document.

'That is the Origin Scroll,' Bhante Rinzen explained from across the room. 'That's not paper, it's Himalayan birch bark. Before paper this is what the ancients used for their important records...' She breathed hard. 'Strips of bark, oiled and polished...and written on with India ink. It took me two weeks to unroll and preserve in the plastic.'

'Bhante, please rest,' Iti advised, and the priest nodded weakly. The girl paused, seeing that Kumar Fourteen had snuggled up to Pujari Nandan's bearded face for a nap. She hoped the priest didn't have any issues with cats. Although Kumar Fourteen was offensive to most things alive...

'Do you want to read or look at the Scroll?' Isaac asked Iti. She shrugged, putting the thought of the priest and the cat aside. 'I'll give the notebook a go, then.' He sat in one of the chairs and started on Bhante's translation.

Under the light of the naked bulbs Iti began inspecting the Origin Scroll. There was a lot of strange writing all along the edges, surrounding one large painted illustration. It seemed like two hills, both with a village on top: it could only be Devagarh and Yakshagarh. Yakshagarh looked weird, though. She could see the village, and the Black Kot with some kind of kingly figure sitting cross-legged on it. The odd part was a strange cone that seemed to shoot up out of the fort, with a golden dome on top. The only thing she could think of, looking at it, was vanilla ice cream in a cone. There were a whole lot of other figures drawn all around as well, very detailed, but Iti had never been great with mythology. Gods? Demons? 'I don't know, it doesn't make sense to me,' she finally confessed to Isaac.

'I'm getting it a bit,' he said, showing her the notebook. 'Bhante has copied some of the illustrations and referenced them.' He pointed at an object on the page that looked like a bell with a hook coming out of it. 'This is an ancient lock and key. The writing on it is a,' he squinted at Bhante's writing in the notebook, 'A Prakrit? The Prakrit writing says "Trikunchika". It means three keys.'

'Okay,' Iti said.

Isaac showed her the notes under the entry. 'Here Bhante makes a note of "the three protectors". Now, Kariba said her uncle is the Rakshas Lord, Guardian of Yakshagarh, right?'

'Right.'

'Well, look at this.' He leaned over to study the scroll for a moment. 'Here.' He pointed at an indigo-skinned demonic figure dancing below the village of Yakshagarh. 'That's the Rakshas Lord. Look at his hand.'

Iti stuck her nose close to the plastic, narrowing her eyes. 'That's the same lock and key. He's holding the ancient key.'

'Yes, now look at these.' Isaac pointed at the village of Devagarh, where another king sat cross-legged on some kind of animal—a wolf? Then he indicated the king sitting on the Black Kot. 'Look at their hands.'

'They're both holding the same key.' Iti pouted, trying to figure it out. 'So what, there are three keys? Keys to what? Is Mister Mer trying to find them? Do we need to find them before him?'

'I don't think so,' Isaac said, flipping to another page he had been marking with a finger. 'Here Bhante translates, "whoever defeats"—"Trikunchika" in Prakrit again—"will open the door", and Bhante put a question mark on the word "defeats". Like she's not sure if it's right. But the word can't be wrong, the writing is too sophisticated to be ambiguous. "Defeats" must be the right word.'

Iti sighed and ran her fingers through her long black hair, beginning to feel frustrated. 'But how do you defeat a key, or three keys? It doesn't make sense.'

'You're right,' Isaac said. 'Which is why the only thing that makes sense to me is not that the three Guardians hold or guard three keys.' He pointed at the king of the Black Kot. 'They *are* the three keys.'

The girl's mouth popped open. 'That's why Mister Mer is trying to defeat Kariba's uncle—it makes sense!'

Isaac waved his hand defensively. 'Hold on, it's just a theory. It may make sense, but there might be another explanation. Which is what we've got to figure. Because another thing we need to know is who these guys are.' He pointed at the two kings. 'There's a Guardian of Devagarh, and a Guardian of the Black Kot, who is referred to as "Aadhiraat Raja".'

'The Midnight King,' Iti said, and for some reason that sent a shiver down her spine. It was a portentous name. 'But the most important thing we need to know is what is in the Black Kot. That's what Mister Mer is after.'

'Right,' Isaac nodded. He sat in the chair and shrugged. 'That's all I've got right now.'

'Okay.' She glanced over at the priests lying on the other side of the room. 'What say we try to revive Pujari Nandan, and then come back to the book?'

He closed the notebook. 'Let's go.'

A moment later they both knelt by Pujari Nandan, chasing a disgruntled Kumar Fourteen away. Bhante Rinzen watched from her bed. It was tough, Iti realized. She still felt spent from healing Bhante earlier. The spiritual healing was significantly harder than healing the body. She remembered Isaac's words, and hoped they weren't pushing themselves too hard. After all, it was only the night before that they had discovered their powers. Except for Safir.

Holding up her hands in front of her, Iti felt a great contentment that Healing was her power. Isaac put his hand on her forearm and murmured, 'You ready?' She nodded at him. She looked down at Pujari Nandan's old, worn, kind face. So many kind people were suffering from Mister Mer's actions. She promised herself she'd help them all, heal them all, all those who had been hurt, who were lonely and helpless.

Iti put her palm on the priest's forehead and started.

21

SECOND AND THIRD PATH

Walking through the jungle to Yakshagarh was everything Shari had imagined it would be. The forest here was thick and wild, and tough to navigate, except for Kariba who seemed to slide through like an eel. The trees, a mix of huge evergreen and oaks and other kinds he couldn't name, were interspersed with large tangly bushes. It was strangely silent here, but Shari told himself that maybe that was normal on Yakshagarh.

They'd been at it for twenty minutes since crossing the bridge. Ignoring the downward path they had taken yesterday, as well as the other path that led crookedly towards the haunted village, they followed a diagonal western direction, down and across the face of the hill. Kariba led them unerringly, saying, 'This is the quickest way to Rabakak's home.'

Rabakak's home, Shari thought, wondering if maybe 'lair' or 'den' might be more appropriate.

Trikaya let out a sudden shriek and danced towards Tal and Shari, who grabbed her and looked fiercely into the trees. 'What, what?' Tal asked.

'Bones! Skeletons!' Trikaya was shivering in their arms. 'So many of them!'

Kariba skipped back to them and hopped up onto a boulder to get a view. 'Oh, that? That's just the remains of his meals.' The three children moved in a cautious huddle to see. In a depression of land was the largest collection of bare white bones they had ever seen: full skeletons, half skeletons, skulls and skulls and skulls, easily fifty or more. 'Mostly sambar and goral,' the rakshasi evaluated. 'A couple macaques, foxes, and a bear.'

'How is that not scary?' Shari declared, trembling at the thought of the appetite that could put away this much meat.

The rakshasi turned with hands on her hips. 'What, don't you eat meat?'

'Yes, we do,' Tal conceded. 'But not this much!'

'Just because you don't see the butcher's work doesn't mean the bones aren't there,' Kariba stated. 'Rabakak lives alone out here, what else should he do with them?'

Trikaya nodded. 'You're right. It makes sense. You're sure he won't, you know, get hungry with us around?'

'He doesn't eat humans, never has. He's not that kind of rakshas.' She gestured. 'Come on, we're right there.'

They steeled themselves and continued.

Sure enough, in some time they reached an area of the hill that looked distinctly lived-in. The trees were sparser here, and some of them showed signs of unusual wear and tear. Shari remembered that bears rubbed themselves hard against trees. It looked like Rabakak might do the same.

'Well,' Kariba said, troubled. 'He's not here. This is his main home, he's here most of the time. He has another smaller residence on the north side of the hill, where it gets more rocky. I could go check it out, but I'm pretty certain he's not there.'

'Should we take a look around?' Shari volunteered. 'There might be clues.'

'Yes, thank you,' the rakshasi said, and wandered off on

her own. Tal thought she looked a forlorn figure, with her pigtails and light yellow frock and bare black feet.

'Come on, let's spread out and look,' Tal said.

'But stay in the area, far from the trees,' Shari added quickly. They all agreed emphatically. They were in a rakshas's home, in the middle of the jungle, in Yakshagarh. Being here was the definition of hazardous.

The ground, Shari noticed as he walked around, had been packed tight, pressed down, no doubt, by the weight of the rakshas who lived here. He saw a tree trunk three times his size that looked like Rabakak used it as a chew toy. There were unmistakable tooth marks puncturing it. The shivers ran up and down his spine, and he moved on quickly from it.

'I found his bathroom!' Trikaya called out, running quickly towards them, pinching her nose. Shari and Tal exchanged a disgusted look between them. They didn't want to imagine what a giant rakshas's toilet was like...

He saw Tal stoop down suddenly, and looked over in alarm. She saw him watching and showed him what she had found: a good rock. Round enough, about two centimetres wide. Tal pocketed it and made a gesture, miming their sling shots. Shari nodded and wondered why they hadn't pulled out their sling shots yet. They were in the boys' Box back at the Lodge, wrapped up and put away. They hadn't used them in some years now, actually. They still collected rocks when they were outside out of sheer habit, like Tal just did. They'd come home and drop them into the rock bucket in the girls' room. Shari gave his sister a thumbs up, confirming that they'd both remember to take them out. If ever there was a time to properly arm themselves it was now.

When Shari looked for Trikaya he saw her aimlessly walking around. He made a beckoning wave, and she and Tal started to walk to him. Kariba was at the other end of the area. Was she talking to herself? The boy moved towards the rakshasi, trying to make out what was going on. No, Kariba was nodding, even gesturing. She was talking to someone who Shari couldn't see, in the jungle. As he approached, Kariba seemed to finish her conversation, turning to greet him.

'Who were you talking to?' Shari asked, as Tal and Trikaya caught up to them.

'My fellow students,' the rakshasi said, scratching her arm. 'I'm part of a rakshas gurukul down the hill. They can't get involved, but they were concerned for me. They can sense something is off with Yakshagarh.'

'Rakshas gurukul?' Shari enunciated, incredulous. 'Like…a boarding school for rakshas?'

'Yes,' Kariba replied, and added, 'It's a very old and prestigious one. You can only come if invited.'

'Cool!' Trikaya crooned. 'How many students are there?'

'About fifty, from all over the Indian subcontinent. There's even one girl from Lanka who claims to be related to Ravana, but everybody thinks she's fibbing.'

'Gurukul means you have to have a guru,' Shari stated. 'Who's your teacher?'

'Everyone calls him the Quiet Father,' Kariba answered. 'But no one knows his name, or who he really is. He hardly ever speaks. And he's ancient, super ancient. And he doesn't look it, so he must actually be *really* powerful. Rabakak treats him like…like he's some kind of saint or something.' She looked around and then leaned in conspiratorially. 'Don't tell the other students, but Rabakak thinks he might be a Maharathi who gave up war a long time ago.'

'Sure,' Tal said. 'What's a Maharathi?'

The rakshasi made big eyes as she explained, 'A Maharathi is a supreme warrior. Arjuna from the Mahabharata was a

Maharathi. Drona, Bhima, Karna, they were all Maharathis. In the classical ranking, a Maharathi can single-handedly take on 720,000 soldiers.'

Trikaya's face was all awe. '720,000!'

Shari was little more skeptical 'That's a bit much, isn't it? I mean, these are all people from legend, and from ages ago too, if they actually even existed. And your uncle's guessing your teacher's a Maharathi. Can you really make that comparison? It's not like he actually fought in the Mahabharata or anything.'

Kariba stared at the boy resolutely. 'The Quiet Father's old. Really, really old. Did he fight in the Mahabharata?' She thought hard, one eye scrunching closed. 'I can't say for a fact he didn't.'

Tal shrugged. 'If you believe it, that's good enough for me. Shari's always doubting stuff that should just be taken in good faith.'

'Good faith?' her twin said heatedly. 'I'm taking everything in good faith, don't talk about me like I'm...'

'We're sitting in a rakshas's lair!' Tal pointed out loudly, 'Kariba's a rakshasi, we've got magic, and devas, and yakshas...'

Shari stepped up close to her, nose to nose. 'Yes thank you, I can see that, but you'll just take what anyone says? Without question? Even *she* doesn't believe her classmate who says she's Ravana's...'

Kariba and Trikaya jumped in between the twins, prying them apart. 'Stop it!' the little one cried in alarm, cheek pressing against the boy's chest, 'Stop it, stop fighting! We can't do this, don't you see we need each other?'

'It's true,' the rakshasi told Tal, gently but firmly holding her back. 'It doesn't matter who the Quiet Father is. What matters is finding Rabakak and stopping Mister Mer.'

Tal was still shivering with anger, he could see. 'Yes, you're right,' she said, blinking hard. She smoothed her hair back into its ponytail, not looking at him. 'Shari, I'm sorry. I shouldn't have said that.'

He felt like he'd just seen a baboon slap a shark. 'You're sorry?' He paused a second, and all the anger left him. 'No, it's okay, I'm sorry. I'm sorry, I...' He didn't know what to do. Tal apologizing? To him? As if that wasn't enough, his twin now put out her hand. Shari solemnly took it, and they had one firm shake. Trikaya also looked like she couldn't believe her eyes.

'Let's go,' Kariba told them. 'Rabakak has a sunning spot nearby, let's go see.' They nodded and fell into line behind her.

Shari was glad how things concluded, after such an ugly turn. He hadn't meant for it to boil over like it did. Sure, Tal had started it, but he was supposed to be the cool one, the one always in control. His sister was the impulsive, irrational one, the reason why the KSS split in the first place. And for her to not only recognize her fault, but to apologize, and be so civil about the reconciliation... It was unsettling. His whole life, he realized, had been in large part defined by Tal being Tal. If she now became someone and something else, what would that make him?

As they moved out of Rabakak's home area Trikaya let out a squeal of excitement. 'Galahad!' They turned to see the yellow-throated marten come running across the open expanse, moving in that beautifully sinuous way as he hopped his way to them. The marten stopped nearby and stood up on his hind paws, arms hanging down in front of him. 'He's with us,' Trikaya told Kariba proudly, echoing her sister's words from before.

The rakshasi bowed to the marten, who watched her

and then bobbed his head. They once again headed off, and Galahad followed, his golden torso flashing brightly.

Rabakak's sunning spot was about a hundred metres away, through a small rock ravine, and then up to a part of the hill that jutted out slightly and was clear of trees. Evidently the Guardian was not there, so Kariba turned around with a shake of the head. Trikaya and Tal made to follow, but Shari stood rooted, staring at the middle of the open spot. He called out loud, 'Wait, there's something...' The others stopped, and he looked at them and said, 'There's something not right here.'

They moved out carefully over the clear spot as he explained, 'I don't know what it is, but something that grew here was wrong. It grew... unnaturally.'

The land dipped slightly, and Shari saw, as they all did, that the earth here looked disturbed. A very large and long expanse, in fact, like when diggers have passed. Galahad stalked through the broken dirt, sniffing here and there intently. 'The dirt's been dug up,' Kariba said, crouching down to inspect the rich, dark loam. She picked up a rock that looked freshly split, the sheared surface glinting in the sunlight. 'And roughly.'

'Something grew here,' Shari said nervously. 'Under us.'

'Under us...' Kariba repeated, and began flitting around the dug up area purposefully, as if looking for something.

'Kariba, tell us what you're looking for,' Tal called to her.

The rakshasi stopped, staring at the ground. 'It's under,' she declared, and the girl in the yellow frock just disappeared...

For a second Shari didn't quite understand what had happened. Then the three of them ran to the place and saw a black hole just wide enough for Kariba to slither into, going almost straight down. Dirt still flew up from inside, and they could hear her soft grunts carrying up to them. Even the marten looked leery of going down there, sending some tense cries after her.

'Are you serious?' Shari said, eyes popping. 'Kariba!'

'Do…do I go in after her?' Trikaya asked, fascinated but also terrified.

'No,' Tal said, putting a hand on Tri's arm. 'I think she knows what she's doing, give her a minute. Just don't move, we don't want to collapse the tunnel.'

The seconds stretched on until the rakshasi exploded out of the hole, and landed next to them calmly. She looked clean as day, not a speck of dirt on her skin or her frock. 'He was here!' she told them excitedly. 'Here, under us! I'm so happy, it smells just like my uncle!'

They paused a second. 'You might not want to repeat that elsewhere,' Trikaya informed her, voicing their common thought.

'Oh, is that not done with humans?' the rakshasi asked, interested. None of them volunteered an explanation, so she carried on. 'The dirt, ten metres deep, has been all turned. There are tree roots everywhere there shouldn't be, all knotted up.'

'That's it, it's the tree roots that are wrong!' Shari exclaimed. And now that he could put it in words he felt it clearly: the massive, thick tangle under the earth was a gigantic knot of roots.

'But he's not here anymore,' she continued, 'the roots are broken and twisted, and his smell goes off up the hill, under the earth.'

'He's digging himself out under the earth?' Tal pronounced. 'But he's huge! Why not just come straight up?'

'The spell,' Kariba said. 'What Shari is feeling is the root spell that trapped him, it's too powerful. He was able to wriggle out of it by digging down, but I guess he just got away in whatever direction he could. I couldn't follow him because there's no tunnel left. The earth has slid in and filled up behind him. But...' The rakshasi pointed upslope. 'There's a tunnel network through most of the hill leading to the village. It's logical that he would have headed there. Once he's found a tunnel it should be easy enough to go up and make his way out to the surface.'

'The village?' Tal said.

'Yakshagarh?' Trikaya trilled.

'The *haunted* village?' Shari specified.

Kariba nodded. 'It's okay, it'll be my first time there too. We rakshas also avoid it because of the ghosts.'

Shari thrust his hands forward. 'And that's supposed to comfort us?'

'You basically just *confirmed* that there are ghosts,' Tal stated. 'And you think it's a good idea to go there?'

The rakshasi nodded, 'Yes. If Rabakak is there, we're going there. He could be wounded, for all we know. Whatever spell this was, it was strong enough to overpower him. And let me tell you, he's no pushover. There's a reason he's been the Guardian of Yakshagarh for the last three hundred years.'

'Three hundred years?' Shari exclaimed, then sighed. 'Why do I even get surprised anymore?'

'Me too,' Tal agreed, shaking her head.

Shari gathered his sister's and Trikaya's gazes. 'This is what we came to do,' he reminded them. They looked as nervous as he felt, but they nodded, agreeing.

22

THE OTHER VILLAGE ON THE HILL

A whole lot of trekking got them back to the path from the bridge to the village, Kariba in the lead, Galahad still following at his marteny pace. Tal was glad they had gotten a nap and a meal, because this was tough going. She wondered how Isaac and Iti were doing.

The path started off dirty and dusty, but after twenty metres became a magnificently flagstoned road, made of the grey-brown granite of the hills. It was strange to be walking towards the ruins they could see peeking through the tops of the trees. The road turned, and as it wound up they passed under a tall and imposing archway with towers on both sides. It was clear what that was for, Tal thought as they went under and saw the narrow staircase leading up. Archers and soldiers would slow down any invading force here.

Beyond the archway the houses sprouted. Ancient structures with collapsed roofs, sunken doorways, and empty windows, like sagging human faces made of stone. They were two- and three-storeyed buildings, gorgeously carved, but a lot of the engravings had been worn down by the elements. Smaller paths began splitting off from the main road, narrow ways that crawled up or down hill between the houses leaning against each other.

They couldn't possibly walk any closer together than they already were, shoulder to shoulder, Trikaya gripping the hems of Tal and Shari's T-shirts. Their sneakers sometimes bumped together, but no one complained. They could feel it now, and they squeezed against each other even harder.

The village was watching them.

None of them had ever felt anything like it. People talked about the sensation of being watched, and Tal had an approximate sense of what that meant. This was nothing like that. This was the unmistakable certainty that hundreds, thousands of faces were crowded close to you, centimetres from your body, breathing on your cheeks, eyeballs about to touch your skin…but the moment you turned your head they seemed to always just slide out of sight. It was maddening.

They began panting as the feeling intensified, the air becoming thick with menace. Tal hardly felt her friends by her, so overwhelming was this sensation. Terror rose in her, and she couldn't hold it back anymore. It was watching, they were watching! She opened her mouth to call out to Shari, blinked…

Tal stood in the middle of the road, alone. Night had set, somehow, a moonless black that was impenetrable. All around her Yakshagarh hung, the buildings like heaped skeletons. Over them all loomed the Black Kot, darker than the night itself.

You're not welcome here.

It seemed as natural as anything for a voice to speak to her. It came from nowhere, but it came from everywhere, all around. It was the voice of Yakshagarh, thousands of voices in a single one. 'I…' she said, a quavering note. 'I'm Tal. I've come to help Rabakak.'

You don't belong here. Go back.

The voice seemed to push her back down the road, away from the Black Kot. It would be so easy to turn and run, cross the bridge, run up the steps of the Lodge, and dive under her bed…

Shaking her head, Tal said, 'I can't leave. Where are my friends? Where's my brother, where's Shari?'

If you stay we will come for you.

Nothing chilled the cells of her brain more than that pronouncement. But she bit her trembling lower lip and stuttered, 'I ca…I can't leave…without them…'

There was a silence. And then she felt something stirring in the village around her, a presence rising in the buildings.

Tal. Tal.

The voice began to chime and echo around her.

Tal. Kandhari. Tal Kandhari. Little Tal. Insignificant. A speck. Nothing. Think you're a Star? Think you shine? Nothing. Go back. We will blow you away. Blow you out. Like a candle.

A Star, she remembered, clutching her fists tight. Tal had always thought of herself as a star. Whatever she did, in school, in sports, in life, she felt she shone. She carried that certainty in her heart. And yet…

Not a Star. You're not. Nothing. We will blow you out. Go back. Insignificant.

'I am a Star,' Tal murmured. But was she? Her family had never said so. Not that they'd said the opposite. It was their silence on the matter that always made her wonder. Doubt. Was she really as great as she thought? Did she really shine to the world? She watched her fists open and stared at her palms. If she really was a Star, she should shine. But nothing came. No light came from her hands.

Nothing. No light. Family knows. Family knows you. Nothing. You are nothing. Go back.

Tears came to her eyes. She wasn't a Star. Or a star. What was Tal, really? Did her friends really even like her, or just follow her because she talked loudly and acted impulsively? The KSS was breaking, they were leaving her. The illusion of Tal the Star was breaking. Of course they would leave. And she would be alone. No family, no friends, nothing.

Nothing.

Her legs wouldn't hold her anymore, she sank to the ground, feeling the shape of the flagstones on her knees through her jeans. 'Alone...' she whispered, staring at her hands, tears plinking as they struck her palms. Yes, alone. With nobody.

Nobody.

Nobody.

Nobody.

Nobody...except herself.

Silence.

Tal looked up. It was true. Even if everybody left her, Tal still had Tal. And what did *she* think of Tal? She was brave. That, she knew. And strong, yes. Was there a flicker of light in her palm? And loyal, absolutely. Did her index finger seem to lighten?

'Alone,' she said, her voice strengthening.

Alone.

Tal lifted her index finger, holding it up. And as it rose so did she, climbing to her feet. And as she stood a gleam emanated from her digit, sparkling in her eyes. 'Alone, but not nothing.'

Her finger ignited, turning into a candle, pushing back the darkness, the whiteness spreading to her other fingers.

'Alone with myself.'

Brighter, brighter, chasing the shadows back, while she curled her fingers, tightening and condensing that light into her fist.

'Therefore: not alone. I always have me.'

She held her fist higher, above her head, and the village turned bright as day, the light forcing even the Black Kot to back off, to lean away from her. How warm she felt, how glorious, shining the way she always knew she should!

'I am Tal!' she told the shadows fiercely, defining herself, 'I'm a *Star*!'

The presence shrunk down to almost nothing, quivered in front of her, bowing down, cracking...

Tal leaned down, seeing it reduce to a speck of black between two flagstones. She pointed her finger at it, that blindingly bright sun on the end of her hand, and cried at the presence, 'Give me back my friends!'

It was like lightning, a blinding flash of light and sound.

Tal stood in the road with Shari, Trikaya and Kariba, all of them blinking in the afternoon. The presence they had felt, the watching, was gone. All of them had expressions of anguish, tears streaking their faces.

'You saved us,' Kariba whispered, wiping her eyes and grabbing Tal's shoulder. 'I felt it. You pushed them back...'

'They tried to make me feel like I was nothing,' Tal said in a husky voice. 'But they couldn't convince me.'

Shari nodded slowly. 'They told me I destroy everything I touch. The KSS.' He squeezed Tal's hand. 'You.'

'They said I break everything,' Trikaya sniffed, rubbing her nose. 'Because I'm too clumsy, I get carried away, and I break it all.'

'Me, they said I'm weak,' Kariba said, steadying her breath. 'That I'm too weak to choose for myself, too weak to change things and make my own life.'

They held each other's arms another moment, then burst into embarrassed giggles. Galahad seemed to have been unaffected by the ghostly ordeal, and watched them with a bemused expression. 'Come on, then,' Tal cheered them, 'Can you smell your uncle here?' Shari and Trikaya tittered.

'I can, actually,' Kariba said, raising her pert nose to the air. 'This way!'

It was incredible how differently Yakshagarh felt now. It was still a ruin, of course, and alienating in that way. Without that presence crushing them, however, it was almost a pleasant stroll, in the middle of the afternoon with the breeze blowing. They hurried on up the winding road, following the rakshasi's nose.

'Oh wow,' Trikaya said suddenly, making them all stop. They had been so busy looking around that they hadn't looked at what was in front of them.

The road ended a hundred metres ahead, and there, squat and solid, was the Black Kot. The four of them stood transfixed, mouths open.

The Black Kot was a prison, a cage, a black mass of unyielding stone. The walls, fifty metres high, were sheer and smooth; the four towers that made its corners were starkly octagonal; there were windows peppered here and there, but thin slits no child could squeeze into. It had been made to be a fortified chest to safeguard whatever was inside, and it had been made well. In the middle of its front wall, facing the road, was a double door of wood that looked thick enough to stop a missile, banded with iron and locked tight.

Shari gulped and gave them a crooked smile. 'I almost feel bad for Mister Mer…'

They hurried on, not wanting to stay in the shadow of the sinister fort. Soon Kariba led them into a large house that seemed only slightly less dilapidated than the others. She found a staircase leading down, and they stepped cautiously into the basement. It was a large storage room still filled with jars and baskets that had gone grey with age and dust. At one end there was a rather grandiose arch that led deeper into the ground, and then another staircase down which they climbed.

By now it was dark, and Tal wished her hands to light. It was awesome, she thought giddily as they went down the next set of stairs. Light was just coming from her hands, exactly like the high beams of a car, and wherever she pointed her palm the light went. The marten seemed thrilled by the lights, running to grab at them as they moved, his eyes glittering with glee.

Another tunnel, this one with arcades along the side. She flashed her hands through the arcades as they walked, and all of them drew in their breaths. The arcades were balconies, clearly the third or fourth floor of some structure overlooking a courtyard or something deep below. They didn't approach the side, fearing that age had made the balconies fragile, but they became conscious of the scale of what was underneath Yakshagarh: another entire city, hidden and unknown.

'There,' she said, slowing down. 'Uncle Rabakak?'

Tal pointed her hands and tried to make out where he was. They had reached another wide and tall hall, the walls covered in intricate mosaics, with balconies and windows stretching above their heads. The wall in front was an oddly plain surface, textured and rough and completely undecorated, which was strange given how everything else here seemed...

The wall moved, quickly, so fast that they couldn't react, rolling out towards them, and then stopped. 'Kariba?' a voice called out from above.

Her heart in her throat, Tal raised her hands and looked up, conscious of Trikaya and Shari also craning their heads back.

This giant tree trunk of a creature hovered above them,

black eyes shining in the dark. Even here, reclining in this hall, it was still towering five or six metres above them.

'Oh my,' Trikaya squeaked, and sat down in the dust. Galahad flowed into her arms, surprising her, and she hugged him close for comfort.

'Uncle, how are you?' Kariba said, jumping forward to press her hands and face to that rough bark-like hide.

'Peeved more than anything,' he said, his voice rumbling and echoing. Tal frowned. Did he have a British accent? 'But yes, exhausted too. I can't stand, I get dizzy.' He groaned and lowered himself back to lie down, a whole mechanism that shook the ground and actually made their feet leave the floor. 'What are you doing here?'

'We came to rescue you!' Kariba sang. 'Are you hurt?'

'Not hurt, no, but weakened.'

The rakshasi turned to her friends. 'Do you think Iti can come and heal him?'

'Sure, we can try,' Tal said. 'I've got the walkie-talkie, hopefully we'll be in range upstairs.'

'No, no,' Rabakak said, gesturing with his odd pincer-hands. 'I'll be fine. You don't by any chance have a tasty cat or two with you, do you? What's that little thing there? Perhaps a succulent feline?'

As if sensing the rakshas's interest, the marten hissed and snuck around behind Trikaya. 'No, that's Galahad, he's not a cat!' she said, cross.

'Ah,' the Guardian sighed. 'No matter, I'm done anyway. It'll take me days to recover the strength to get upstairs, and even after that I would need roots and trees. That's where I get my energy, but down here?'

'Roots?' Shari said. 'There are trees in the village. Roots must extend down nearby.'

'Too far,' Rabakak said, his voice growing faint.

Tal saw her brother make a fist. He said, 'Not for me.' Shari stepped away from the rakshas and closed his eyes.

'Is he…?' Trikaya whispered loudly to Tal, who nodded.

For many long seconds they waited, and then Shari said, 'Got it.' He pointed his finger up above them, at an angle. 'Now…' More time passed. Tal moved a little closer to Shari and realized he was sweating, and panting. Was he alright?

A distant sound, as of something clattering, reached their ears. 'What's that?' Trikaya said.

'That's me,' Shari hissed. He was pale.

'Shari, wait, don't…' Tal began, worried. 'Don't push too hard.'

His hand was still pointed up, but it was shaking. She could see him working his fingers, as though he was guiding something. Another moment passed, and he suddenly gasped and began to keel over. Tal shouted and jumped to catch him, managing to get him just in time. Trikaya crawled over, and Kariba came sliding to them.

'Stop!' Tal yelled at him. 'Stop, it's too much!'

Shari nodded. 'Yes. But I have to.' He coughed, rolled to his side, and with their help managed to kneel. 'We have to stop Mister Mer.' He raised his hand again, his entire arm shaking. 'I'm almost there.'

They sat around him, Tal praying that he would be okay.

And then they heard it. A rustling, a whisper of movement. Galahad stood up on his hind paws, alert, and they knew it was there.

Out of the darkness they came, like a dozen snakes, roots thin and black, crawling along the stone floor. The roots seemed to grow faster as they came closer to Shari, speeding along in straight lines around and under all their legs to reach the rakshas. The black lines curled up under Rabakak and climbed his dark hide, then stopped.

'Shari?' Tal whispered at her brother now that it was over. He opened his eyes, smiled, and said, 'I did it.'

She threw her arms around him, as did Trikaya and Kariba. 'You did it!'

'Okay, I need to lie down,' he said. They helped him down, resting his head on one of the roots he had just grown.

Rabakak drew in a long breath and raised himself onto an elbow. 'Oh ho,' he rumbled. 'Ask for some roots, and Bob's your uncle!' He smacked his huge cracked lips. 'But that's the stuff, no doubt. Give me an hour and I'll be running laps around this place!' He chuckled. 'Well done, Kariba. Looks like you went and found the only yakshas worth something around here.' He peered down at them, one at a time. 'Aren't you all interesting... Glad to see some of you around, finally.'

'Thanks,' Tal said, a little surprised at how comfortable they now felt around the monstrous creature. 'But we're a little pressed for time. Do you know what Mister Mer's up to?'

Rabakak's face became grim, and he snorted. 'Mer. I knew I recognized the voice...'

'I tried to come tell you in the morning!' Kariba piped, waving her arms with passion. 'But you were trapped already!'

'Mer's grown strong,' the rakshas stated, 'And masterful. He's playing with things better left alone. I must admire his strategy, however. Finding and trapping Rabakak the Treeborn is no mean feat.'

'What happened?' Trikaya asked.

'It was a manipulation spell,' Rabakak explained. 'Making the trees think of me as their enemy. Simple enough, but difficult and powerful to execute. But it was how he got the spell to me that leaves me...'

'How did he get the spell to you?' Trikaya pressed, fascinated.

'I was hidden by my vast and intricate sorcery, you see,' the rakshas said. 'And when Rabakak hides, none can find him.'

'I can find you,' Kariba said.

'Well, yes,' he retorted, annoyed, 'When I say none, it's obviously a slight exaggeration for dramatic purposes. You're a rakshasi, and my niece, it's different for you.'

'I'm just saying, be precise,' the rakshasi said, shrugging.

'All right, all right, when Rabakak hides, very few can find him. Happy? Most importantly, Mer can't find him. Which is why Mer spelled someone who could find him.'

'Who? Who?' Trikaya was hopping with anticipation.

'A Listener, of all things! Rabakak can hide from all— from most things—but a Listener can hear the universe.'

Tal and Shari stared at each other. 'I'm sorry, what did you say?' she asked. 'A Listener?'

'Yes. In fact you know him, he was with you yesterday, with the cat. Little boy, glasses? Doom and gloom sort of chap?' Trikaya's eyes were wide with disbelief. 'Imagine my surprise, this morning, when he just appears at my sunning spot, and can see me! I introduce myself, polite-like, and the moment he hears my name, sure enough it's the trigger for the spell. Opens his mouth, Mer's there on the other line, and hey presto! I'm buried in the ground.' He sighed, and paused, looking at them. 'You're all looking a little peaky suddenly. A nice little cat would do you good right now, rolled in puff pastry, with a walnut butter glaze...'

The three children gathered together, their faces grim. Kariba joined them and said, 'It's him, isn't it?'

Safir.

They had to get back to the Lodge.

23

PURSUITS SCHOLARLY AND OTHERWISE

Safir sat on the window ledge, heart racing, looking down at the drop below. He couldn't believe what he was about to do. But left behind twice in one day… It was too much for one boy. He pushed himself off, plummeted down one metre, and landed in the dirt, miraculously unscathed.

The bush behind the boys' room had often been used as a secret exit point for Shari over the years, but Safir had never dared follow him down. Until today. What a day it had been… He peered out from the bush and saw the coast was clear. Crouching down, the boy stalked around the house, staying well under the level of the windows.

He stopped at the front corner of the Lodge, between the row of rose bushes Auntie Sophie cultivated and the wall. His heart was running like a jackhammer. Never before had Safir disobeyed his father. The consequence loomed in his mind, dire and unimaginable. To him, though, the alternative was to sit at home while his friends were in danger and risking themselves. Between disobeying the Brigadier and letting his friends down, it was an easy choice.

Although actually doing it was proving tough as nails. Safir was having difficulty getting his sweating, trembling body to move. The final run was across the front of the Lodge and to the village. Anyone looking out the windows would clearly see him. And if Abba were to see him…the boy shivered.

And then jumped up and skedaddled at top speed.

He was doing it! Past the door, around the trunks of the few slender trees dotting the property, and then out in the open. Come on, he told himself, gritting his teeth. It was a long run to reach the village, but he didn't feel safe out in the open like this, especially with the thought of the Brigadier spotting him. So Safir, who could usually only manage a haggard trot and at most a five-metre sprint, ran and ran, and ran some more, until he turned the corner into Bazaar Round.

Back at the Lodge, standing tall at the first-floor window, Brigadier Safdar Idris watched his son struggle down the path and reach Devagarh, his face carved in stone.

How strange, Safir thought, as he slowed down to a walk. He thought he would collapse and have to lie down for an hour or two, but he actually felt all right to walk. Sure, his legs felt like they'd gone under a steamroller, and his lungs were filing for bankruptcy, but he was still up and moving.

Bazaar Round was buzzing, he saw, which was a whole other kind of fun. By now, middle of the afternoon, most people in Devagarh were out here, along with the tourists who had made it this far to see the Barbarika Festival. That giant Barbarika statue even seemed to be smiling; Safir was certain that wasn't its usual expression. He could see street performers through the crowd, walking on wires and turning back flips, and vendors hawking some of Devagarh's specialties, freshly fried. For a second he wished he could hang out here a bit and take a good look. But then he refocused. If there was a place he wanted to be, it was with the KSS.

'Safir!'

The boy looked around, hiking his glasses back up his nose. People thronged, making it difficult for him to see. He craned his neck, trying to figure.

'Over here!' There, sitting comfortably at Bintu's, was Dr Negi, waving at him.

Safir couldn't possibly get out of it, especially not after the doctor's intervention last night, so he hurried over hoping it would be done quickly. He liked Dr Negi, but there were more urgent matters at hand. 'Hi Dr Negi,' he called out, and the doctor put out his hand as usual for him to shake.

'Hello hello, young Mr Idris!' Dr Negi chanted, an ordinary-looking older man with flashy glasses and a brown tweed suit. He was sitting at one of the plastic tables, in the company of an elegant-looking European man and Constable Dobal, the one policeman in Devagarh. 'What are you doing running around like this? You should be in bed!'

'Actually we're all fine,' Safir said quickly. 'Really, we've been up and around all day.'

'Those aren't the doctor's orders,' Dr Negi scolded good-humouredly.

'And one really should take the doctor's orders seriously,' the foreigner said, an Englishman. He was in a white shirt and brown suit, dressed modern, but with his neatly styled brown hair and large sweeping moustache he also looked like an army officer of the British Empire.

'I concur,' Constable Dobal declared, eyeing the Englishman. He was a large-bellied man in his forties with a moustache hanging over his mouth and the beginnings of a combover. The policeman's passion for order and karaoke were established facts in Devagarh, but often clashed. The policeman organized the town's only karaoke event once a week, but no one ever came because of his authoritarian ways. Every Sunday evening one could hear Constable Dobal's marvellous falsetto soaring through the village and scaring away man and beast. 'Things must be done correctly. Otherwise all sorts of shenanigans can be expected, from all sorts of parties.'

Dr Negi leaned forward. 'Safir, this is Mr Robert Charles, he's visiting from England and has come to see the Barbarika Festival.'

'Charming town,' Mr Charles said, grinning at the policeman. 'A little bit of a trek, but certainly worth the effort.'

'We try hard to keep things in order,' Constable Dobal stated. 'And we expect all our citizens, and visitors too, to do their bit, Mr Charles. Where in England did you say you were from?'

'Pooley Bridge, in Cumbria. Have you ever been to the Lake District?' Mr Charles asked back.

'No, we have a lake here,' the policeman retorted. 'Are you here on business?'

'Mostly pleasure,' the Englishman said, smiling broadly. 'Although I can never rule out the opportunity to invest on my travels.'

Dr Negi cleared his throat, and said, 'Anyway, it's my professional opinion that you, and your friends if they're around, should return to the Lodge immediately. Better to rest one day than risk illness for a week. And that fever you all had, I've never seen anything like it. I almost called in for a helicopter to evacuate you!'

'The priests are sick,' Safir blurted out, 'All four of them!'

The doctor blinked. 'The priests? All four? Sick how?'

'I don't know, but it seemed serious, you really should take a look at them.'

'Come on,' Dr Negi said, grabbing his medical bag

(which never left his side) and standing up energetically. 'Take me to them!'

Safir paused. 'Me?'

'Why, yes!' the doctor said, and turned to his companions. 'If you'll excuse me…'

'May I be of help?' Mr Charles said, getting up. 'I have had some experience in nursing.'

Constable Dobal leaped up. 'I will be coming too! To make sure there was no mischief. Four priests at once? Sounds suspicious. Who knows, someone may have done this to them?' He narrowed his eyes at Mr Charles, who looked like he would burst out laughing any second.

So Safir led the doctor, the Constable and the Englishman to the stupa, wondering how he had gotten into this mess.

As they walked, Constable Dobal continued to press Mr Charles for information, like his identity papers, his profession, whether he was married with children, and what kind of visa he had used to enter the country. The Englishman responded with increasing hilarity, supplying all the answers and documentation from his breast pocket, but all his actions served only to rile the policeman.

Dr Negi soon snagged the Constable, pulling him back so he could stop harassing the Englishman. Mr Charles lengthened his stride to come up with Safir, and smiled kindly at him. The boy thought for a second, and asked, 'Do you know the knight Fierabras?'

The Englishman looked perplexed. 'Fierabras? Well, yes. Knight of Charlemagne, giant and champion, King of Spain. Are you interested in medieval Europe?'

Safir shook his head. 'Not really. I mean, maybe now. Fierabras is my ancestor.'

'Ah!' Mr Charles exclaimed. 'I'm in the presence of royalty!' He made a nimble little bow in mid-stride.

Safir laughed, shaking his hand. 'No, no, I'm just a kid...' They were reaching the stupa, and the boy quickened his step, jogging in and calling, 'Hello, it's Safir, with Dr Negi!' Hopefully that would give Isaac and Iti a heads-up.

The four visitors entered the inner chamber and looked around.

'Dr Negi!' Iti said, skipping up to him. 'Thank you for coming! They're here.' She hustled the doctor away, followed by the policeman and the foreigner. Safir looked around for Isaac Shroff, and saw him sitting at a desk on the other side, carefully shifting papers around. Isaac saw him, winked and nodded. Safir went to join him, glancing over his shoulder and seeing Iti distracting the others. Dr Negi made a bit of a ruckus, trying to chase Kumar Fourteen away from the patients, and the cat skulked around the chamber in a foul mood.

'How's it going?' Safir asked softly.

'Slow,' Isaac said. 'We have a working theory, but Bhante Rinzen and Pujari Nandan are out, they can't help us.'

'Are they doing okay?'

'They're awake, Iti healed them. But they can barely do anything but blink.' He tapped the chair next to him. 'Sit down, you're looking a bit out of it. How did you get away? You managed to convince your father?'

The boy sighed and sat. 'Not really...'

A slow smile formed on Isaac's voice. 'You snuck out? You disobeyed him?' He pressed his knuckles to Safir's shoulder and nudged him. 'Good for you!'

'I...I mean,' Safir stuttered, 'Yes, but, it's not really a good thing, is it? Disobeying?'

'I think you did the right thing,' Isaac said, reaching out to pick up a red notebook from the table. 'But the important question is whether you think it's the right thing. After that it's only a matter of managing your father's reaction.'

'I guess,' the boy mused, fiddling with his glasses.

'Now that's quite a map,' a voice cut between the two of them, and their heads whipped around to see Mr Charles standing right behind them, inspecting the table. 'May I?' He reached forward before they could say anything more, and brushed papers aside to reveal a plastic sheet within which were preserved several sheets of some sort of paper.

'It's Bhante's,' Isaac said nervously, slapping his hands down on the papers and stopping the Englishman. 'It's confidential.'

Mr Charles looked Isaac in the eye, and both of them remained locked like that for three long seconds, while Safir squirmed in his seat. 'I see,' the Englishman said casually, leaning back. 'My sincere apologies, I didn't know this was a private matter.' He turned, slid his hands into his pockets, and ambled back to the other side of the stupa.

The moment the Englishman seemed out of earshot Isaac leaned over and whispered suspiciously, 'Who's that?'

'Some tourist. He was hanging out with Dr Negi and Constable Dobal at Bintu's.'

'Most strange,' they heard Dr Negi declare as he walked towards the entrance, looking distraught. 'I have no diagnosis.' They looked up to see Iti escorting the visitors back to the entrance. 'The best I can say is to wait. If there are no other symptoms, they should get better. Where are the other priests?'

'In their quarters, at the church and the mosque,' Iti said.

'All right,' the doctor said. 'We'll go check on them. Constable?' The policeman nodded.

'I'll stay,' Mr Charles announced. 'Just a bit to make sure they're alright.'

Dr Negi nodded and exited quickly. Constable Dobal scowled, not wanting to let the foreigner out of his sight, but his sense of duty prevailed and he scuttled out after the doctor. Iti raised her eyebrows at Isaac and Safir behind the Englishman's back, asking what she should do.

'Now,' Mr Charles said as he turned, his voice resounding in the chamber. 'Can any of you tell me who is the Guardian of Devagarh?'

The children froze.

'Anyone?' the Englishman said.

'The what of who?' Iti replied, exaggeratedly blinking her large brown eyes. She surreptitiously scooted around closer to her friends.

'We don't know what you're talking about,' Safir declared woodenly. 'We're just kids.'

Isaac raised his hands helplessly. 'We're just helping Bhante organize some papers, we don't know anything.'

Mr Charles looked the three children over. 'Right. Of course.' Safir was trembling, sensing the tension in his friends. 'I'm actually looking for someone here. Heard he was visiting. A bit of a strange fellow, about two metres tall. You haven't seen him around, have you?'

Safir couldn't help glancing at Iti and Isaac, then realized how suspicious that must seem. Mr Charles was looking for Mister Mer...as an enemy, or an ally?

'No,' Isaac answered defiantly. 'None of us have.'

The Englishman approached slowly. He didn't seem aggressive or anything, but the children naturally drew together, Iti putting tight hands on the boys' shoulders. Mr Charles stopped right before them and pointed at the desk. 'Is that a tower?'

The children glanced down and realized a large part of the Origin Scroll was still showing. Safir recognized it instantly: it was a representation of Yakshagarh, with the Black Kot at its peak and some man sitting on it. From the Black Kot rose a strange image, looking like some kind of triangular spinning top.

'We don't know,' Isaac answered, his voice tight.

Keeping an eye on them, Mr Charles leaned over close to the desk. He switched his look to stare intently at the Scroll. 'Is it a tower or...?' he muttered to himself. He got closer, face as near as it could be to the map, nose touching the plastic. 'Good God,' he breathed after two seconds, his face turning shockingly pale. 'Surely it can't be...a Gate?'

'What?' Isaac said. 'A gate?'

Mr Charles practically jumped back from the table, whipped up his left arm, pulled back his sleeves, and scanned his watch frantically. 'Is there still time...?' he mumbled, stepping towards the entrance of the stupa.

'Wait!' Iti said, 'What do you mean?'

The Englishman began striding away urgently.

'Mr Charles!' Safir hollered.

That seemed to get his attention. Mr Charles stopped, already half into the tunnel leading out. 'Whatever it is you think you're doing, stop. This is no game for children. Go home, pack your bags, take your families, and leave. Not in ten minutes, or five. Now. Tell your parents whatever you need to, but leave Devagarh now.'

The Englishman turned on his heel and sprinted, as fast as they had ever seen an adult run, and was gone. A few seconds later Kumar Fourteen sauntered into the spot where Mr Charles had been, raised a leg, and began licking himself intently.

The children looked at each other. 'Okay,' Safir said shakily in the wake of the warning.

'A gate,' Isaac uttered, peering at the Origin Scroll where Mr Charles had been looking. He scooted his chair back and began pulling open the drawers in the desk. 'Ha!' he crowed, and plucked out a magnifying glass. He leaned back in, adjusting the glass slightly. After a few seconds he handed the magnifying glass to Iti and cleared the space. 'Check it out.'

Iti inspected the Origin Scroll for a moment, then handed the glass to Safir. Impatient, Safir pulled his chair close and leaned over. Finally he could see: the Black Kot jumped out at him. The man sitting cross-legged on it was clearly a king, crowned and holding a…what was that, some kind of bell? Above the fort that triangular top became clearer. It was actually like a weird yellow tower, tiered terraces one on top of another, and a tiny yellow palace at its peak. Where was the gate? He blinked and looked closer. Right at the intersection of the Black Kot and the point of the triangle was a window. Like the top had come out of it, except that the perspective was so out of whack, but still…

'There is a gate,' Safir concluded, meeting the others' eyes.

'Yes,' Iti said softly, looking nervous.

'I see it too,' Isaac agreed.

They sat in silence. Mr Charles had told them to go home, to go the Lodge, and get everyone to leave. They couldn't possibly deny that he knew far more about this than any of them: in one glance he had identified the subject of the Origin Scroll. And he had told them to leave, with such insistence.

'What do we do?' Iti whispered.

'I don't know,' Isaac replied.

Safir nervously pushed his glasses back up his nose and cleared his throat. 'I think I know. What to do, and where to go.' They looked at him with wide eyes, and he told them.

24

A SENSE OF INNOCENCE

Shari ran over the bridge to Devagarh with Tal and Trikaya, consumed with the urgency of getting back. Tal was working the walkie-talkie endlessly, trying to get a signal across to Isaac and Iti. They had left Kariba to tend Rabakak. The rakshasi planned to stay a short while and then join them in Devagarh for the Barbarika Festival.

They were almost at the Lodge, Galahad in tow, when static broke out and Isaac's voice came across: 'Isaac here, uh…over.'

Tal stopped, and the others also pulled up, panting. 'Isaac, we found Rabakak, he's fine. Kariba's staying with him in Yakshagarh village. Shari, Tri, Galahad, and I are almost at the Lodge, we have to talk to Safir. What's your 20? Over.'

'Fantastic!' the boy's voice came through, excited. 'Yakshagarh village? Like, the haunted village? Okay, okay, later. Um…what's twenty?' There was a garble of voices as he found out. 'Oh, uh, our 20, we're almost at Mademoiselle's. Iti and I, and Safir's right here, should I put him on? And Kumar Fourteen. Um, over.'

Tal's mouth opened and closed, caught short and not knowing what to say. Shari waved his hands to catch her attention, and mouthed words for her to repeat. 'No, no, it's okay, we'll meet you there in twenty minutes. Over.'

'Okay. Er, copy that. Over. And out. Over and out.'

Trikaya giggled, 'It's so cute when they first learn how to use a walkie-talkie…'

'Safir's with them,' Tal said, tense.

'It's okay,' Shari reassured. 'We don't know if he's still spelled or not. Isaac sounded okay, so he's probably acting normal. All we have to do is get to Mademoiselle's.'

'Is it five yet?' Trikaya asked exuberantly. She grabbed Tal's left wrist and held it up to read the time on her friend's red plastic watch. 'Almost. Yes! Mademoiselle's!'

Shari couldn't help but smile. In the middle of all this, there was Trikaya with her priorities in firm order. It felt funny to be heading to Mademoiselle's. There should be somewhere else more important to go…but there wasn't really, right now, was there? So Mademoiselle's was as good a place as any, wasn't it? He caught Tal's eye, and from the embarrassed and eager smile forming on her face, he knew that she was thinking the same thing.

'Okay,' he grinned and put his hand out palm down. 'Even heroes need their macarons.' The girls giggled and slapped their hands over his. Galahad eyed the hand stack and combed his triangular head with his front paws in response.

The trek from the Lodge to Mademoiselle's was particularly arduous this time, after all the running up and down Yakshagarh they had done. Bazaar Round was full of people, and they had to make their way through slowly. Trikaya spotted R2R at a distance, and they traced a wider path around to avoid them. They didn't have time to waste with the likes of them. Even Dharm Square was filling up. Shari wondered if Bhante Rinzen and Pujari Nandan were all right, but knew that they couldn't stop to check on them.

Besides, he felt that Isaac would have told them on the walkie-talkie if anything were wrong.

Down the avenue, along that line of ominous black poles, and then a couple of turns, and there was Mademoiselle's, an oasis in… well, not that Devagarh was a desert, but at this moment the patisserie was just that much more brilliant. Shari could tell that the girls wanted to hurry up the slope, but they were all exhausted. Mademoiselle's would be a total restorative.

They could see through the French windows their three companions, sitting peacefully at a wrought-iron table. The three companions saw them at the same moment and threw their arms up, and now Shari, Tal and Trikaya felt a little burst of giddy energy. As they reached the door Trikaya cried out, 'Galahad!' and sure enough there was the marten rejoining them. He had balked at entering the village, with this many people gathered, and bounded off to the side. Evidently he had traced his own path around or through quieter streets, and now reunited with them at destination. Poor guy, Shari thought, he also looked out of breath. He was actually a young animal, Shari realized, and new to the wide world and people. But how could Shari know that? He wasn't a biologist. Unless it was another skill that came with being a Gardener…

They opened the door and there was a joyful and noisy reunion. The group of six moved to one of the larger tables away from the window and sat. Galahad seemed particularly intrigued by the inside of the patisserie, its smells, and by Kumar Fourteen, who himself seemed rather distressed at being in the vicinity of so paramount a predator. Shari and Tal groaned loudly as they sat, making a show of their leg fatigue to the others, while Trikaya went straight to Iti and snuggled up for some quiet hugs.

And yet through it all, Shari and Tal quietly stole glances at Safir, looking for odd expressions, listening for odd words. Who knew whether Mister Mer still controlled him. Was he even Safir at this moment or just an expertly controlled puppet?

'Bonjour!' the greeting sang out before they even saw her, but everyone turned in anticipation.

Mademoiselle Fulara swept into the room. She had changed to a candy-pink salwar kameez, and topped it with a lovely grey woollen shawl, and had evidently done her hair, which was even more resplendent than usual. Shari looked at his sister. Tal always got a special twinkle in her eye when she was near Mademoiselle, and behaved much more elegantly and soberly than usual.

'Bonsoir!' they all chorused, and she went around the table planting kisses on every cheek, making both boys and girls giggle. Shari had to amend his earlier thought: when Mademoiselle came in, everyone got a special twinkle in their eye.

'My heart is whole!' Mademoiselle said, shaking her head with glee and making her wonderful wavy hair fly. 'I love seeing you all together again. This calls for a celebration!' She sailed back into her kitchen, and everyone sat back, impatient.

She was back in hardly a minute, and by then they were all boiling with expectation. In her arms was a tray larger than seemed possible, and on the tray was a treasure trove of plates.

'Summer Bummer!'

Fat brioche sandwiches rained down on the table, stuffed with poached eggs and bright red bell pepper hollandaise.

'Dizzy Fizzy!'

In a spherical glass as big as their heads was an effervescent yellow soda, banana and mint.

'And…the Electric Choc!'

A platter landed full of cigar-shaped wonders: a dark-chocolate shell encasing a milk-chocolate layer, a crackling praline shell, and in the centre a chilli dark-chocolate ganache that stung the tongue.

They all practically had tears in their eyes, except Safir, who had actual tears in his eyes. Mademoiselle hummed a happy French song as they began their industrial consumption. 'Ooh!' she cried suddenly, and knelt down to the floor. 'This one I know,' she said, gently flicking Kumar Fourteen's nose, 'but you, sir, are new.' She settled down in front of the yellow-throated marten.

The marten stood close to her, sniffing the air and showing his pink mouth. 'He's dangerous!' Tal hissed in warning.

'His name's Galahad!' Trikaya chirped from her chair.

Mademoiselle smiled. 'Hello Galahad.'

And Galahad lowered himself, sniffed her fingers, and curled up in her lap.

'I knew it,' Safir said nonchalantly around mouthfuls of food. 'It's Mademoiselle.'

Mademoiselle fetched little plates and a bowl for the cat and the marten, with small portions of the meal. While she was gone Shari and Tal exchanged looks. He bobbed his head, indicating he'd take care of it, and she nodded.

It took fifteen minutes for the eating to finally wind down, for plates to be wiped or licked clean, little tongues doing the final work. One by one the members of the two KSSes pushed their plates away and sat back, bliss on their pink-cheeked faces.

With a few sweet words Mademoiselle cleared up the table and as she did so, Shari gently kicked Isaac Shroff and Iti's shoes. They were confused, but got his message, and when he got up saying, 'I'll be right back,' they followed suit.

Tal and Trikaya began chatting Safir up at that moment, just like they had planned.

The three stepped outside onto the wide patio of golden sandstone. The sun was already on its downward path, burning its patch of sky to ochre. Devagarh looked beautiful from here, peaceful and lively. They could faintly hear the music from Bazaar Round. A few people were still crossing the village, heading towards the festivities.

Shari told them in a few quick whispers what had happened between Rabakak and Safir. He concluded the story with the plan they had in mind: for Iti to heal Safir. Rabakak had confirmed that it was within a Cure's power to remove spells from a person.

Iti looked particularly distressed, gripping her hands so tight that Shari reached out to hold them. 'It'll be okay,' he told her. 'You're brilliant, you already healed practically everyone.'

'It's true,' Isaac agreed. 'You can do this in your sleep.'

'Yes,' Iti said, squeezing Shari's hand. 'I have to. It's Safir.'

They walked back in. Shari craned his neck to make sure Mademoiselle was still in the kitchen. She had taps running, and some kind of machinery. There was no way she'd be able to hear them.

'Hey Safir,' Shari began.

'Hi,' the boy said. He looked around the table, at everyone staring at him, and his expression shifted, becoming anxious.

'Listen,' Shari said, but now that they were getting into it he wasn't sure how to continue. How could he just tell Safir that Mister Mer had possessed him with a spell and used him to bury Rabakak under Yakshagarh?

'Safir,' Trikaya announced, grabbing his hand. 'Mister Mer possessed you with a spell and used you to bury Rabakak under Yakshagarh.'

Or he could just let Tri take care of it.

'What?' Safir said, chuckling nervously. 'Is this a joke?'

'No,' Tal said, surprising everyone with the gentle tone of her voice. 'It's true. This morning, somehow, Mister Mer put a spell on you. You went to Yakshagarh, alone I guess. Rabakak was hiding with his magic, but your Listening power is stronger than that. Mister Mer wouldn't have been able to find him by himself, so he used you to find him. He spoke the spell through your mouth. That's why Rabakak was missing all morning. We just rescued him. Well, Shari did, he was amazing.'

Shari couldn't help a surge of pride at his twin praising him. 'Iti will heal you,' he picked up the argument, comfortable now that the worst was started. 'Rabakak says she should be able to remove the spell, if it's still there.'

'I can do it,' Iti said, looking into Safir's eyes. 'I know I can.'

'Do you remember this morning when Kariba came?' Trikaya reminded him gently. 'She said Rabakak's name for the first time, and you cried. It's because you knew what Mister Mer made you do, inside, even if you didn't remember.'

They waited a moment, letting Safir take it all in. 'Okay,' he finally said. 'I don't remember any of it, but if you say it happened, I trust you.'

Just like that. Shari had to tuck his lower lip up to keep the tears from his eyes. He was the doubter of the group, Shari was. How much of a fight would he have put up? Denied, argued? Everyone would have, he reckoned. And here was Safir willing to go with them, because he trusted them.

'All right,' Shari said, blinking to clear his eyes. 'We're all here. Let's do it.'

Isaac put his hand on Iti's arm, and Iti reached out to hold Safir's hands. All six sat around the table, quiet. Shari watched intently. He hadn't seen Iti's healing yet, not the big things she had done like Reva's wound or Bhante Rinzen or Pujari Nandan. He wondered if it would take a long time...

'Done,' Iti sang, and let Safir's hands go. That was fast.

The first thing Safir did was sigh. A big, big sigh. Then he squeezed his eyes shut, rubbed them hard a few seconds, and looked up. 'Oh yes, I remember. Bits and pieces. I remember Rabakak. It was horrible. I just watched him get buried and didn't do anything...'

'It's not your fault,' Isaac interjected quickly, leaning in to put a hand on Safir's shoulder. 'It was Mister Mer controlling you.'

'But if it was any of you guys you would have fought it, you might have stopped it,' Safir said softly, cynically.

'No they wouldn't,' Mister Mer stated. 'And no they couldn't, not any more than you could.'

The children spun around in their seats, stunned to silence.

There he sat at one of the tables by the French windows, as if he had always been there. Tall and thin, his face as haughty as ever, smiling condescendingly at them. 'You are completely innocent, Safir, if that's the kind of thing that matters to you. I needed your help. Thank you for that. And well done, Miss Pillai. A Cure indeed. The spell was done anyway, but its residue was there. To remove it in such an efficacious manner... But what am I doing? Thanking and praising you, when really all of you would be nothing next to the one who really matters.' He leaned forward, his entire body extending like a giant spider relishing the approach to its trapped prey. 'The one who deserves the thanks and praise, really, is...Isaac, isn't it?'

25
THE LURE OF POWER

'You're all tolerable right, to be fair, but that's it,' Mister Mer continued, making a dismissive gesture with his hand. 'Miss Pillai, you heal bruises and headaches. Yay, here's a trophy! Girl Kandhari, you might be useful during a power cut. Until I find a candle. Boy Kandhari, you can grow flowers. Egad! What godly might! Well done with Rabakak, though. I genuinely didn't think you'd make it on your own. Miss Pillai junior, you're a joke. Where's your power? Your confederates are rubbish enough, but you don't even belong with the rubbish. Safir, you have something interesting. Had it for years, in fact. It's still derivative, however. Useless, in fact, for what really matters.' He held out a fist and pointed that long index, like a cue stick, at Isaac. 'But you, Mr Shroff. You are something special.'

Isaac didn't know what to say, transfixed. Here he was, here was their enemy, the man who had put the mighty Guardian Rabakak under the ground. And what could they do against him? The casualness of his presence told them how insignificant they were next to him. And Mademoiselle, if she came out of the kitchen, could they protect her if Mister Mer was moved to act? He prayed with all his heart that

Mademoiselle would stay there long enough for this scene to play out.

'It's a sad thing,' Mister Mer continued, rising slowly and clearly becoming engrossed in his own oration. 'To lose one's mother, and so young.'

The others stole quick glances at Isaac.

'I did too,' the magician intoned, his face becoming melancholic. 'Not that my mother was of any value, really. Genevieve Kent, however, was an angel. And that is truly a loss, one that I can genuinely sympathize with.'

Isaac whispered raggedly, 'How do you know my mother?'

A crooked smile slashed across Mister Mer's face. 'See, Safir? You're not the only one stumbling blind in a labyrinth of family secrets and lies.' His eyes seemed to become sad, wistful. 'How do I know your mother? Ishan wasn't even there when you were born. Who do you think was the first person to hold you in their arms? Not even Genevieve. It was I, Isaac. And I who laid you next to Genevieve, reuniting you with your mother. I was there at your beginning. Now, this is the second beginning for you. And here I am.'

Tal put a hand on his arm, but Isaac hardly felt it. He didn't even know what he was feeling. He wanted to not believe it, to stand up and shout at Mister Mer that it was all a lie, to defend his mother. But defend her from what exactly? It was true that Isaac hardly knew anything. His mother had died when he was four, and Ishan Shroff soon evaporated. Isaac didn't have a memory of his own of Genevieve Kent. Or even what her voice sounded like. Only photographs. Forever silent.

'There are things you can't do anything about, Isaac,' the magician emphasized bitterly. 'When Genevieve left us… It was her time, I suppose. She would have stayed, if she could, I don't doubt. There were other things, however, that could have been done after her time.' He raised a finger. 'Telling the truth.' A second finger. 'Taking responsibility.' A third. 'Not abandoning your child who has lost his mother, and sending him to grow up an orphan in a dark castle somewhere.'

There was a storm of upset in Isaac, more than he could bear. Was it true? Had his father abandoned him from even before, from the very moment of his birth? Was Mister Mer, this strange and powerful villain, really a friend of his mother, and the first person to hold him in his arms? He felt sick in his stomach, a tight ball of hurt.

The magician pressed on, caught up in his speech. 'Ishan Shroff, Doctor of Philosophy! What a father. I know your sadness, Isaac. Your anger. It is a tragedy, and unfair. You grew up with no one. No one to watch you, no one to listen, no one to take your side. No more. I am here. I can help you be strong, teach you to be strong.' Mister Mer approached the table slowly, each step making the children turn their heads up higher and higher. 'What do you want? To take revenge on Ishan Shroff? To control him? To make him proud? To make him love and admire you? Whatever you want, I can give that to you. You just have to join me, be on my...'

'No,' Isaac barked instantly. His mind was awhirl with thoughts and feelings, but this much he knew: Mister Mer was an enemy. The rest could be figured out separately. 'Join you? You call my friends names, and praise me, and you think I'll join you? You expect me to turn my back on them to come with you?'

'It's the price you pay to become who you're meant to be,' Mister Mer countered. 'These "friends" were strangers to you yesterday, Isaac. What are they to you? Are they any different, really, from those other three wretches I sent to secure you today, that Rudra and his lady flunkies? Hear me when I say this: staying with fools will only make you a fool yourself. Staying with them is turning your back on yourself.' He pressed his knuckles into the thick glass of the table and leaned his weight down, making the wrought-iron legs creak. 'You think I don't know what you went through? I had the same choice as you, years ago, in this very place. I had friends, family, neighbours, people who knew me. All of them wanted me to remain weak, to be the strange, tall kid who they could keep pitying and mocking forever. It was either being loyal to mediocre friends and unexceptional people, or being loyal to me and everything I wanted to become.' The magician stabbed his finger into the tabletop for emphasis. 'In the end I chose to be loyal to me. I became stronger. And what did these friends do? Shun me. Talk behind my back. Despise me.' A smile creased his craggy face. 'Fear me.'

'It's true,' Mademoiselle's voice declared, clear and pure as sunlight. The children turned in alarm, to warn her to stay back, but they stopped, stunned. Mademoiselle stood in the kitchen doorway, hands resting on an ancient-looking sword that stood point to the ground. 'You became a bully. The very thing you hated and feared yourself when you were young and vulnerable. Not everyone abandoned you, even in the last days before you left. I was there. I would have remained your friend, if you hadn't chosen to become like this.'

'Mademoiselle Fulara,' the magician pronounced, smiling. 'Lies from your beautiful lips are still lies. You talk loyalty? My destiny was always to walk this path, and you would have always chosen to be loyal to your duty rather than to your friend.' Mister Mer drew the children's glance back with a gesture. 'Do you think she would choose you, or you, or you, over her duty? The Wolf Queen of Devagarh?'

The children turned slowly back to Mademoiselle, as if seeing her for the first time. The way she stood there, with that broad-bladed sword, her wild brown hair framing an expression fiercer than they could ever imagine on that sweet, pretty face...a she-wolf in her kingdom. 'It's you,' Tal stated with dumb wonder. 'You're the Guardian of Devagarh.'

'Mister Mer is here to fight you!' Iti cried out. 'And the other Guardians too!'

'I know,' Mademoiselle intoned, moving her hands quickly to snatch the sword handle and swing the blade up to rest on her shoulder. Isaac gulped. The swiftness of the movement pointedly communicated that her ease with the sword was not recreational. 'I am the First Guardian,' she declared as she daintily settled into a chair between the children, and opposite the magician, her eyes stern. 'Vira Devi Fulara, the Wolf Queen, rightful ruler of Devagarh.' She flashed the children a brilliant smile, picked up a tissue, and affectionately wiped a little chocolate from the tip of Safir's nose. 'And pâtissière. So, unless you're here to try a portion of Electric Choc and have a friendly chat, I suggest you leave this town.'

'Yeah,' Trikaya punctuated with a sneer and a snap of her fingers at Mister Mer.

The magician burst out laughing. 'This little vaudeville is meant to intimidate me? Mademoiselle Fulara, I have seen things, been to places, that you wish you could not even imagine.' He paused, flustered, and tried again. 'No, wait: that you could not dare imagine, and if you did you would then wish that you had not imagined them in the first place. I mean, that you *had* imagined...' He smacked his palm on the table. 'I've been to places that would scare the make-up off your face!' The magician turned on Isaac, shaking his finger at him. 'And you, you will want to reconsider my offer. If you're not with me, then you're likely to become my enemy, given the kind of company you keep. And believe me, you would not like to be my...'

Standing up suddenly, his chair almost toppling over, Isaac interrupted him with a solemn, 'Mister Mer. I don't know if what you've told me is true. I also can't say it's false. It's important to me, and I'll find it out one day. But it doesn't matter right now. You're asking me to betray my friends. It doesn't matter what you're offering me, because I won't betray them. I stand with them. With the KSSes, both of them. And with Mademoiselle.' The boy put his hands on the table, nervously playing with his fingers. 'I don't know what happened to you. You're older than me, and you've done way more stuff. But whatever bad things happened to you, whatever bad things you've done... All that can stop. Just stop. I mean, right now, you can choose to leave it, to stop going after the Guardians. Pull up a chair and sit down with us. Have some cake. And just not be... whatever you've been for so long that's been making you do these things. I've admired you for as long as I can remember. I wanted to be a magician because of you. Maybe you could tell us about that, the performing. I mean... You could have been anything else, and done your magic privately, secretly. It couldn't be for money because you've got real magic. If you wanted to perform...maybe you wanted to be with people, to make them laugh, or make them feel something. Like I felt watching you. Because I didn't just admire you. I liked you.' He drew in a deep breath, winded. 'Would you consider it?'

It was the strangest little stand-off. Mister Mer, peering down from the top of his two metres, and little Isaac Shroff, eleven years old and neck craned back, looking into each other's eyes. It lasted only a few seconds, but everyone watched the magician, and they all sensed that, for a small moment, he contemplated the boy's words, and even wavered...

'I think not,' Mister Mer said, stepping back leisurely. 'And I think I hear my assistants ringing the bell. The curtain is about to rise. I'm sure I will see you soon, Mademoiselle, and doubtless the little whelps too. In the words of the masters,' he declared, pulling something out of his breast pocket and flinging it straight at Mademoiselle's mouth: 'Abracadabra!'

Whatever it was moved faster than they could blink, except for Mademoiselle's hand, which was even faster, a barely perceptible blur snatching it out of the air in front of her. The children jumped after it was all done, shocked.

Mister Mer was gone. The door of the patisserie remained closed, untouched. There was no one outside, for as far as the clear view over the village allowed them to see.

They looked to see what the magician had hurled at the pâtissière. She set it down on the glass tabletop, spreading it out calmly with her elegant fingers.

It was a red ticket, with the magician's face on it, printed in bright gold: *The Mesmerizing Mister Mer.*

26
WE ARE THE GUARDIANS

'That was so cool!' Trikaya gushed, grabbing and shaking Isaac Shroff's hand. 'You almost had him!' Everyone was hanging to their chairs despondently, Shari even face down on the table. The girl didn't understand what was with everyone. 'Why are you so low?' she demanded to know. 'We faced down Mister Mer!' She grabbed Mademoiselle's hand and hugged it to her. 'Mademoiselle is the Wolf Queen! Guardian of Devagarh! She's a princess *and* a warrior.'

One by one the others seemed to stir, looking up, nodding in agreement. She was glad they could see the sense in her words. 'We need the KSSes together for the fight,' she told them, going around the table to put an arm around her older sister. 'All of your powers together.'

'Absolutely not,' Mademoiselle announced, standing up. 'I don't know how you got mixed up with all this, although for some reason I'm not surprised. But I couldn't in good conscience allow you to continue.' She reached out and gently held Tal's chin between her fingers. 'You're children. And this is not a fight, this is going to be a real battle, a war even. Mer is more dangerous than I had anticipated.' There was sadness in her eyes, so much so that Trikaya had to hop around the table to hug her by the hips. Mademoiselle laughed fondly, rubbing the little girl's back. 'I'm sorry, it's my fault. I should have done more to find Mer myself, to stop him. I might have been able to help the Rakshas Lord, but I thought…' Her lower lip tightened against the upper. 'I hoped that Mer had changed. That going abroad, and being a famous magician, and travelling the world had healed him, of whatever it was that had wounded him. He wasn't like this. A long time ago. He was my friend, once.' Her eyes were distant, lost in a time that she seemed to realize for the first time was irretrievably gone.

Then she shook her head, tossing the superb glossy brown curls of her hair, and once again she was the Wolf Queen. 'It is sad, but it is done. And now the Guardians must rise to meet him.'

'But what does he want?' Iti practically yelled. They all looked at her with wide eyes, amazed to hear that tone coming from her. 'I'm sorry,' she mumbled, blushing. 'It's just, we've all been trying to figure it out, and nobody tells us, so… What is Mister Mer after?'

Mademoiselle hesitated, clearly considering whether to tell them or not, and then sighed. 'He wants to conquer the Black Kot. It was built aeons ago to guard the Secret, a secret no one could know…'

'Yes, we know,' Trikaya jumped in, waving her hand impatiently, 'It's a gate, but a gate to what?'

The Wolf Queen's mouth stayed open for a few seconds before managing to say, 'Oh. Well. Yes, it is a Gate, but…' She puckered her fuchsia lips into a resolute pout. 'I can't tell you. For you to know this much is already perilous.' She wrapped her hand around the handle of her sword. 'You stay here. The patisserie is guarded with spells, you will be safe.'

'No.' Safir's voice rang out. He scrambled to his feet. 'We're coming. We're the Kumaon Secret Society, True and Real.'

Tal also stood. 'And the descendants of yakshas.'

'Doesn't that make us Guardians too?' Shari affirmed, he and Iti getting up at the same time.

'I'm a Catalyst,' Isaac said quickly. 'I can multiply power. I don't know how, but I can do that for you. And Shari's a Gardener. Iti's a Cure, Tal's a Star, Safir's a Listener, and Trikaya's... she's...'

'I'm a hero!' the littlest one declared, 'Because I don't have any powers and I'm *still* going to war!' She stared hotly at Mademoiselle who, in spite of the smile that she struggled to mask, nodded.

'I see,' the pâtissière said, 'And I agree. But don't get in if you don't have to. The Guardians are born and trained to this duty, but you are not.' She turned to Iti. 'Safir was spelled from the very first time he met Mer, and likely you all are too, to a lesser degree. I think he blindly spells everyone he runs into, just a seed of magic which he can then cultivate. You're the Cure, Iti, make sure you heal everyone now. We leave as soon as you're ready.'

'Can I see your sword?' Tal jumped to Mademoiselle's side eagerly, as Iti nodded and reached for her sister to start the healing.

The lady laughed, and laid the weapon down on the table. It was a metre long, with a heavy black hilt and pommel, the handle bound with worn leather. The blade, a light blue tinted metal, was unlike anything Tal had ever seen. It wasn't the kind of thin or curved blade shown in movies and on television: instead it was five centimetres wide at the base, widening and thickening all the way to the end, and instead of tapering to a point it cut in abruptly to a tip. A black spike jutted ten centimetres straight out from the bottom of the handle. 'This is Uttaradanshtra, the Fang of the North,' Mademoiselle explained proudly, although it felt more like an introduction. 'This style of sword is called khanda. Prithviraj Chauhan forged three such blades with his own hand, one for himself, and one that he gave to my ancestors to protect the Black Kot.'

The children oohed, their eyes sparkling. 'What about the third one?' Tal asked.

'I don't know,' was the reply, 'He didn't tell me. Although if he sent one to guard the north, my guess is that he sent the other one to guard the south.'

'What's in the south?' Safir wondered.

Mademoiselle shook her head and smiled. 'One thing at a time, little ones.'

They began gathering at the door, looking out of the windows, until Iti snapped, 'Trikaya!'

Trikaya and Safir had snuck behind the counter and were stuffing one pain au chocolat after another into a paper bag. 'What?' the girl cried back. 'We need to keep up our energy for the battle!' Some of the others rolled their eyes, but Mademoiselle herself went to help them to hurry things up.

The western sky was rich with colour as they stepped out. The whisper of music from the Barbarika Festival drifted to them. Another day in Devagarh was coming to a close, one that should have been only joyful and harmonious. 'Do you feel that?' Isaac spoke in a low voice.

The others nodded solemnly, and Trikaya shuddered. There was a heaviness in the air, an ominous charge as though something momentous was about to happen. 'Stay close to me until it starts,' Mademoiselle told them.

The group began climbing down the path that would lead to the central avenue. Trikaya had only gone a few steps when Safir nudged her, looking perturbed. 'Tri, I...I'm remembering stuff. Like meeting Mister Mer in the jungle, and before. We were at the Lodge, and then you left, and

I meant to tell you but I forgot...' He rubbed the tip of his finger up and down his nose, embarrassed. 'I know your power.'

'Hold up!' Trikaya hollered, making everyone jump. 'You knew my power all along?'

'I forgot it,' the boy answered quickly, 'It was Mister Mer...'

'That's okay,' she said, jumping to excitement. 'What is it? Tell me, tell me, tell me!'

'You can join stuff together,' Safir replied. 'You were playing with the blocks this morning, and after you left I picked them up. They were fused together.' He bent down to pick up the first two rocks at hand. 'Here, try it.'

Everyone crowded close to watch eagerly.

Trikaya looked around at her friends, impatience and nervousness warring in her. She had tried out almost all the cool superpowers they had listed this morning, and none of them had worked out. Safir said she could join stuff... The girl held up the two rocks, one smooth, oval and yellowish, the other roughly shaped and red-brown. Two very different types of rock. Now that it came to it, she felt the urge to throw them down and run. What would it mean to have a power? And this power? Joining stuff? What would she do with it, fix the broken toys belonging to cousins way younger than her?

A hand on her shoulder made her head turn. Tal stood close, grinning. 'Go on, just do it.'

Breathing deep, Trikaya steadied her racing heart. Tal was right. Just go on and do it, and then she would see. Yellow stone, red-brown stone. The little girl gently made their ends touch and whistled quietly, hardly knowing it, 'Fffyyuuuw...' She let go of one of the stones, and it stayed. It just stayed hanging there, just touching, but now both rocks were as one. 'Ha,' she breathed, and everyone else whooped and clapped hands on her arm. 'Nice,' she said softly, turning the stone this way and that, showing it around. 'But...what can it do?'

Mademoiselle crouched in front of Trikaya, looking her in the eye. 'Trikaya, you are a Bond. You bring things together, and join them in such a way that they can't be separated ever. Think on that.' She tapped the little girl's chin with her index. 'Your power will be as small or as great as what you can figure out what to do with it.'

They continued onwards. Trikaya stared at the joined rock in her hand for a moment more, then let it slide out onto the path. She knew Mademoiselle was being kind, that's what she did, who she was. Her power was useless.

She didn't notice Iti, four steps behind her, bend down to pick up the joined rock and tuck it into her pocket.

They got onto the avenue and hurried down it, the house lights of Devagarh beginning to show as the sun dipped further into the horizon of high hills. Trikaya began to pant at the pace, and looked back to check on Safir and Iti, who always had a tough time keeping up. But there they were, right on her heels. They both flashed smiles, and she produced a jovial thumbs up, overjoyed to see them running with ease. This was how the KSSes should be, heading into whatever it was together!

A bizarre cacophony of sound erupted from everywhere, startling them and the few stragglers who were hurrying to join the festivities. It was as though a thousand accordions had suddenly started up, drowning out all the local musicians instantly.

'What's that?' Shari warned, pointing ahead at Dharm Square.

A dozen Devagarhis stood watching a strange figure

capering oddly before them, some kind of contortionist flipping himself over and over…

'More are coming!' Iti shrieked. Trikaya and Tal turned, seeing more and more of these creatures leaping out of side streets.

'They're not human!' Isaac yelled, terrified. The figures were too fast, they couldn't even tell what these things were! All angles and sharp edges flashing, the figures rushed the little group, while the accordions grumbled a melodious but jittery din.

27
THE MESMERIZING
MISTER MER

Eight of them they were, coming from all directions, unnaturally fast, and in the waning light Safir drew back in horror, realizing these things were not even alive. They were misshapen origami clowns, made of multi-coloured sheets of huge paper. Their bodies were paper thin from one angle, but tall and wide and menacing from the other, without hands or feet but balancing on pointy corners or rounded curves. They all bent sharply at unpredictable joints, moving in grotesque flips and slides, their contorted faces flashing sometimes high, sometimes low, sometimes upside down…

And then Mademoiselle was there. Her circular steps were almost casual as she moved from one side of the little group to the other, and everywhere she went she flicked Uttaradanshtra as though it were a reed she had plucked instead of a heavy ancestral weapon. Everywhere the sword swung the origami clowns went down, each neatly sliced in a way that completely impaired it. They didn't get up again.

'Come on,' the lady told them before they could even react. They obeyed her instinctively, trotting forward on her heels.

Where were these accordions? Safir wondered. It was impossible to hide so many of them, not when they were blaring like this from everywhere.

'Not all of them are attacking,' Isaac told the group. It was true, in the crowd the origami clowns were handing balloons and candy to children, performing magic tricks, or capering around comically.

'Watch out!' Iti grabbed at Tal, and they turned to see...

All the poles that had lined the main avenue of Devagarh, easily forty or fifty of them, were ceremoniously marching towards them. The nearest ones were still uprooting themselves, neatly stepping out of their holes on two smooth black legs. They waded into the crowd, drawing small screams and laughter from the revellers, five-metre tall giants with long dangling filaments that, as they walked, still purposefully dipped and bobbed, looking to just touch people's heads.

'They're doing something,' Shari told Mademoiselle, grabbing the sleeve of her pink kameez. 'The way they're touching people.'

'Yes,' the Wolf Queen said, realizing the objective of the poles. 'They're drawing out spirit and magic. That's what they've been doing all day.'

'They must have been draining all the priests!' Iti said.

'The priests?' Mademoiselle wondered.

'Safir!'

'Oh no,' Trikaya moaned.

All their families appeared one by one, coming out of the crowd, Mr Idris first. He stood with fists on his hips and elbows out, looking as stern as usual. 'I saw you this afternoon, hotfooting it into town. Do you remember me explicitly telling you to stay at home?'

The sound of the accordions brayed in Safir's ears. He

thought he mumbled, 'Yes, Abba,' but he couldn't tell, his head felt so light with terror. Of course the Brigadier would catch him. That's how it worked, wasn't it?

The other parents were still engrossed in their own conversation, although Mrs Idris had seen and was moving quickly to hear what her husband was telling their son. However she was cut off by a tall figure diving in to stand at the Brigadier's elbow.

'Ah, Safdar Idris,' Mister Mer drawled, 'tormenting your son again... Well, we all have our hobbies.' Mr Idris turned sharply, and blinked. He was used to looking down on people shorter than him. To have to raise his head to look the magician in the eye was a disconcerting experience. 'I seem to recall the older Mr Idris, Safir's grandfather, persecuting you in mostly the same way. Didn't learn your lesson, though, did you?'

By now the parents had circumvented the little scene and watched with trepidation as the Brigadier's face seemed to go from stern to a superhuman version of grim. 'You are the *magician*, aren't you?' he stated, his words ice and disdain. 'You really should keep your nose in your own business before someone sticks it back in there for you.' Their eyes bore into each other's stony gaze, the conflict palpable.

Safir's trauma had evaporated in the face of this astonishing sight. Never before had he seen someone tower over his father like Mister Mer. And as he watched, a darkness seemed to fall around the two. The hems of the magician's black coat suddenly began to tremble from an unseen wind. The boy felt a new fear jolt through his heart. He could hear it, the sound of Mister Mer's magic gathering, a river of silk sliding over vast sands. He could feel it, that uncanny pressure building, the weight of it like an elephant about to drop from the sky...on his father.

'No!' he cried out, his voice breaking. 'Mister Mer, please, don't!'

The two men's locked stare broke as both looked at Safir. The boy was virtually in tears. Rolling his eyes, the magician sighed, 'Oh very well, consider this repayment for your splendid work with Rabakak.' He waved his hand dismissively.

Behind him two of the giant poles stepped up, their antennae lightly springing here and there, touching people in the crowd. One filament whipped out and tapped Mr Idris's cheek, and the Brigadier toppled over like a marionette with its strings cut. Mr Kandhari was close enough to catch him, but Mr Pillai and Mrs Kandhari had to join in to help him down. 'Safdar!' they called out in alarm.

'Mer,' Mademoiselle challenged, the sword rising out at her side.

'Not yet,' the magician laughed, prancing away, waggling his fingers. 'It has barely begun.' He put his hands around his mouth and howled a laugh that overwhelmed even the accordions, instantly drawing the attention of everyone in Dharm Square. Mister Mer pounced, a leap that made him fly five metres into the air and alight to stand comfortably at the very top of one of his poles.

Iti jumped past Safir to grab Mr Idris's hand. She didn't even have to close her eyes anymore, she realized. Just a touch and she knew that he was unharmed, only asleep, and of course drained of spirit. The parents fussed over him, which allowed her to come back to the boy and whisper, 'He's all right, he's sleeping.'

'Welcome!' Mister Mer greeted, his voice seeming to come from everywhere. The Devagarhis stared at him in awe, standing on top of that five-metre pole. 'I am Mister Mer. Most of you remember me, I'm sure.' He seemed to casually step out, but that step was another jump, hopping to the tip of the next pole, drawing out nervous cries. As he soared overhead he flung out his arms, and constellations of firework sprang from his hands, spreading into the shapes of fantastic animals for a few flashes before fading away. The villagers had never seen anything like it, and many craned their necks to look for wires and other contraptions. 'I have toured the world for over thirty years. Climbing unseen peaks, diving to unliveable depths of the ocean…'

'He just keeps yapping, doesn't he?' Tal muttered as their group shoved its way through the crowd, trying to keep up with Mademoiselle.

Trikaya held Safir's hand, pulling him along. He was still distressed at the vision of his father falling senseless like that. And yet he was relieved. He knew the unnatural violence Mister Mer was about to inflict on his father in that moment, and he had been able to save the Brigadier from it. 'Can we leave them there, Tri?' he asked.

'We have to,' she grunted back at him. 'It's better if they stay out of it.'

The crowd began to pour into Bazaar Round, following Mister Mer. He leaped from the poles to the roof of the church, frolicking down its length, and then on to other poles beyond. His words were lost to the children, struggling through the adults. It was clear he was doing the introduction to his spectacle, however. And that meant things were going to get hairy soon.

They were still mostly in Dharm Square, Safir could tell. He jumped up to try to get a good look ahead. The poles were pushing through the crowd with little concern for safety, and people were getting shoved aside and bruised. Things were coming to a head, he felt. The fireworks raining from Mister Mer's hands were doing their job distracting people, but Safir could sense the spell that was forming above the exploding lights. The air up there was filled with, he didn't know the words to describe it…textures, thickness, swathes of pressure rolling in like the tide.

'Safir!' he heard someone yell, but when he turned he couldn't see who. He realized instead that Trikaya and he had been separated from the others. There had been space to manoeuvre before, but now that everyone was packing into Bazaar Round to see the performance, the crowds were becoming even denser. The boy tightened his grip on his friend's hand, and they forged a way forward resolutely.

'And now,' Mister Mer declared as he came to a halt at the top of a pole, standing with his back to the giant statue in the middle of the square, 'The venue!' He made a grand sweeping gesture.

From the outside of the stores and restaurants of Bazaar Round jumped expanses of cloth and ribbon, gushing up, wrapping together, soaring high above everyone's head to join together at the top: a giant tent had formed out of nothing, and within ten seconds almost a thousand people stood under its striped ceiling. The people began to clap, astounded.

Until someone screamed, 'There's no exit!'

A restlessness passed through the crowd, too many unsettling feelings connecting. The people surged this way and that, echoing the cries, 'Not here!', 'There's no way out!' and 'Where's the door?'

All under Mister Mer's widening grin. 'And now that we're all here, let us begin…' He clapped his hands sharply.

'Get back,' Safir warned Trikaya, shoving her up against the wall of a clothing store and protecting her with his body.

The poles stopped, shuddered, and then went crazy. Whipping their filaments around so fast and hard that the tent was filled with the sound of zinging, they tapped person after person, and whoever they touched wilted and fell to the ground unconscious. A few dozen were already laid low before the crowd understood this was a trap, and began to stampede in every direction, trying to get away from the poles.

'Safir, there!' Trikaya hollered, pointing from under his arm. There was Shari, crouched down, and from the ground around him tree roots shot up and out, tangling up the legs of one of Mister Mer's poles.

A flash of light caught their attention. Almost on the other side of the statue Tal was sprinting, flinging shards of light so hot they sawed through the metal that the poles were made of. She managed to finally chop off one leg, and that pole toppled onto a sweet shop, sending roof tiles spilling everywhere.

More and more people fell, dozens, hundreds. Some people had climbed the fence that ran around the statue, hoping to hide under its legs, but the poles leaned over and sent filaments to them. They dropped like flies. Constable Dobal appeared, hopping around, surprisingly nimble with his round belly, yelling at the villagers to stay calm and trying to arrest the poles.

'Let's go!' Trikaya whooped, and ducking from under Safir's hold she barrelled towards two poles that were busy putting a whole knot of people to sleep. The boy had no time to think, he just ran after her, not knowing what he would do if...

Whistling, 'Fffyuuuww!' Trikaya slapped one hand on one pole leg, and reached out to point her finger at the other pole's body, and the two poles lurched towards each other. As though suddenly magnetized, the places that the girl had selected slammed together and welded into one whole. Lopsided, neither one's legs nor filaments matching up, the two poles lurched around before falling over and writhing between two buildings.

'There's Mademoiselle!' Safir said, having spotted the pâtissière cleaving a pole in half with her sword. Isaac and Iti were behind her, and Shari and Tal gathered to them soon enough. Reunited, they faced the one unmoving pole: Mister Mer's.

'Mer!' the Wolf Queen shouted, pointing Uttaradanshtra at him.

He glanced over his shoulder, noticed her, and smiled. 'Glad you could join us, Guardian. Now do your duty.'

'Stay back,' Mademoiselle told the children, and this time it was a command. They watched her walk forward, her grey dupatta whipping about her. All around the poles chased people, while greater and greater mounds of sleeping bodies piled up. 'I don't want to fight you,' she called up to the magician. 'Please, don't do this. I'm begging you, as Vira, as your friend. If you stop I'll put my sword away. You can stay in Devagarh with me, with us, like we used to. Or you can go, if you want. But please, please…don't do this. Don't make me do this.'

Mister Mer's expression was contemptuous. 'Only the weak beg. I thought this would be a challenge. Why don't you just give up, and I'll move on to Yakshagarh.'

From where they stood the children couldn't see Mademoiselle's face, but when she put up her hand to brush at her face they knew it was to remove tears. They saw her toss her hair back, straighten her spine, tighten the grip on her sword. She took one moment to look behind and make sure the children were at a safe distance, and then faced the magician.

'You want war?' the Wolf Queen cried out. 'You will have it.' She whipped her sword up, pointing the blade straight at the statue that stood in the middle of Bazaar Round, and articulated unknown words.

Five metres tall, the statue blinked, and then hurled itself at Mister Mer, who watched it come with a wicked grin across his craggy face.

28

DEFIANCE AND DEFEAT

Tal watched the living statue with her mouth open. 'It wasn't a Barbarika statue,' she murmured. 'It's a deva...'

It looked like it had stepped out of all the old comics of the Mahabharata, magnificently proportioned, wearing a golden breastplate and a green dhoti. On its head was an intricate golden crown studded with jewels. Its face, frozen in an eternal expression of proud majesty, had a thin moustache, the large painted eyes fixed in place. A round golden shield protected its left arm, while in its right it held one of those large maces with an absurdly round head and a spike at the end. It may have been made of stone, but it moved like an animal, smooth and fast, swooping on Mister Mer instantly. Tal had never imagined something so big could move with that speed.

Not that the magician seemed to care. The pole he stood on began to bend and weave with impossible dexterity, avoiding the statue's swings of the mace with apparent ease, while Mister Mer stood casually on top, arms crossed. 'Tiresome and predictable,' he derided, before continuing in a mocking falsetto, 'What's that? The statue in the middle of the village? A Guardian? Of course not! It's just five metres tall, no one knows when it was built, or where it came from…' He laughed as the mace missed him by millimetres, making his hair fly.

'Where does he have the power…?' Mademoiselle breathed. The magician hardly seemed troubled by the statue. Tal saw the pâtissière gritting her teeth, and glanced at Isaac, who was already clearly thinking the same. She gestured at the others, and the group of six scampered over to the Wolf Queen in a huddle.

Tal poked Mademoiselle, and nudged Isaac forward. The boy looked a little embarrassed as he reached out to squeeze the lady's forearm in his fingers. The Wolf Queen paused, and then an expression of astonishment transformed her face. Tal grabbed Isaac by the shoulders in excitement, asking, 'How is it?'

Uttaradanshtra's point rose up again and she giggled with glee. 'He won't be happy.' The Wolf Queen began to move her lips quietly, frowning with concentration.

'It's a spell!' Trikaya whispered, excitedly pawing at anyone next to her.

And what a spell. The statue stopped in mid-swing, startling Mister Mer, and from its back exploded two masses: two more arms, exquisitely muscled, one holding a sword and the other a spear.

'Isaac Shroff!' the magician shouted, 'I am most displeased with you!' He made his pole retreat as the statue surged forward, weapons ready.

By now all the people in Bazaar Round had been put to sleep by the poles. The monstrous contraptions had just finished pushing the piles of dozing bodies into the buildings or around the edges of the tent, clearing the people away from the centre. Mister Mer crowed a harsh laugh, and beckoned to the poles with both arms. Before the statue could come any closer, the forty or so other poles had charged and leaped at the magician, crashing together with a mighty noise.

'Oh no,' Safir moaned, blinking through his glasses. 'All those poles are full of spirit and magic...'

The wriggling mass of black metal stopped, revealing a cage bristling with spikes raised on forty limbs, like a grotesque spider. 'I also have a turbo mode,' Mister Mer called out merrily. The spider rushed forward, each limb spiking the ground and tearing up chunks of dirt. Dozens of the other limbs shot forward, and the Guardian statue began working its own four arms furiously to ward off blows.

'The statue won't make it,' Shari said, seeing that each limb that made it through chipped away substantial chunks of the statue.

'Not alone,' Mademoiselle agreed, and ran forward. She sprinted towards the fight, Uttaradanshtra in hand, and jumped, up, and up, and she was flying straight at, and into, the statue. There was no impact as she hit it, just a sudden merging.

Immediately the statue became even faster, and the spider's limbs no longer hit it. Mister Mer manoeuvred his machine sideways frantically, but limbs began to fall as the statue's sword and spear sheared through the black metal easily. It was clear that the Wolf Queen was in perfect control. The statue now moved like she did in combat, skilfully smooth, stepping constantly in small semi-circles to keep its enemy off guard. Tal could see that the statue's eyes moved and blinked. They were Mademoiselle's eyes, hazelnut in colour and soulful, but at this moment fierce in battle.

The cacophony of the metal hurt the children's ears, but they wouldn't back away. The statue and the spider tumbled across the open square of Bazaar Round, stepping on the round fence and crushing it underfoot like it was aluminium foil. There was nothing they could do to help, Tal realized, furious. The battle was too hot and epic, the giant antagonists moving and clashing too fast.

'She's winning!' Trikaya exclaimed, clapping her hands together.

It seemed like it at the moment. None of the spider's limbs could come close, and more and more of them were dropping, massive black bars clanging to the ground. The statue suddenly dropped its shield and grabbed three of the limbs, holding the metal spider in place so it couldn't dodge anymore. The children knew the Wolf Queen was moving in to end it. Up and down, in and out, the spear and mace and sword worked, cutting in closer and closer...

And then the massive spider leaped forward. Mademoiselle wasn't able to keep her footing, startled. The statue crashed on its back, making the ground shake, and then Mister Mer was on top, multiple limbs pinning his opponent down. One of the statue's arms spun away, shattered at the shoulder.

'No!' Trikaya cried, and Iti grabbed her tight to keep her from running forward. 'No, no, Mademoiselle!'

The magician roared with triumph and laughter, standing in his cage, making the limbs tear the statue apart. He stopped it suddenly, one spider limb poised high overhead. Then that spike dove sharply, cracked the chest of the statue, and ripped the golden stone breastplate away.

From where they watched, horrified, the children could see Mademoiselle cocooned inside the stone, unconscious, her hair wild, covered in dust and shards of rock. Shari and Isaac fought to hold Tal back, the girl screaming, terrified for the pâtissière.

The one spider limb slowed, then, shifting its shape. It gently, almost tenderly, scooped Mademoiselle out from her space. It lowered her down and deposited her on a clear patch of ground far enough away from the scene of the final conflict. The spider cage then dipped down, and finally that horrendous black beast stopped. The jagged bars of the cage uncurled like living hairs. Mister Mer stepped out and rushed to the Wolf Queen, kneeling by her and raising her head with one hand.

'Come on!' Tal screamed. The children ran, pelting the ground with their sneakers, to come to Mademoiselle's rescue.

'She's all right,' Mister Mer announced as they came, words that made them pull up short. He sounded relieved. 'She's just in shock. Iti, you can ease her distress, but she's unharmed. She's unharmed,' he added softly to himself. They watched him, one hand under her head, pulling sheafs of her lush brown hair from her beautiful face, murmuring words they couldn't hear. He sighed, and laid her head back down slowly. 'Iti,' the magician called as he stood and walked away, not even acknowledging them otherwise.

The children jumped in, Iti putting hands to Mademoiselle's cheeks instantly. Tal looked on anxiously for a few seconds, until Iti nodded reassuringly. Then she stood to glare at the magician's back. He was still walking away, towards the west end of the tent. 'Mister Mer!' she shouted, pointing furiously at him. 'You won't get away with it. They'll stop you. Rabakak and the Midnight King, they'll stop you!'

Mister Mer leisurely turned, strolling sideways for a few steps to call back, 'Rabakak may try. The Midnight King? Not him. Not anymore.' He waved his hand, and with a loud pop and whirring of cloth, the tent broke apart, massive stretches of cloth rolling and snapping together. The sun's red rim was still visible over the hills, gone down considerably since the tent had gone up. A fresh hill breeze scattered the heat and dust haze that had gathered from the crowd's anguish and the monster battle. The magician walked on, turned the corner, and disappeared from sight, heading down the path to the Lodge and from there to Yakshagarh.

'What's wrong?' Shari asked anxiously as Iti kept caressing Mademoiselle's slender hands. 'Why isn't she waking?'

'She will,' the girl replied. They had moved the lady so her head lay on Iti's lap. 'See?' The slightest flutter of Mademoiselle's eyelashes made them all breathe with relief. Tal put her arms around Iti, who rested her head on her friend's shoulder. 'I feel strong,' Iti said, for Tal's ears only. 'I felt weak and useless for so long... It's like, becoming the Cure, I've finally become what I've always really wanted to be. I can heal, I can help. I don't have to be the fastest, or the one who shoots the slingshot best. This is what I do.'

Tal smiled at her dear friend. 'And no one else can do it,' she affirmed.

A little later the children spread out. Isaac and Shari scouted the area quickly, and confirmed that no one seemed to have been hurt seriously. Their parents were all near each other, asleep and uninjured, so they left them there. There was nothing more to do, at this point. Mister Mer had won. Rabakak was weakened, and if the magician seemed so certain that the Midnight King wouldn't stop him...

'I can hear it,' Safir told them as they sat around Mademoiselle, heads hanging low. He stared in the direction of Yakshagarh, eyes distant. 'The hills...They know the first Guardian has fallen. They sense Mister Mer approaching the Black Kot.'

'What do you hear?' Isaac asked.

The boy brushed back his longish hair. 'The voices of the hills of Kumaon, but like a deep vibration, from deep in the earth. And the trees, like...rivers rippling through their leaves. We hear leaves in the wind, but that's their language, their words passed along from branch to branch. And Yakshagarh. It's creaking, breaking. The ghosts who live in the village are terrified. They have one purpose: to guard the Black Kot. But they know they're going to fail.'

Tal felt the frustrating emptiness of failure gnawing her own insides. How foolish they had all been. With their new powers, they thought they were superheroes. And the real Guardian, the Wolf Queen, with a legendary sword and a giant statue? The magician had blown her aside and stepped over her like an afterthought. What could they do?

'Here you are,' Trikaya said abruptly. They glanced up to see Kumar Fourteen sauntering over, his one ear flicking this way and that. He sat at Mademoiselle's feet, closing the sitting circle they made. 'Where have you been all this time?'

'Sucking on a skeleton in someone's trash,' the cat replied. He shook his head around, thrashing his tongue as if to get the taste of something gross out of it. 'If Rabakak only knew what this creature eats he'd stop craving cats all the time... Anyway,' Mr Dangwal said, scrutinizing them with his evil eyes. 'Looks like a right pretty sob party happening here. Any particular reason why you all look like someone used your teddy bear as a plunger?'

Trikaya screwed up her nose at the expression. 'Nice. But we lost.'

'Mister Mer is on his way to Yakshagarh,' Shari intoned.

'And Rabakak's barely had time to recover,' Isaac added.

'True,' Mr Dangwal said. 'But it still doesn't explain why you're sitting around like this.'

'Because Mademoiselle was beaten!' Tal pointed out.

'We're just kids,' Iti said. 'What can we do with our new powers? Against someone who can defeat the Wolf Queen and trap Rabakak?'

'It's over,' Safir murmured, summarizing it all. 'We failed.'

Mr Dangwal emitted a sharp noise that seemed strangely like a dog's bark, and then sighed. 'The sun has almost set. I've barely got a minute, so I'll be brief.' He cleared his throat and eyed them fiercely. 'Failed? You haven't failed. And I'm here to tell you why.'

29

THE RESOLVE

'Failure,' the cat continued, 'is what? What is it?'

Iti saw the other children looking at each other, puzzled and unsettled. For some reason she didn't feel as perturbed as they seemed. It was weird. They had already lost, they were at the lowest point. But she felt oddly composed, almost peaceful? 'Failure,' she said, surprising even herself with how spontaneously she spoke, 'is two things. One is a fact: you tried something and it didn't work out. That's just a practical thing. The second is when you carry it with you, and you let it become a definition of you.'

'Listen to the Cure,' Mr Dangwal told them. 'You didn't stop Mister Mer here. That's a fact. It happened. But now you're sitting here, beating yourselves up about *being* failures. And that is a crime against yourselves.'

'But what can we do?' Shari exclaimed.

Mr Dangwal shrugged. 'You're asking me? I'm just a cat that talks. Who am I to tell you what you can and can't do?' An all-too human smile played on the cat's mouth. 'Bad enough you define yourselves as failures, now you'll let this dreg-dredging feline tell you what you can do?' He shook his head. 'My time is up. Remember what you are. Gardener. Cure. Listener. Star. Bond. Catalyst. And now go make yourself who you want to be.' The cat sneezed, blinked, and was Kumar Fourteen again. His slitted eyes observed them warily, and then he slunk off in search of more garbage to slobber over.

'Children!' someone's voice cried out. They turned to see Imam Azlan rushing towards them, a young man in a white kurta-pyjama and cap, his beard gracefully styled. Behind him came Pujari Nandan and Bhante Rinzen. 'They're here! With Mademoiselle Fulara!'

'You're all up!' Tal exclaimed, seeing the youthful Father Ewan bringing up the rear in his black cassock.

'We all got up ten minutes ago,' Bhante confirmed.

'We were coming here, and saw that tent,' Pujari Nandan added, 'And then it disappeared!'

Mademoiselle stirred and spoke then, lifting herself with an effort. 'Bhante, we can speak openly, the children know I'm the Guardian. You take care of the people. Children, the four priests know a bit about our real task. Pujari Nandan and Bhante Rinzen have been translating the Origin Scroll for me. Now I hate to ask this of you, but please go and help Rabakak. Isaac may be able to multiply his power. Whatever we can do to stop Mer, we need...'

'It won't be enough,' a new voice interrupted. Everyone looked to see Mr Charles striding up to them. A spectacular-looking rifle was in his hand, carved and gleaming. 'Mer is far trickier than you can imagine. If he's come out in the open like this it's because he's certain he can carry out his plan to the end.' He nodded at the priests and crouched down with the children. 'Robert Charles,' he introduced himself to the Wolf Queen with a charming smile, 'at least in most places. I apologize for being so late, Mademoiselle. I might have been of some assistance. Although I daresay not enough to have alter the current course of events.'

'How do you know Mer?' the pâtissière asked.

The Englishman considered his answer carefully. 'I, and some like-minded persons, have been tracking his activity for some time. His trail went cold after he flew into Delhi last week. In the absence of a lead, I came here. It was a providential decision, since I found him.' He nodded at the children. 'And you lot of little adventurers. When I realized what Mer was after I hurried up to the pass to send a message to someone who should be able to help. That's why I couldn't be here in time.'

'Someone?' Mademoiselle repeated intently. 'Who? Who could stop Mer?' Her eyes widened. 'Not...*him*?'

'Someone in Mumbai,' Mr Charles confirmed. 'He should be here in about an hour.'

Iti and Tal exchanged looks. Someone in Mumbai who should be in Devagarh in about an hour? What would he do, fly in on a jet fighter and parachute down into the hills? The Wolf Queen addressed the children urgently, 'This changes everything. We don't have to stop Mer anymore. Just stall him, for one hour, until *he* comes. You can do this. Mer thinks he's already won. He'll be taking his time. It's been decades of work. If I know him he'll be relishing every minute and making it stretch.'

'Wait wait,' Trikaya interrupted, raising her hand as if in class. 'Who's *he*?'

'A friend,' the Englishman answered. 'A powerful friend. He has many names, but in the hills of Kumaon they know him as the Last Son.'

'The Last Son?' Isaac frowned. 'Of who?'

Mr Charles stood up and slid the strap of his rifle over his shoulder. 'Of Shiva.' He peered in the direction of Yakshagarh. 'We should get going.'

Pujari Nandan stepped forward. 'Mr Charles, you can't go.'

'He's right,' Bhante Rinzen concurred. 'Yakshagarh is waking as the magician comes closer. Only the high blood can climb the hill. It will be dangerous for you, a human.'

'I have to go,' Mr Charles insisted. 'They're only children.'

'The children *are* high blood,' Bhante said. 'Yaksha, deva, rakshas, asura. Are you any of these?'

The Englishman looked ready to protest further, but stopped when Safir tugged on his coat. 'We'll go, Mr Charles,' the boy said.

'We're the Guardians of Yakshagarh too,' Tal declared.

'And the KSSes,' Trikaya added.

'True and Real KSSes,' Safir clarified to the Englishman.

Mr Charles was clearly mystified, but his large moustache crept up anyway as he smiled at the clear resolve in the six children. 'Well, when you put it that way...'

30
TO BUILD A BRIDGE

It was not fully night when the children ran down the path from Bazaar Round to the Lodge. They were halfway there when a low black shadow streaked out of the grass towards them, and the only warning they had was a now-familiar squeal. 'Galahad!' Iti cried, and the marten skipped between them to take a place in the middle, running with the group.

'Lodge first!' Tal yelled as they reached the corner of the building. 'Shari: slingshots! I'll get the rocks.' Her twin nodded.

'I have to change,' Iti said.

'Who needs the bathroom?' Trikaya demanded. 'Because I do!'

'All right,' Tal called out as she hurdled the three steps up to the porch, 'Meet in three minutes in the living room!'

The yellow-throated marten stopped and sat just short of the steps to wait for them outside. Inside the door the six children split, each running to their respective duty.

Shari blew into the boys' room like a storm and dove over the beds straight for the Box. The lid flew off, and out came all the toys and games. He felt excited and hopeful now that they had a feasible plan. Whoever this Last Son was, Mademoiselle and Mr Charles were confident he could stop

Mister Mer. And if all they had to do was delay him… Well, at least they would do their best.

Right at the bottom was a plastic bag wrapped and tucked a way neatly into a corner: the four slingshots. He unpacked the lot and pulled them out. How long had it been since they'd used them? Iti hadn't wanted one, which was why they had only gotten these four. There had been that one summer when they had shot rocks all up and down the town and the maidan. After that they had used them less and less, until they were permanently put away in the boys' Box.

It was strange, he realized as he hurried back to the living room. He didn't feel scared at all. Yesterday at the waterfalls when Rabakak had lurched out of the trees he had been petrified. Since then they had learned so many terrifying things about Devagarh and Yakshagarh's epic and dark history. And they had seen Mister Mer in action just now, so they knew just how powerful and frightening he was. But Shari wasn't scared. None of them seemed to be. They had all grown since yesterday, he reasoned, and through the events of today. Even Safir had been unwavering, just now when they decided to go to Yakshagarh alone. Shari smiled, proud of himself and his friends. It didn't matter now whether he led the KSS or not, and he doubted Tal would lead it either. The KSS didn't need a leader, not anymore.

A chorus of low giggling reached his ears, and he entered the living room to find everyone watching Safir. He must have gone upstairs into Mrs Idris's make-up kit, because he held a stick of kohl and was in the process of drawing thick black stripes on his cheeks and forehead. Shari grinned at the scene as he jumped into the sofa with them. 'See?' Safir said, turning this way and that. 'Just like in the army. It's called camouflage.' He handed the stick to Trikaya, whose hands were already eagerly out. 'Camo for short.'

They did that for a little over three minutes, long enough for them to mark up each other's faces with black. Trikaya insisted on drawing smileys on everyone, protesting, 'It's for luck!'

Galahad jumped up when the six children shot out of the house, even Iti and Safir. The marten raced alongside, yowling excitedly, as they headed for the bridge.

'Oh, whoa,' Safir gasped. 'Do you see what I'm seeing? The colours on the hill?' The children exchanged quick looks and said no. To Shari the black shadow of Yakshagarh lay outlined by the indigo of the night sky. There was an imperceptible layer of clouds, evidently, since the stars weren't visible. It was evident, however, that the Listener was perceiving far more than they could: 'It's like pillars of green and purple light, curtains actually, running all up and down the hill. And geysers of red shooting up, there! And there!' His eyes were bright and filled with wonder as he ran, and Shari made sure to move closer to him so he didn't trip. 'And the stars...the stars...' They could tell that words couldn't begin to describe everything he was sensing. 'The stars are *screaming*.' Safir shivered. 'Mister Mer is getting closer, we have to hurry.'

'There's someone,' Tal pointed. 'At the bridge.'

'Kariba!' Trikaya hooted.

The rakshasi stood up ahead, arms stretched towards them. 'The bridge!' she cried mournfully as they came closer, and they skidded to a stunned halt.

The bridge to Yakshagarh was destroyed.

'What?' Tal yelled in disbelief. A few stones jutted out from this end and from the far end on the other side. The entire structure, wood beams and stone slabs, was gone, probably cluttering the dark streams far below.

'I saw him do it,' Kariba told them, in tears. 'I had

just crossed when I saw him coming, and I…I hid. I know he had defeated the First Guardian, I sensed it from the forest.' She lowered her head in shame. 'I think everyone could sense it, you can't hide that kind of power. I couldn't face him.'

'It's okay,' Trikaya chirped, wrapping the rakshasi in her arms. 'We lost to him in Bazaar Round. But the next round is ours!' She looked quickly at Safir to see if he got her jest, and he gave her two thumbs up.

'So how do we cross?' Shari stepped in. Safir had said they needed to hurry, they had precious little time to waste.

'That's the thing,' Kariba sniffed, rubbing her eyes with her palms. 'You can't. We can't. The ghosts are awake, and the hill is in a, I don't know, a spiritual lockdown or something. Maybe it's part of the defence system. In this state, the only way to cross is the bridge.'

'She's right,' Safir confirmed dully. He had crept up to the edge of the cliff and was peering up and down the ravine. 'Everything is fractured. There's magic and coloured energy stuff everywhere. Even if we could climb down we really shouldn't.'

'What'll it do?' Tal asked, wondering if they could still press through.

'I don't know,' the boy said truthfully, pressing his glasses up nervously. 'Maybe melt us or blast us or something.' He held up his hands to show them. 'But I can feel it so bad my palms are sweating.'

Shari shook his head. 'Right, that's not an option.'

They stood in silence, while Safir continued to stare at the hill, transfixed by everything the others couldn't see. 'There has to be a way,' Tal said intensely. 'There has to be.'

Shari peeled away from the group to step carefully up to the jagged end of the bridge. Galahad was pacing restlessly back and forth nearby, emitting rough cries of frustration. 'I know,' the boy told the marten, who stood on his hind legs to commune with him. 'We'll get across.' Galahad blinked, seeming to understand his words, and resumed his impatient trot.

'How's your uncle?' Isaac asked Kariba as they sat on the ground, taking a break.

'He's all right,' the rakshasi replied. 'He got up and was walking around, but he hasn't recovered fully. Mister Mer hasn't actually faced him head to head, though. The Rakshas Lord is no pushover.'

'Neither was the Wolf Queen,' Trikaya said despondently.

'Did you find out what he's trying to do?' Kariba asked.

Isaac nodded. 'The Black Kot was built to guard a gate or something. There's this Englishman, Mr Charles, he saw the Origin Scroll and identified that. But a gate to what, we don't know.'

'And the tower,' Iti reminded. 'A tower on top of the Black Kot, drawn on the Scroll but that isn't actually there. And then he ran off.'

From where he stood, Shari saw Kariba straighten up noticeably. 'A tower?' the rakshasi said sharply. 'What kind of tower?'

'I don't know,' Isaac said, trying to remember. 'Like a cone.'

'Or a yellow top balanced on the Black Kot,' Safir added.

'How many storeys was the tower?' Kariba asked intently.

'How many storeys?' Iti shrugged. 'Four, or five?'

'Could it be five mountain peaks?'

Isaac, Iti and Safir made uncertain expressions. 'It looked more like a tower than a mountain…'

'I know what it is,' Kariba said, jumping up. They could all sense how upset she was, and waited tensely as she walked to the cliff edge. 'I know what Mister Mer is after. The Guardians defend the Black Kot. The Black Kot was built to protect a Gate.' The rakshasi turned to face them. 'And the Gate leads to Mount Meru.'

'Mount what?' Trikaya said, screwing up her face in confusion.

'Mount Meru is the centre of the universe. A five-peaked mountain a million kilometres high. It's usually depicted as a tower with five storeys, with a golden palace on top.'

'There was a yellow dome on top of the tower,' Isaac added quickly.

'The golden palace is where the gods and the devas live.' Kariba began pacing as she thought out loud. 'There are very few Gates out there in the world. Some simply lead to other worlds and dimensions. You can't just cross over, however, there's usually some spell or magical mechanism that opens and closes it. So this one leads to Mount Meru. But what's in it for Mister Mer to open the Gate?' She looked at the others. 'What can he do with a path to Mount Meru?'

'I don't know,' Shari said, kneeling by the ruined edge of the bridge. 'We'll figure that later. Right now, though, I can get us across.' He gestured at Isaac Shroff. 'Can you back me?' Without waiting, Shari faced the gap between them and Yakshagarh, already concentrating. Why hadn't he thought of it sooner? Fifty metres from here to the other side.

He reached out with his mind and immediately felt the roots, all around. The tiny tufts of roots that grass used, the longer tough roots of bushes. Those wouldn't work. There! There were some trees up and down the slope with roots that extended deep and wide. On the other side there were plenty of trees, the jungle of Yakshagarh creeping right up to the edge of the sheer drop. Fifty metres.

Isaac's hand fell on Shari's shoulder, but another set of

fingers gripped the other one. He glanced over that shoulder and saw Tal was there too, holding up an enthusiastic fist. 'Come on, Shari, show them what you can do,' she whispered to him.

Oh, yes he would.

The roots of the trees leaped towards him, racing through the earth, shoving and packing earth aside. In a year tree roots normally grew about a metre, Shari knew. Right now, with him coaxing them and Isaac multiplying his strength, it took a minute for the root networks of thirty nearby trees to dig through twenty metres of dirt. Faster and faster they came. He could feel them. Both his hands were out and his fingers played the air as he guided them over rock or around. He then moved one hand towards the other side of the bridge, feeling the far more powerful root network there. Could he do it? He had to.

The others felt the earth shift under their feet, and with the sound of shattering rock a knot of tree roots leaped from just under the bridge edge, flying out, growing fast, practically horizontally. Shari's eyes were fixed on the other side, and though he couldn't see that far in the deepening twilight it was like he could see them, another mass of roots soaring across the space towards him, reaching to meet in the middle.

Both ends flagged after ten metres, and fell, drooping, into the ravine before twenty metres, unable to overcome the pull of gravity.

Black graininess swarmed in Shari's vision, and he wobbled where he knelt, but Isaac and Tal were already holding him. It took two minutes for his head to clear. His neck felt hot and thick. 'It's too much,' Tal said anxiously. 'It's too far, Shari. The strain is too much. We'll find another way—'

'I have to do it,' Shari retorted, his voice hoarse. 'There's no one else, nothing else.'

Safir crouched down by them. 'Can you make pillars down in the stream? Grow it from down up?'

'Yes,' he replied. 'That's a fantastic idea.' Shari looked at Isaac, who nodded, and then at Tal, who tightened her lips but didn't say no. 'Come on,' he said to everyone but mostly to himself.

Roots, he thought. They were everywhere. Most of the trees had roots extending about ten metres deep, these were the ones he sensed were the strongest and used them. Safir was right. If he could get the tree roots down the cliff, under the stream…

With a deep breath Shari started, gripping the knots of roots he had already grown on both sides of the ravine. Down, he spoke in his mind, and they began to dig down, deeper, the earth becoming rockier as they reached close to the bones of the hills. He had to leave some where they were, emerging into dead ends of stone that would go nowhere. Thinner, he figured, shaping the roots into slim tendrils that could more easily wriggle into the cracks and wrinkles between tons of rock.

It was tough. Shari could feel the mass of the hills pressing up, resisting the roots. He abandoned more roots, focusing on the more successful paths. Down, deep enough to go under, and then bending beneath the water. The earth there was moist and cold, watered by a thousand leaks from the gushing streams above ground. But it was working. He could feel the roots getting closer to each other. Twenty metres apart. Ten. And there, now…they joined.

His fist pumped and then he extended two fingers up. The roots exploded from the middle of the streams, far out of sight below, in the depths of the ravine. It was lucky the water didn't move too fast here. He sent out tendrils in all directions, locking deep into the bedrock. The shoot rose up, fragile at first, buffeted by the rushing waterfall. Then it thickened, spread, and rose. Quickly he shaped three more sprouts, so that there was one every ten metres.

How much time was going by? He had no idea, and that made him nervous. Mister Mer was already ahead of them on the other side. Come on, Shari, he told himself, gritting his teeth. Just a little more, just a little faster.

The four sprouts in the streams stood out clear in his mind as he pushed and pulled the root networks from the bridge ends. This time he went with just one thick strand from each side. They connected quickly, jumping from sprout to sprout until he had, riding just a metre above the stream, a rope of root extending from one end to the other.

'Now we push,' Shari muttered, reaching behind to grab Isaac Shroff's jacket. The new boy's hand tightened on his shoulder.

They pushed.

Hard and fast the bridge rose, the four sprouts becoming slim tree trunks, thicker pillars. He had never done this before, and had no idea how big they should be, but there was no reason to hold back now. The stone under the streams shook and split, tearing as the roots underneath dug down to anchor the four growing trees. And while they rose, Shari thickened the main roots above, the path they would walk on.

'I see it!' Trikaya called, leaning out over the edge, Iti and Safir holding her desperately. 'It's huge!'

Shari wouldn't have been able to see even if he was there at the edge. His eyes were wide open but all he saw was black swarming in his vision. He could hear his blood rushing in his ears, dimming all other sound. He knew if he let up for one instant he would pass out. No, he told himself, not before it was finished. He clung on, focused on the one task, getting that root bridge up to their level, and it was almost there.

To Tal, who stood helpless while her twin grew a bridge out of the waterfall between the hills, what she saw was nothing short of magnificent and miraculous. It was like a horizontal path of rough and damp wood, three metres wide, fifty metres long, rising up out of the darkness below. If she leaned over she thought she could make out the pillars that held up the bridge, thick and strong trees, sprouting branches and leaves within seconds. It was unbelievable. How strong was Shari in his power, to be able to do this? And after what he did for Rabakak too? Tears shimmered in her eyes, but she let them stay there. They were tears of pride.

When the bridge was there, and he knew it was steady as the earth they walked on here, Shari let go and slid down to the ground, knowing Tal would catch him. His twin and Isaac laid him out, fussing over him. He could hear them distantly, but it didn't mean much to him. Iti was going to stay with him, he heard their voices like a whisper, but it was all incidental.

He had done it. He had built the bridge to Yakshagarh.

31

RABAKAK'S BATTLE

Isaac ran close to Tal, Trikaya on the other side of her. Leaving Shari and Iti behind was tough, but they had no choice. Mister Mer was getting closer to the Black Kot. Safir was on edge, barely able to stand in one spot from anxiety. Isaac glanced back once at Shari, lying there unconscious, his head in Iti's lap. Galahad squatted by the Cure, staying back to guard her, but his little black eyes keenly watched the others pass to Yakshagarh.

'Three bridges in ninety years,' Kariba muttered, 'I'm starting to feel old.'

They crossed Shari's incredible tree bridge in barely a minute. As wide and sturdy as the wooden path clearly was, there was still a slight apprehension at being the first ones to ever cross it. The lack of handrail also made the crossing slightly daunting, with the edge just falling away into the black noise of the waterfall.

'Get behind me,' Kariba instructed loudly, her bare feet carrying her to the front of the group. 'All sorts of beings are coming out, stay close and tight.'

'Oh,' Safir pronounced, voice trembling, looking all around. 'Oh…' His face was pale.

Trikaya wrapped one of Safir's arms under hers, guiding him forward. 'What, what are you seeing?'

He shook his head and gasped, 'Don't want to know.'

'Keep your head down,' Isaac placed himself on the other side of Safir and grabbed his sleeve. 'Don't look, we just follow Kariba.' Tal was right in front of them, eyes fixed ahead, slingshot in hand and a rock armed, just one step behind the rakshasi.

They ignored the left path that led down by the waterfalls, and took the path up. There was no question that something was wrong with the world. There was no wind that Isaac could tell, but odd pressures seemed to buffet them, shoving them this way and that. The trees of the jungle were stirring, giving rise to a din of leaves and branches.

'Kariba!' Safir screamed ahead. 'Something's coming!'

'I know,' she replied over her shoulder, calm. She slapped her hands together, making an unnaturally thunderous sound, and shrieked, startling them all. It wasn't just a cry, but instead a long string of varying sound. It was half-screaming and half-guttural, but whatever she said seemed to have an effect. The moment she finished there was a loud sound off the path, as if something large and unseen was fleeing. Safir took a deep breath of relief, and fixed his eyes again on Tal's heels.

The darkness was not absolute, since some moonlight seemed to be drifting down through the clouds. He could see the path well enough, running through the forest and up. The ruins were dark titans, their angular, broken shoulders looming suddenly out from the trees. A strange ululation reached Isaac's ears, low but definite.

They were in the village now, he realized, as he saw the lines and bulk of fragmented buildings. 'Not far, one more turn,' Kariba told them.

'What's that sound?' Trikaya finally asked, as that oddly melodic howling became louder.

'It's Rabakak,' the rakshasi told them as they turned the last corner. 'It's his war song.'

What they saw made them slide to a stop and crash into each other.

Little more than a hundred metres away the Black Kot sat at the end of the path. Between them and the fort were Mister Mer and Rabakak the Treeborn, locked in battle, lit by a multitude of lights the magician kept about him.

A separate swirling storm of blackness engulfed the two combatants, like innumerable crows or bats thickening the air. The giant Rabakak was on one knee, arms forward, mouth open, screeching that alien howl they had been hearing. Mister Mer stood unperturbed before him, one hand raised behind into the tempest of black, and the other hand forward and pressed against the strange limbs of the Rakshas Lord.

Kariba curled up her little hands in fists, and streaked forward.

'Hey!' Tal cried, and grabbed Isaac's arm.

'Stop her!' Safir yelled.

The four children chased after the rakshasi, but she was faster. Up ahead Rabakak was labouring, straining to keep his arms forward. Whatever strange combat this was, human hand to giant rakshas hand, he was losing it. 'Give it up, Rabakak,' Mister Mer called up. 'You're done.'

It was only because Kariba slowed down to try to find a way to get into the fight that Tal and Isaac were able to catch up and wrap their little arms around her. 'Kariba, stop!' the girl told the rakshasi, who began to struggle.

'We need a plan,' Isaac said in Kariba's ear. 'If you go in now you might break Rabakak's focus.'

'I have to!' the rakshasi growled. 'Let me go!'

The boy pulled back to look her in the eye, his face close to hers. 'You know it's not the right move. If Rabakak falls *we're* the last line of defence. He needs you there, not here. *We* need you there.'

Kariba turned her face away, furious and distraught, but she stopped fighting them. Trikaya and Safir had caught up by now, and the group shuffled off to the side of the street, tucking themselves behind a corner to watch.

There was no doubt that Rabakak was weakening. His war song was faltering, and he suddenly dropped one hand to the ground to hold himself up. That was the end. Mister Mer swept his hand away, smacking the Guardian's outstretched arm to the side, and then made a cutting motion in front of him. A massive impact smashed Rabakak aside, and his giant body crashed into and crushed a building, throwing sheets of debris and dust into the air.

That done, the magician turned to face the black cloud twisting above him. 'Back, ye ghosts and spirits!' he crowed. From his open palm shot a sudden flurry of blinding lights. The shadows scattered instantly, slipping this way and that, and the magician was free of them.

Mister Mer took a moment to straighten his coat, and sauntered down the street. He didn't even look at the brown giant fighting to rise in the shattered building to his left. 'Stop,' the Rakshas Lord called out weakly, knocking a section of wall down so he could see the magician. His English accent made Isaac's eyebrows rise in curiosity. 'You may have defeated me, Mer. But you go to your doom if you enter the Black Kot. The Midnight King is beyond you. You will never defeat him.'

'The Midnight King?' The magician's laugh echoed from the broken walls of Yakshagarh. 'Tell me, Rabakak, when was the last time you saw him? The fabled Third Guardian?' There was no answer. 'Exactly. You thought, you *hoped*, that he was just a very discreet gentleman this whole time, or maybe meditating or something.' Mister Mer paused. 'Eight hundred years. That's how long the Midnight King has been absent. He put a steward in his place. Or, probably more truthfully, a steward had no choice but to step up after the King deserted his post. But even the steward is long gone. The Black Kot is empty, Rabakak, and has been this whole time.'

'No,' the Guardian whispered, desperate. 'No, it can't be.'

'Haven't you figured it out?' the magician derided. 'With all your wisdom and power, you don't know, do you? The old Midnight King died last month. Or, who knows, maybe he found a way to be free of the Black Kot, crafty old codger.'

'How can you know this?' Rabakak groaned.

'I know because I felt it. With the old Midnight King gone, the mantle falls to the heir.' A smile slashed wickedly across Mister Mer's face. 'And who do you think that is? A cadet branch of the yaksha kings of the Black Kot, mixing with the local folk, living in Devagarh. Forgotten. Cast aside. Until I reclaimed my destiny.' He struck a dramatic pose, and gestured at the fort down the path. 'Until I reclaimed *my* throne. I am the descendant of the Midnight King who was. I am now the Midnight King. And you know what that means.' He turned and strode off, leaving Rabakak lying in the ruins. 'The Black Kot belongs to me. And if the Black Kot belongs to me…then so does the Gate.'

The magician walked on, and the children didn't dare come out, still holding Kariba back. The fortress loomed high over Mister Mer, dwarfing him with its blacker than black walls. Even the double doors, locked tight, striped with thick bands of black iron, made the magician seem like a mouse sniffing defiantly at a monster. What would he do? Blast the doors with fire? Cut them down with some other awesome magic? The children peeked around the corner and peered through the darkness, waiting.

Mister Mer put his hand to the old, polished wood of the doors and declared, 'I am the Midnight King. Open.'

The doors produced a single thunderous sound, and then swung open on eerily silent hinges, revealing a quiet darkness. Mister Mer stepped into that shadow and vanished from their sight.

Still the children hesitated, until Safir said, 'We should go. The ghosts are freaking out, and the Black Kot is about to explode.'

They trotted out swiftly then, following Kariba who raced to her uncle. 'Rabakak,' she called to him softly, and the giant rakshas turned his head.

'Kariba,' he whispered, his voice low with defeat and despair. 'Little yakshas,' he greeted the four who came after. 'I have lost, and shamed myself.'

'You did what you could against the heir of the Black Kot, the new Midnight King,' Isaac reminded him.

'It's a failure, but it doesn't make you a failure,' Trikaya lectured him, remembering what Mr Dangwal had told them. 'You only fail if you don't try.'

'Your words are kind but by the by,' the Guardian said with a heavy voice. 'If Mer is the descendant of the Midnight King then he can easily open the Gate.'

'The Gate to Mount Meru?' Kariba asked.

Rabakak stared at her and the children for a long moment before nodding. 'Yes. And he must be stopped. The old power of the King of the Black Kot is kept on the other side. If Mer were to reclaim that power, he would become a god. There is nothing this side of the Gate that could stop him.'

'The Last Son is coming,' Safir said abruptly. 'Can he stop him?'

'The Last Son?' Rabakak seemed to revive for a moment. 'From Mumbai? When?'

'Soon,' Kariba told him. 'But we have to stall Mister Mer in the meantime.'

'If he's coming, then we have a chance!' The Guardian reached out a two-pronged hand to grab the far edge of the building, tried to pull himself up, but the ruined stone crumbled and he fell back hard, shaking the ground under the children's feet. 'I can't...' he panted, frustrated.

'It's up to us,' Isaac stated. 'We're the Guardians too.'

'Unfortunately, little ones, you are,' the Rakshas Lord said. 'Opening the Gate takes some time, it requires magic and spells. It was meant to stay locked, so it will take Mer some effort. His power is far greater than it should be, for a human yaksha, but well within what is required to open the Gate. There is another danger. Mount Meru is a spiritual world, completely different from Earth. It is native to beings of unfathomable spiritual intensity. As such the atmosphere of Mount Meru is toxic to Earth, and the moment the Gate opens it will force itself into our world.'

'So we have to make sure he doesn't even open the Gate,' Tal noted. 'That's our task,' she declared to the others. 'Until the Last Son arrives. But...' she hesitated, turning back to Rabakak. 'Is he really that strong, the Last Son? Can he really beat Mister Mer?'

'Mer is still human. The Last Son is a *demigod*. It's pebbles before the Himalayas,' the Rakshas Lord answered. He waved a hand, moving on. 'The ghosts of Yakshagarh are all the spirits of past yakshas, and the spiritual blood that reinforces the Black Kot. You are yakshas. They will side with you against Mister Mer. Take their help.'

Isaac pulled the slingshot out of one pocket and a round rock out of the other, following Tal's example as they stepped out of the ruins onto the flagstoned path. How did he end up here? he suddenly thought. Yesterday he had just arrived in Devagarh, unenthusiastic about a long holiday in some remote town in the hills. And today he was standing with these other kids in a haunted village, in the company of rakshasas, and about to take on Mister Mer, his favourite magician who turned out to be a real magician and an evil tyrant. And he had powers, of a kind.

'Pretty weird, huh, new boy?' Tal chuckled, nudging him.

'How'd you know?' he asked, studying her dark brown eyes.

'I can see it on your face. Plus, we're all thinking the same,' she nodded at Safir and Trikaya, who both smiled sheepishly. Her hands quickly and efficiently tightened all the loose spots in her ponytail. 'When we get home, after this is done, I'll teach you how to shoot that for real. For now, just point and release.' Tal made a fist with her left hand, and it began to lighten and brighten. 'Are you ready to conquer the Black Kot?'

'No,' Safir quacked. 'But we should go in, because the ghosts are about to attack him. He's started his spell to open the Gate.'

'Come on then,' Trikaya cheered, thrusting her slingshot hand into the air. 'For Mademoiselle and Rabakak!'

They ran for the Black Kot.

32
THE BLACK KOT

For all her bravado, Trikaya's tongue knotted up with fear as they approached the Black Kot. She had seen old forts and palaces here and there, visiting with her parents, but nothing like this. The menace that emanated from its high walls was palpable, making it difficult to put one foot in front of the other.

The thick doors opened onto a tunnel six or seven metres deep lined with slitted windows, even in the ceiling. Trikaya could see some light playing ahead, since Mister Mer was illuminating his own way, but couldn't quite make out where they were headed. Tal wasn't lighting things up yet so as to not give away their position. They slowed down at the exit and peered around.

The Black Kot was nothing more than four high, thick walls surrounding a large inner courtyard of grassy dirt about a hundred metres wide. There was a keep at the far end, but it seemed more like living quarters than an inner fort. Twenty metres in front of them was a large decorated throne on a modest dais, fronted by a long rectangular fountain from which fresh spring water still ran.

What had pride of place, in the middle of the courtyard, was a magnificent construction of stone. It looked at first like a huge dome, but then Trikaya realized it was actually like a hand fan spread out. In the play of Mister Mer's floating lights their eyes began to adjust, and the girl realized it was actually a huge depiction of a peacock's tail, carved and inlaid with glinting jewels, gold and precious stones. And in its centre, facing the magician, and them, was a gigantic double door made of stone, intricately sculpted to show five mountains each of a different colour teeming with animal and plant life and human activity, each peak higher than the other, and a brilliant golden sun rising above them all. The Gate.

Mister Mer was already droning unintelligible words to the Gate, and as they watched they saw small sections of the stone doors beginning to gleam. The entire surface was covered in inscriptions, sentence upon sentence of that old Brahmi script hidden in the five mountain carvings, now revealed in the foliage of trees, the movement of people, the shapes of the animals. It seemed like an opening mechanism, unlocking little by little as the gold-lettered spell advanced.

'Don't be scared,' Kariba warned them, 'I'm changing into my rakshas war form.'

'Your what?' Safir whispered.

The rakshasi stepped away from them, and as she moved the black dirt or dust that perpetually coloured her feet began to slide up her legs, rapidly turning her entire body dark as charcoal. Her yellow summer frock disappeared. She grew like an inkstain, spreading taller and sleeker, feet planting talons into the earth, a slash of black becoming a long tail, her hands sprouting claws. Kariba's head also shifted, thickening and elongating as a swathe of soft fur emerged from her skin.

She looked back and down from her impressive new height at her friends whose mouths had dropped open. Her head was like a panther's, and when she spoke her long canines stuck out like white daggers. 'Come on, what did you expect? A penguin?' The rakshasi slunk away along the wall, vanishing into the darkness.

'She's got to teach me that trick,' Trikaya breathed to the others.

'Let's spread out,' Tal instructed. 'Isaac and I will take centre, Tri take right, Safir take left. I'll get his attention first. Wait for me to start shooting, and we'll give him everything we've got.'

They nodded and split immediately. Trikaya crouched down as she headed to their right, glad the dirt underneath was silencing their approach. She saw Isaac and Tal scoot to the stone dais with the throne and climb stealthily around it. Safir was on the far side, fiddling with his slingshot. He was a good shot, really, when he wasn't so nervous.

They crept closer quickly, and when they were only ten metres away Tal raised her hand, and a flash of light shot out erratically from her palm. It totally missed the magician, instead striking a part of the peacock-tail formation with a hiss. Trikaya grimaced, knowing how furious Tal would feel about missing.

Mister Mer whirled around, stunned, interrupted in the middle of his incantation. 'You simian simpletons,' he snarled. 'It was all right in Devagarh. I let it go because you're children. Now you're meddling with adult matters. Turn around and leave before I actually do something about you.'

'We're here to stop you,' Tal announced, standing up straight, both her hands glowing with light.

'Are you?' the magician retorted, turning to face them. 'Then do your worst.'

The children stood rooted in place. Trikaya expected Tal to send off a shot any minute now… But no, they just stood and stared at the magician, who stared back.

And then laughed, a scornful sound that echoed in the space. 'Really? That's your weapon? Just stand and look at me sternly? Is that the best you can do?'

When Kariba came, it was from behind the peacock sculpture, sprinting with the speed of her war form and launching herself at the magician with all her claws out. Mister Mer sensed her just before she reached him, and he ducked and windmilled his arms madly. The rakshasi's claws had him in range, and crashed down towards him...but then bounced off the air just centimetres from him, repelled by some invisible shield. Kariba flipped her body sinuously to land on her haunches just metres away.

'Aah!' Mister Mer howled. 'Aha ha! The rakshasi!' He grabbed his arm where she had been aiming. 'Well done, you seem to be...'

And now Tal sent off a shot. The rock pinged off the shield, drawing the magician's attention to the side. Immediately the other children began shooting, pulling out one stone after another.

Kariba leaped at Mister Mer again, climbing all over his shield and laying into it with tooth and claw. The magician shrieked at the sight of her carnivorous attack so close to him, but he was safe from it. He gestured and the rakshasi flew back with a yowl, but she was already turning her body in midair to readjust herself.

One rock got through. It hit him on the thigh above the knee, making him howl and start hopping around. Trikaya looked to see who had got him.

'He can't cover everything!' Safir yelled triumphantly.

Good job, Safir! she thought, and they all adjusted their shots to try to hit different parts of the magician.

Now Mister Mer danced, waving his hands around frantically to ward off stones coming for his feet as well as his head. Kariba came in again, only this time she wasn't slashing but ramming him, shield and body together. The shield took most of the impact away, but Mister Mer still staggered backwards, away from the peacock wall.

Trikaya huffed, and jammed her slingshot into her pocket. It wasn't working, she figured. Stones and Kariba were fine, but the magician was too powerful, and the surprise attack would only last so long. She sprang forward with an Amazonian cry.

The other three froze, seeing the smallest of them hurtle forward. Trikaya hopped up onto the dais supporting the Gate and jumped. She hit the smooth stone right next to Mister Mer, sliding on her jeans, and slapped his boot with her hand with a whistled, 'Ffffyyyuuuww!' before rolling away frantically.

The magician's boot became instantly fixed to the ground, joined to the stone. He was in the midst of backing away, and with his foot unwilling to follow he folded right over and smacked to the ground hard. Kariba was on him instantly, but he managed to snap a small shield over himself, keeping her at bay.

'Power me up!' Tal ran to Isaac with her arm up. He caught her other wrist, and the girl shot off her attack.

Everything went stark white, everyone's vision wiped clean. For a whole minute all of the people in the Black Kot stood blind, blinking wide eyes, arms splayed out.

'Not quite what I intended,' Tal muttered at Isaac, glad that he was already holding her so they wouldn't go bumping around. 'I'm getting the hang of it, though. A little more of this, a little less of that.'

Trikaya climbed to her feet, and stared at Mister Mer. 'Look at his hair!' she yelled at the others, and began hooting with laughter.

The magician frowned, seeing the children quickly all double over with laughter. He sat up, his foot still caught in his boot, and looked for that wild rakshasi. She prowled nearby, but even her bestial mouth was curled up with mirth. 'Nice look,' she growled at him.

Mister Mer reached into the pocket of his coat and pulled out the hand mirror he carried to check his make up when he performed. The children saw it and burst into even greater peals of laughter. His ears burned with embarrassment, but he shut them out and inspected himself. Face fine, eyebrows, hair...hair? He had to turn his head slightly to see what had happened.

Tal had burned a neat line along the backside of Mister Mer's head, leaving a huge, bright red bald patch. 'My hair...' he stammered, 'my beautiful hair!'

'Give up, Mister Mer!' Trikaya shouted, walking back to her friends. 'We'll get Shari to grow your hair out again, like Safir. Otherwise Tal will burn all your hair off, and you'll be bald as an egg!'

The magician stood slowly, striking off the shoelaces with a slash of his hand. His foot came free, wrapped in a purple sock with a hole where his toe poked out. Kariba jumped at him again, but Mister Mer was done playing. He spat out some words, pointed his fingers at her, and the rakshasi crumpled down to the stone, held there by magic. Another flurry of words, he pointed at the children, and they also fell, their limbs and bodies held down by some invisible pressure.

They watched with dread as he walked to them, stepping off the stone dais and onto the dirt. His face was serious, cold, and the spell words that tumbled from his tongue now were harsh and cruel. Mister Mer raised his hand, standing over Tal.

From where she lay in the dirt Trikaya saw, in a flash,

Galahad flowing through the grass towards the magician, and Shari behind the marten. Shari was pointing at Galahad, focusing his Gardener's will on the animal.

With each step forward the yellow-throated marten grew, his glare fiercer, his claws longer, his teeth sharper. The biggest martens grew up to seventy centimetres, but Galahad surpassed that in a flash. When he finally flung himself forward he was a metre long, a monster marten, and brought all the savagery of his species to the magician.

Kariba was a rakshasi, and a warrior-in-training, but Galahad was a force of nature. Every single part of him was a weapon, and with Shari having given him unnatural size and strength, it was no wonder that Mister Mer decided to run shrieking from the frenzy rather than face it. And so he hopped in frantic circles while Galahad harried him around the courtyard, growling ferociously.

Shari trotted up to Tal and Isaac, followed by Iti. 'What are you all lying around for?' he asked, confused.

'It's called magic,' Tal said sarcastically.

'Shari, you're okay!' Trikaya trilled.

Tal rolled her eyes. 'Of course he's okay, Iti's there.'

Isaac, who had been oddly silent this whole time, suddenly rolled to the side and got up.

'How did you do that?' Trikaya demanded, still struggling against the magic that held her down.

'I don't know,' he replied, crouching by Tal and searching the air with his hands. 'I thought if I can increase magic, maybe I could also weaken it, and I got free.' Tal's hands snapped up, and a moment later the rest of her was free.

'Me, me!' Trikaya called, and Isaac come over to release her too. 'We're winning!' she sang, rubbing her hands as Isaac went over to Safir and then to Kariba.

'We are,' Tal said, picking up her slingshot from the grass.

She aimed at Mister Mer, still cavorting with Galahad, who was relentless in his chase. The rock shot off and smacked the magician in the back, making him yell and prance away.

'Filthy brats!' Mister Mer roared.

'Whoops-a-daisy,' Shari chuckled, and pulled.

The grass around the magician's boot and purple-socked foot whipped up about his ankles and sent him sprawling.

Mister Mer flipped over quickly, and saw the yellow-throated marten bearing down on him, fangs bared. There was no choice left. These children were proving more difficult to deal with than he had anticipated. Grimacing, the magician uttered the old Sanskrit spellwords and delved into the spirit he had harvested from the Devagarhis.

It was as though a huge hand grabbed the marten and flung him away, his black and yellow body spinning haplessly through the air.

The magician rose, spitting spellwords and sound, gesturing at the children, and one by one they froze, stuck in mid-motion.

Mister Mer walked towards the Gate, and sat down on the step of the dais. 'It's over now.'

33

THE LAST MOMENT

'You're all fools,' the magician stated, wiggling the toe peeping from his purple sock. 'Lucky fools. You actually made me use some of the magic I gathered from Devagarh, which I was saving for the Gate. But luck can only take you so far. And when it's over, all you're left with is your foolishness. The foolishness of going up against me.'

Safir had initially pushed against the vice that held him, but stopped. This was a different spell from the first one, he knew. To his eye the first one had been light, a translucent hand pushing them down. This was something else entirely. The magic was thick and almost opaque, seeming to encase them all from head to toe.

'Oh, Isaac,' Mister Mer lamented. 'If only you had agreed. This would all be over by now. I'd have crossed over, and you'd be home with your friends, and your family. Well, if one Aunt Jyoti can be called family.' He leaned back, resting after his scuffle with the marten. 'It's not too late, however. We're both here. The task is still at hand, and the night is...'

'Never,' Isaac stated curtly.

The magician pouted, rocking himself on his elbows. 'Oh dear,' he mused. 'Guess I'll have to change your mind.'

He stood up and ambled over to the six children and the rakshasi, statues in the courtyard.

Safir felt the nervousness blooming through all of them, as Mister Mer approached. He didn't know how much of what he sensed was visible to them, but if only they could see the Gate like he did: constellations of light flickered like filigree all up and down its surface, flows of magic that pooled here and there before spilling out in different directions. The others didn't realize it, but the Gate was already half unlocked. They had to stop him from opening it, Safir repeated in his mind. Anything, any trick, whatever it took to stop the magician. Just long enough until...

'The Last Son is coming!' Trikaya shouted abruptly, and Safir's heart shrivelled at the words. 'So you'd better stop and run!' What was she thinking? To scare him into leaving? Didn't she realize it might also make him hurry?

'Tri!' Tal interrupted, panicking.

The magician didn't seem to react. 'The Last Son? What is that, some kind of medical balm?'

'The Last Son of Shiva, from Mumbai!' Trikaya continued defiantly.

'Trikaya, stop!' Iti admonished.

'Oh, that Last Son,' Mister Mer chuckled. 'The urban legend? Some mysterious person no one has ever seen?'

'He's coming, any minute now, and he's going to stop you!' the girl screamed hotly.

The magician walked past Shari and Iti, and stopped before Isaac and Tal, who were standing frozen near each other. 'Yes, yes, I'm sure he is,' he murmured wryly. 'Any minute now, riding a unicorn.'

'You're lying,' Safir declared, surprised.

'What's that?' Mister Mer spoke softly, his tone dangerous.

The boy continued, gripping his courage with both

hands. 'You're lying. I can sense it. You can speak the lies, and speak them well, Mister Mer. But I'm a Listener. I know the truth. You know the Last Son is real, I can feel it in you. And you're terrified that he's coming, but for whatever reason, you're pretending like you don't know. Maybe you want to look brave to us, but we know you're afraid.'

'Yes!' Trikaya said triumphantly. 'We know you're afraid. We know you're trying to get to Mount Meru. We know everything! Your name is Mahipati. Mahipati Me-er!'

Mister Mer stood impassive. 'Is that it?'

'Mahipati!'

'Because if he is coming, which may or may not…'

'Maaaa…hipati!'

'May or may not be true, it doesn't change anything. In fact, it makes one thing clear.'

'Mama-hi, mama-mahipati!'

The magician snapped his fingers at Trikaya, and Safir saw the thick magic block stop her lips. 'That I need to finish this little distraction now, and get on with my work.' He settled his coat again over his black kurta-pyjama and turned back to Tal and Isaac. 'Now, Isaac Shroff, I'm going to ask nicely: won't you raise my power? As they say, pretty please with a jamun on top?' The boy was about to reply when the magician's arm came up swiftly, and his fingernails came to rest on Tal's slim throat. 'You might want to consider your answer carefully before you speak. I won't ask again.'

Never before had danger come this close to Tal. Fighting with R2R today, when Rudra was out of his mind, it had been terrifying in a wild way. But this was cold and final, a different kind of fear. The girl's eyes went automatically to Shari, who stared at her speechless, not daring to say a thing. Then she turned to Isaac. The new boy. He was looking at her steadily, into the rich chocolate colour of her eyes, large and round. He didn't hesitate.

'Of course I will.'

Mister Mer flicked a finger and Isaac's right arm fell free. 'If you would be so kind.' He extended his own arm, and the boy reached out to touch his wrist.

From where he was, Safir had a direct line of sight with the magician. He saw the man's eyes widen. Even worse, he felt the man's power multiply. Twice. Thrice… Mister Mer pulled away, gasping. For a second he stared at Isaac, almost wondering whether the boy was trying to do something sneaky. Then he shrugged, realizing it didn't matter.

'My thanks, young master Shroff,' the magician said. 'And now, back to work.' He walked to the stone dais of the Gate, but the moment he stepped on it, a thick black wall formed before him, barbed and shivering. 'Oh, for the love of… You again?' Mister Mer looked annoyed.

'The ghosts,' Safir told everyone. 'They've come.'

'Get away!' the magician shouted, and punched the wall. It was blasted back, shuddering apart, but held. The man was livid, frustrated. 'Ah, don't make me waste it!' He slipped his other hand next to his fist, muttering spellwords, and pried the wall apart. Pieces of the darkness flew here and there, but it almost seemed like it would… With a final roar Mister Mer tore the wall apart and leaped forward to slap his palm against the stone of the Gate. 'Now!' he shouted, and continued his interrupted incantation, feeding magic into the stone as fast he could.

'Mer!' a woman's voice shouted. Mademoiselle! She tottered through the group of children, reaching out to them as she did so, and with each touch the sorcerous bonds dissipated and they wobbled down to their knees. The Wolf Queen couldn't stand anymore after that, and sagged down to kneel in the dirt.

Safir looked back to the doors of the Black Kot, wondering how she could have come all this way in such a state. He saw a huge shape half out of the doors and realized that Rabakak had also crawled to them in the meantime, dragging his huge body over the flagstones and into the tunnel. 'Please stop!' Mademoiselle pleaded, 'You don't know what you're doing!'

Mister Mer sang out the last Sanskrit spellwords and stepped back, a beatific smile on his harsh face. 'I know exactly what I'm doing, Mademoiselle Fulara, and why.' He raised his arms and roared. 'I am the Midnight King, and I command you to open!'

And the Gate opened.

Quietly, smoothly.

As each door swung open, every millimetre that opened to that other world let out a ghastly thick blue light, a strange illuminated substance that was something far from natural to Earth.

'Tal!' Mademoiselle called weakly, 'Your Star power can negate the atmosphere of Mount Meru.'

Still on all fours, Tal pushed herself back to sit and raised both hands. Her Star light blasted out, and wherever it touched the blue light it shimmered, and nullified it.

But the doors were opening still.

The more that horrid light came out, the harder it became for Tal to shine. She knew how to make a quick flash, that was easy, but sustaining something this strong, for so long…? She didn't know if she could do it.

And then it was suddenly easy. The light from her hands intensified, becoming just as robust as the light coming through the Gate. Tal glanced over her shoulder. Isaac had crawled up to her and grabbed her ankle, and was multiplying her power. Yes! With Isaac aiding her she should be able to resist it for longer.

'Call the ghosts!' Mademoiselle instructed. 'Make them help you!'

Safir could see the ghosts, their masses spinning this way and that. For as far back as he could remember he had been hearing and seeing things, and desperately trying to ignore them. Kariba was the first time he had addressed one of them. And he had done it just yesterday. He hesitated at first, but then a thought struck him. If these were the ghosts of the yakshas who had served on Yakshagarh, weren't they his ancestors? His people? His family? It wasn't like talking to unknown strange creatures, not at all. The boy stood up, pushed his glasses back up his nose, and reached out to the ghosts. He had spent years Listening. Maybe now they could listen to him? 'Family!' he yelled to the sky.

The ghosts went still. Listening.

'We are the Guardians of Yakshagarh,' Safir shouted at them. 'Your descendants. Now is the time to be strong, and to stand with us. So…uh…stand with us!' He made a face at Trikaya, who just grinned and shrugged. Not the best of speeches, he judged.

But effective.

The ghosts of Yakshagarh poured down from the sky, thicker and more substantial than ever, and pushed against the doors of the Gate. And pushed. And the doors began to shut.

Brighter and brighter Tal became, feeling her mind slide into greater and greater expanses of space as her power grew. She felt strong now, stronger than ever, and stood. Her arms were light as air. With the ghosts pushing, and her Star power, they were winning!

Mister Mer put his hands to the doors and began pulling them open, straining against the ghosts. That sick light poured over him but didn't seem to affect him. The doors were caught between the massive pull and push, and a curious groaning sound seemed to come from them. Safir could feel the strain in all the parties, everyone putting all their might into this last action. And then a section of the massive stone door Mister Mer was gripping snapped off, sending him tumbling, and crashed thunderously to the floor!

'Come on!' Mademoiselle cheered, seeing that.

And Mister Mer struck back.

He leaped to his feet and pointed at the ghosts, those black clouds, and roared, 'I am the Midnight King, and I command you to back down!'

Bound by duty to the kings of the Black Kot, the great black clouds instantly went quiet, and faded away.

The doors began to open again, and the entrance to Mount Meru yawned before them, letting out that frightful blue atmosphere. So much of it... Tal pushed her Star light up, hotter and faster, but the more of that blueness came out, the weaker it made her light.

Mister Mer walked to the edge of the dais to address Mademoiselle and the children with the satisfaction of victory: 'And this is how it ends.' He turned his back on them with a flourish and stepped purposefully towards the open Gate to Mount Meru.

Something small and hard as a mountain slapped down between the magician and the Gate, cracking the smooth stone.

A sword, buried to the hilt.

Safir saw Mister Mer turn, look up high with an expression of disbelief turning to dismay. The boy looked up, and then everyone else did.

Out of the sky he dropped, like a speeding arrow, and when he landed in the dirt before the dais the earth split and thundered. A man, as normal as could be, in jeans and a brown kurta, and white sneakers, hands casually in his pockets. That's what most of them saw.

To Safir's eye it was as though the sun had abruptly risen and stood right in front of him. The light and power and sheer effervescence of presence that the man radiated made his mind numb. A distant realization echoed in his thoughts: that's what a son of Shiva is like.

'So you're Mister Mer,' the Last Son said. 'I hear you're pretty mesmerizing.'

The magician was stiff and tall, his eyes wary. 'You should see my show.'

'I gather tonight's performance is a fiasco. Maybe you should have stayed abroad pulling rabbits out of hats.'

'The Gate is broken,' the magician stated. 'You won't be able to close it anymore.' He huffed out a word, and all of a sudden he became diffuse, intangible, his outline wavering. A breeze picked up and Mister Mer fell into it, drifting into foggy pieces. The children could feel him looking at them, however, and hear his words whisper in the wind: 'You have made yourselves my enemies, little yakshas. For what is to come, you have no one to blame but yourselves.'

And he was gone.

'Nifty trick,' the Last Son said, and began to move as if to chase the magician.

'No! Wait, please!' Mademoiselle called. 'The Gate!'

The demigod paused, considering. The doors of the Gate were still opening, that blue atmosphere pouring out, and Tal was barely keeping it back. The Last Son decided, and sped to one door. The children watched in amazement as that one man easily began pushing back that huge slab of carved stone. He jumped to the other door, pushed that in, and then stood in the gap with one hand on each. With the blue light cut off Tal was able to direct her Star light better, just as she was reaching the end of her energy.

With a final push the demigod slammed the doors together and paused, leaning against the Gate and running his eyes over its surface. 'The Gate is not locking,' he pronounced. 'It should lock on its own but it isn't.'

The others were slowly drifting in to the stone dais on shaky legs, holding each other up. 'It can't be,' Mademoiselle said. 'The Gate must lock. If it doesn't... The atmosphere of Mount Meru is far stronger than Earth, it'll keep pushing the doors open.'

The Last Son continued to study the Gate, frowning in concentration. Safir could see him following the circuits of light running all along the stone, the mechanism of the spell that none of the others could see. The boy knew nothing about spells and magic, but his Listening told him the locking would not happen if the door was not whole. 'We have to fix it,' he said, approaching the piece of stone that had broken from the structure. It was a small piece, but he realized now it was a massive chunk of the door. He doubted all six of them could lift it.

'Let me get it,' the Last Son said, stepping over quickly to grab that slab and lifting it like it was styrofoam. The moment he had let go of the doors they had begun to swing open, but he was back immediately and holding the piece over the gap.

This close to the Gate, Tal only had to shine her Star light on the blue atmosphere that speared out of the hole, easy enough even without Isaac's help. The children sat around while the Last Son ran through a number of spells and chants, but none of them worked.

'What is it?' Mademoiselle asked. 'Why is it not working?'
'An outside spell won't hold it in place,' he explained.

'The Gate's working naturally repels other magic. And I don't dare try anything stronger than the Gate itself lest it break entirely. It's too large and intricate. I'm afraid the magician was right, we won't be able to close it.'

'Can I try?' Shari said, already pulling roots from outside the Black Kot. They snaked, dark and thin, from the dirt outside the dais and towards the doors.

'A Gardener,' the demigod recognized with a smile.

It didn't work. Shari built the roots into place, but the atmosphere seeping through the cracks poisoned and melted them instantly, and the block fell out within moments.

All this time Safir was watching Trikaya, and he finally edged closer to her as Mademoiselle and the Last Son conferred about what to do. He gave her a meaningful look, and the little girl sighed and nodded in acknowledgement. 'What's wrong?' he asked her softly.

'Well, see...' she began hesitantly. 'I'm always the last one. Youngest, smallest, slowest...'

'Not anymore,' he noted with a friendly nudge.

'True, but it's like I'm always the one behind. And I've hated that. I always wanted to be up there with everyone else.' She paused and looked up at the sky. The clouds seemed to be clearing somewhat. A hint of moonlight was tinging the night. 'And now I can, I can do it, but...what if I can't?' Her eyes sparkled in the light of Tal's Star power. 'What if I try and it turns out I'm still behind?'

Safir shook his head. 'I don't know what you mean. Everywhere I look you're at the front. I've never seen you behind. Trikaya, behind? It's not possible. I can't even put you and behind in the same thought. You know?'

The girl watched him carefully, reading his face, hearing the honesty in his tone. A smile grew on her impish features. 'I know.' Trikaya jumped up, brushed her hands on her jeans, and called out, 'Okay, my turn. Isaac, please?' She marched up to the Last Son and Mademoiselle and squeezed in between to get to the Gate. 'Excuse me, I'm a Bond...'

The other children perked up, suddenly remembering. If there was one person who could fix the Gate, it was a Bond! It was what a Bond did: join things seamlessly until they became one. Isaac scrambled up to join Trikaya. He put his hand on her shoulder, and she put her little hands up against the stone.

'Please step back, Mademoiselle,' she advised to the Wolf Queen. 'Mr Last Son, can you hold it better in place?'

The demigod obeyed her, squeezing the stone in as precisely as possible. 'The original spell of the door has to pass through this piece seamlessly,' he specified, 'or it won't work. It must be made exactly as it was before. We won't be able to break it off and try again.'

'It's a one-time thing, I get it,' Trikaya chirped. 'Here we go.'

Everyone held their breath.

Humming her favourite cartoon song, Trikaya put both fingers together at the middle of the diagonal crack. She studied the stone, both the piece and the door, and all of a sudden slipped her mind into it. She didn't know how she did it, but it didn't matter how.

The spell was an inseparable part of the stone, she saw, which was why that critical piece missing meant the spell was incomplete. How unbelievably complex it was. It was like trying to keep track of every single swirl and twist of water in an entire wave crashing on a beach. Which was why she didn't bother with it. All she knew was what she had to do.

The Bond gathered her power and began with a whistling 'Ffffyyuuwww...' accompanying the fusion of the stone.

The others watched in awe as Trikaya's fingers separated,

unerringly tracing the line of the crack in both directions. Where her fingers had been the stone reappeared, whole, unblemished. Safir couldn't believe his eyes as he saw the flow of the spell begin to pass through the stone she had healed.

It took hardly fifteen seconds, and when she reached the edges of the door she said, 'One sec,' and quickly did something with her fingers on the stone. 'Pschiii! Finished!'

The Last Son stepped back, eyes running up and down the Gate, and let the doors go.

It did not open.

Half of the group collapsed in relief, the other half jumping up to grab and hug Trikaya. Safir stood with a huge grin deforming his cheeks as he watched Tal and Trikaya hold hands and jump up and down with glee. He turned and saw the Last Son watching the doors, still studying the spell. 'It's good,' he told the demigod, who glanced down at him. Then Safir felt a little foolish reassuring the son of Shiva.

'It is,' the Last Son spoke with a nod. He reached out a finger to tap the stone where Trikaya had done the last manipulation. 'I was afraid this might break or alter the spell, but it works just as well.' Safir leaned in to peer at the stone Trikaya had touched in the end.

A smiley face was carved deep into the rock, placed over the spellwords and carvings that were who knew how many centuries old. The boy shoved his glasses up into place and proudly said, 'That's Trikaya.'

34

KINGS AND QUEENS

The Last Son gripped the handle of his sword and slid it out of the stone. Tal eyed it keenly, wishing she could see the weapon and feeling it might be impolite to ask.

'Can I see your sword?' Trikaya asked, direct as usual.

The demigod held the handle to her, amused. 'Don't look too closely at the blade, it's... It's magic.' Shari stepped in with a responsible air and took the sword before Trikaya could get her small fingers on it.

Tal clustered with the other children over the Last Son's weapon. It was a regular-looking sword, unlike the Wolf Queen's khanda, the straight blade flaring out slightly at the end before curving to a quick point. Simple and inexplicably beautiful. 'Oh!' Safir exclaimed, leaning away. 'Oh, yes, uh... don't get too close to the blade.'

'Why not?' Trikaya asked, frowning.

The boy looked spooked. 'There's something living inside it. Not something nice.'

Mademoiselle's hand came from over their heads to snatch the weapon from their scrutiny. 'Swords are generally not meant for children, and this one in particular is one you should stay away from.' The Wolf Queen handed it back to its owner respectfully.

The Last Son took the sword, and it went swiftly back into a plain scabbard that hung from his belt. 'Who's this then?' he asked cheerfully.

Tal looked and saw that Galahad had come over to see them. Iti gave the marten a quick touch, clearing him of whatever bruises he had suffered from Mister Mer flinging him out and away. He was hu-u-uge, Tal saw with some trepidation. Shari had grown him far beyond the natural size of any yellow-throated marten. Galahad looked quite pleased with his newfound strength, however. And he seemed even friendlier than before, rubbing Iti's leg with his head for almost a minute before beginning his usual perambulations.

'Welcome, Son of the Destroyer!' a deep, rough voice called out to the Last Son. Rabakak had managed to wriggle through the tunnel and crawl up to them. 'I am Rabakak the Treeborn, Guardian of Yakshagarh. I'm ashamed to meet you in the failure of my duty, but I thank you wholehear—'

'Did you say Rabakak?' the Last Son interrupted casually. 'Aren't you the cousin of Tomofarish the Foul?'

The Rakshas Lord's mouth made a jagged grin. 'Yes, yes! You heard of me?' His expression soured. '...from Tomofarish? He's a liar. A distorter of truths.'

The demigod gave a mischievous smile. 'He did go into quite a lot of detail about you and...'

'Lies, lies, all of it!' Rabakak cried out indignantly.

'Do you really fly?' Trikaya asked the demigod, peering up at his face.

The Last Son clarified, 'It's not really *flight* flight. It's structured magic, and kind of old, it's a bit difficult to explain...'

Safir cleared his throat urgently. 'Ah, the ghosts are coming.' He gestured towards the Gate. 'I mean, they've been here all along, but they're, I don't know, um… appearing to us now?'

Tal and the others turned to the Gate. Four shadowy figures, two grey queens and two grey kings, slipped into view. They all wore faded crowns, and each held a differently shaped spear. With a start Tal realized they felt exactly like the presence from earlier in the afternoon, when they had been assaulted on the path before the Black Kot. 'You're the ones who attacked us!' she accused angrily.

The foremost of the shadowy figures, a king with a beard, whispered, 'You invaded Yakshagarh. We were doing our duty. We knew you are yakshas, our kin, and so we never harmed you. Only showed you the fears you harm yourselves with.' He faced the Last Son and inclined his head. 'Our thanks to you, Son of the Destroyer. Our guardianship has weakened over time, regretfully. That is the way the world has been shaped.'

The demigod gave the four figures a deep, deliberate namaskar. 'I greet you, kings and queens of yore. I am grateful to have been able to aid you when you needed it.'

The ghostly king raised a hand in ritual blessing. 'We cannot allow the heir's villainy to go on. It is in our right and power, as the ancestors and spiritual protectors, to elect a new Midnight King. The heir's right will then be rescinded. And we can reform the Trikunchika.'

'I failed you,' Rabakak declared, his voice tormented. 'I failed my duty. I could not stop Mer. If you wish it I will leave my place for a new Guardian.'

'I failed too,' Mademoiselle said, stepping forward. She knelt and offered Uttaradanshtra with both hands, head bowed. 'If you wish it I will step down and also leave my place for another.'

The king swung his spear sharply in negation. 'We

acknowledge your humility. But we also failed, Guardians. You did all you could, as did we, and we all failed. Which is why we need a new Midnight King.' He moved forward, legs immobile, drifting over the stone to hold his spear out to the Last Son. 'Would you take this duty, Son of the Destroyer?'

The demigod looked genuinely surprised at the offer. He paused, considering, and then again saluted with a namaskar. 'I cannot, respected ones. A yaksha must rule the Black Kot, and I am a deva. I am not entitled.' The Last Son turned to look over the children. 'But we do have some yaksha blood here.'

'The laws may be bent, but you are right, a yaksha should rule,' the ghostly king agreed. 'I do have some misgivings, however. They are a bit innocent. And...small.'

'Wait, wait...' Trikaya was the first to get her voice back. 'You're not saying...?'

'One of us can be king of the Black Kot?' Shari uttered carefully.

'One of you *must* be the Midnight King,' the demigod corrected. 'Or Mister Mer will remain so, and can come back anytime to open the Gate.' He frowned. 'He will not be happy to be replaced. Be certain that he will come at you with a vengeance.'

Tal looked around at the others uneasily, then shrugged. 'Didn't he say he's going to do that anyway?'

'He did, it's true,' Iti confirmed.

'So...who will be King?' Isaac hazarded.

The silence lasted a few seconds before, as Tal expected, Trikaya yelled, 'Tal!'

Another moment, and then Iti said, predictably, 'Shari is worthy.'

And there they were again. The discomfort of their split

had reared its head again, ugly and hateful. As if by some chance Tal realized they were standing separate, she with Trikaya and Isaac behind her, and Shari with Iti and Safir by him. She could see in their eyes they had all had the same thought as her. Tal knew it was up to her to steer them in the right direction.

'No.'

They all looked at Tal with surprise. She shook her head and continued, 'Not just Shari, not just me. You all are worthy. We all are. Iti, you're the Cure, you've healed everyone! Trikaya, you fixed the *Gate*! It would have all been for nothing if you weren't here.'

'Safir, you see things we can't,' Shari said, putting his arm around his friend's shoulder. 'You knew Mister Mer was bluffing. You snuck out of the Lodge against your father's orders! And Isaac, you...' He held out his hand. 'You belong in the KSS. You're one of us.'

The new boy took Shari's hand and shook it, knowing he wasn't the new boy anymore. 'Then can I suggest...?' He looked around at the others. 'Maybe all of us can be the Midnight King?'

They all immediately began to clamour, Trikaya screaming yes, Safir clapping, and it took a minute for the ghostly king to interject, 'That is absolutely impossible! One Midnight King only.'

'Why?' Safir asked. 'Why only one?'

'It's...' the king began, looking flustered. 'I mean, it's obvious, it's the Midnight King, not the Midnight *Kings*. That sounds...silly.'

'Like a poorly named rock band,' the Last Son mused.

'But is there a real reason?' Tal persisted.

'Yes,' Iti said, 'A logical, practical reason?'

The ghostly king looked from one face to the other,

sputtering, 'Logical? Practical? There's one throne! One Black Kot! One Gate!'

'That's not a real reason,' Iti ruled immediately.

'There's four of *you*,' Isaac pointed out.

'Yes, but *I* lead!' the ghostly king blurted out. Behind him, the other three figures stepped back and stared at him very pointedly. The king's expression turned contrite, and he stammered to his companions, 'No, I mean, I don't *lead*, I just, er, happen to speak on all our behalf...'

'Is it yes or no?' the Last Son interrupted. 'Because the young yakshas look pretty decided.'

Tal crossed her arms and set her feet. At her side, all in a row, were her five friends, equally determined.

The ghostly king looked at the resolute six. 'This is... unprecedented. You would refuse the duty?'

'We refuse nothing,' Isaac told him. 'You're the one refusing to, how did you put it earlier when you asked the Last Son, a deva...? Refusing to bend the laws?'

'Well,' the king stammered, caught with his own words, 'there's bending and *bending*, if you know what I mean...'

'I think we all know what you mean,' Tal said sarcastically.

'There will be consequences we cannot foresee,' he warned.

'Will be or *may* be?' Iti specified. 'Because either there *will* be consequences that you *can* foresee, or there *may* be some consequences that you *can't* foresee. Or maybe you're just trying to scare us because you think we're dumb because we're kids.'

He blinked rapidly and conceded, 'There *may* be consequences. If all six are Midnight King, we don't know if that would mean that only one of you has to be defeated, or all six.'

'We'll figure that out,' Shari stated.

'Then…' the ghostly king hummed, about to agree.

'Just one question?' Iti piped up. 'You keep saying Midnight King, but three of us are girls. Is that a problem?'

The ghostly king seemed genuinely perplexed. 'Why would it be a problem? King is just a word to indicate a position. Why would a girl be any less worthy to rule the Black Kot than a boy? You could call yourself Midnight Queen if you wish.'

'Or Midnight Princess?' Trikaya called out, raising a finger. 'Midnight Queen is a bit…oldish, no? Ooh, ooh, how about something more superheroine-y? Miss Midnight? Or the Midnight Rogue?'

'Little girl,' the king begged, running a wispy hand over his faded forehead, 'I don't have a head anymore but you all give me a phantom headache. You can call yourself the Pink Pumpkin if you want, at this point I just need someone sitting on that throne so we can go back to our spirit world.'

With the Last Son tittering uncontrollably in the background, the ghostly king quickly explained the procedure, which he lavishly called coronation ceremony.

'Easy enough,' Tal mouthed a few minutes later around the brisk wet rub of Mademoiselle's dupatta. The pâtissière had sat the children on the edge of the fountain so she could clean the black mascara off their cheeks and foreheads, dipping her dupatta in the clear water every once in a while. They had protested, of course. The camo was their war paint and the mark of a warrior! But the Wolf Queen had been firm about not letting them become Kings and Queens of the Black Kot with dirty faces.

The six scrubbed children came before the throne. It was a large thing made of black iron, once beautifully carved and decorated, but the detail of it had faded from centuries out in the sun, the rain and the snow. They climbed up one by one: Tal and Shari standing and leaning against the backrest; Isaac and Safir sitting on the armrests; and Iti and Trikaya sitting on the seat itself, the younger wrapped up in the arms of the older. It felt weird…but as they exchanged excited looks, Tal realized that it also felt inexplicably natural.

Rabakak was recovered enough to sit cross-legged, and Mademoiselle stood holding her cheeks in disbelief, the biggest smile on her face. Kariba sat on the grass by her uncle, changed back to her 'little girl in a bright frock' form, black toes wiggling as she watched with shiny eyes. Next to her stood Galahad, arms hanging down his front, peering at the proceedings with interest. The Last Son crouched at the corner of the dais, an amused expression on his face.

In front of the throne the four ghostly figures lined up. They raised their spears as one, straight up to the sky.

What was it that made the clouds part at that very moment, and allow the moon to illuminate the scene? Tal and the others looked up, saw the stars glittering fiercely in the night, saw the giant silver disc shining down on them.

'We are the people of the Black Kot,' the ghostly king announced to the dark hills of Kumaon, and though he alone spoke there were hundreds, thousands of voices in his. 'The yakshas of Yakshagarh. Kings. Warriors. Defenders of the Black Kot. Protectors of the Secret.' The four figures extended their insubstantial spears to point at the six children. 'We see you. Tal Kandhari. Shari Kandhari. Iti Pillai. Trikaya Pillai. Safir Idris. Isaac Shroff. Our distant sons and daughters. We offer you the throne of the Black Kot, its duties and its responsibilities, and with it our allegiance and loyalty, for as long as you rule. Do you accept?'

The children, embarrassed to speak too loudly in this

formal moment (except for Trikaya's earnest yell), mumbled yeses. The king sighed a spectral cloud, and continued.

'Then no longer are you children. No longer are you human. No longer are you yaksha. You are from this moment, now and forever, the Midnight King...*s* and will be known and acknowledged as such by the world and its people until the end of this age.'

'Aren't we supposed to be super-secret kings of a super-secret fort?' Safir whispered in Trikaya's ear, and she stifled a giggle. 'How are the world and its people supposed to acknowledge us?'

'A-*hem*!' the ghostly king coughed and made stern eyes. Trikaya and Safir both shrugged apologetically. The king stepped forward, and his three companions followed suit. They held the spears out to the children.

The children reached out for the spears, one for Safir, one for Isaac, and the other two shared by the twins and by the sisters.

'Rise now, defenders of the Black Kot!' the king roared, the air vibrating with the voices of all the ghosts of Yakshagarh. 'Rise now, Protectors of the Secret! Rise now... Midnight Kings!' The four ghostly figures bent over in a deep namaskar... And then the children saw, and their throats caught.

In the moon-infused night, there weren't just the four ghosts—there were thousands, tens of thousands, hundreds of thousands of them. Diffuse but individual figures in endless numbers, filling the Black Kot. Lining its walls. An uncountable throng extending beyond the tunnel into Yakshagarh and, they knew, all over the hill, down into the jungle, to the waterfalls... All the ghosts of Yakshagarh, the dead generations of countless millennia, their ancestors, gathered here, bowing to them in respect.

One by one the children stood. The spears they had held melted away into the air, allowing them to join their palms together and bow back to their new people in a silent and respectful namaskar.

They were the Midnight Kings.

35

THE KUMAON SECRET SOCIETY

'I don't feel any different,' was the first thing Trikaya commented as she clambered down from the throne, sounding a little peeved.

The ghostly king snorted a puff of white. 'What, did you think you'd suddenly get a whole lot of superpowers? Being crowned king doesn't give you anything new. You were crowned king because you already have it.'

'Maybe none of us are any different,' Iti stated, jumping off the throne, an unusually enthusiastic action, 'But I do feel plenty different!'

'My Kings and Queens,' Mademoiselle said dramatically, making a deep curtsey.

The children immediately became flustered. Trikaya curtsied back automatically and awkwardly, while Tal grabbed the pâtissière's arm and pulled her back up in a panic. 'No, no!' the girl giggled nervously. 'Please, Mademoiselle, we're still us!'

Mademoiselle hugged Tal to her and said, 'I know that. But you're far more than that now. I am in your service, as is Rabakak. The First and Second Guardians are bound to the throne in the Black Kot, just as much as the ghosts of

Yakshagarh.' She winked at Safir. 'I guess that means free patisseries for the Kings and Queens in perpetuity…'

The Last Son, who had been observing with a smile, rose and said, 'It's past time I take my leave.'

'Won't you stay for the Barbarika Festival?' Shari asked quickly, before realizing there may not even be one to celebrate…

'I can't. My wife is expecting me for dinner.' He pulled back the sleeve of his kurta to glance at his watch, and froze with fear. 'I'm late. Are there any flower shops on the way? Oh right, I'm flying. Oh, please let there be good weather…'

'Look what the kids dragged in,' a voice called out. Mr Charles stumbled into the group, rifle under his arm, panting and sweating.

The Last Son looked delighted and vigorously shook the Englishman's hand. 'Geoffrey Gordon,' he declared, 'Where have you been all this time?'

'There was a small matter of getting an inheritance from myself,' the Englishman replied, smoothing his ruffled moustache. 'Apparently the investments I made before I died were rather shrewd. Two hundred years of compound interest worked some minor miracles. There were some relatives who were none too pleased about my return, but apparently I have DNA that matches—whatever that means.' He shrugged. 'In any case, I'm what you call a "billionaire" these days.'

'Hold on,' Tal said sternly. 'You told us your name was Robert Charles.'

'Yes. I lied,' he responded cheerfully. 'My real name is Geoffrey Gordon. Robert Charles is a useful nom de guerre.'

'A what?' Safir inquired.

'Pseudonym. False identity. Fake name?' The Englishman explained.

'Excuse me, but did you say you *died*?' Iti asked cautiously.

'It's a rather long story.' Mr Gordon harrumphed, exchanging a meaningful look with the Last Son. 'The important thing is that I'm back. I have come into a little money, and I now busy myself with certain esoteric matters like Mister Mer. He is a vindictive and vengeful fellow. He will come for you, especially now that you are the Midnight Kings.' He smiled at the girls. 'And Queens.'

'Wait, how do you know we're the Midnight King?' Tal noted suspiciously. 'You weren't here!'

'The priests knew,' he replied. 'The moment the kingship switched, the ghosts calmed down and I could cross the bridge. I ran here, but it was all over already.' He actually looked a little regretful about missing the extremely dangerous action. 'Anyway, I want to extend an invitation to you all. I will be investing in a little patch of land in Devagarh, and I would love to have you over so we can…discuss things further.'

'Discuss things further?' Isaac repeated. 'Like what?'

'Your future,' the Englishman said.

'What future?' Trikaya chirped. 'We're kids. We go to school, we play games, we're cute. What more do you want to discuss that we don't already know?'

Mr Gordon sighed. 'I apologize. I'm used to dealing with people who speak in cryptic ways.' He slung his rifle over his shoulder and let it hang by its strap. 'I'm inviting you so you can train your powers.'

The children nodded at each other. 'That sounds cool,' Shari answered for all of them.

'All right,' the Last Son cut in nervously. 'Everyone's safe, everything's fixed. Can I go now? If I reach home any later I'm going to get it.'

The Englishman shook the demigod's hand again. 'Give my regards to the lady of the house,' he said, grinning at his friend's distress. 'I'll be in Mumbai soon enough.'

The Last Son nodded, delivered a friendly slap to Rabakak's thick hide, and exchanged bows with Mademoiselle and Kariba. The demigod finally came to the children. 'You might be the youngest Guardians these hills have ever seen. Remember, Mister Mer will be watching from the shadows. The only chance you have is to be his match. Become stronger. More importantly, become smarter.'

'We'll do it,' they promised. The demigod reached out to shake hands with all six children. I'm shaking hands with the son of Shiva, Shari thought, not quite able to fathom the idea.

With a final salute the Last Son trotted out to an open patch of grass. He looked up to the sky, spoke some unintelligible words, and...was gone, as though he had never been there. They felt a gust of air stir their hair, and then the night was still.

'I can't see him,' Trikaya protested, squinting at the stars.

'That's because it's night,' Iti teased, grabbing her younger sister to reorient her, 'And you're facing west. He's gone south.'

Rabakak said he would spend the night and lock up the Black Kot in the morning, as though it were someone's cabin he was borrowing. The children high-fived his two-pronged hands in farewell and the Rakshas Lord watched them go, the six excitable creatures skipping and chattering as they were escorted out by Mademoiselle, Mr Gordon, and his niece Kariba.

When their silhouettes had disappeared into the night he turned to the dais of the throne and rumbled, 'Good evening, Quiet Father.'

The bearded man with the unlined face and the ancient eyes had been sitting there all along, invisible to everyone.

The Rakshas Lord asked, 'The Last Son knew you were

here, didn't he?' The man nodded in response to Rabakak as he got up with exceptional grace, carefully manoeuvring his metre-long beard to the side. 'If the Last Son hadn't come, you would have stopped Mer, right?' The man didn't reply, peering at the Gate with studied interest. 'What do you think of all this, Quiet Father?' the Second Guardian wondered.

The man turned his eyes to the luminescent moon. 'Six Kings and Queens for the Black Kot. Who would have thought it? It's a new way they have created. A new world.' He began to walk away.

Rabakak was stunned. In the more than three hundred years since he had been Guardian, this was the most words he had ever heard out of the Quiet Father's mouth. Stammering, he tried to capitalize on the man's uncharacteristic volubility by asking the age-old question of any parent to a teacher: 'How's Kariba doing in school?'

'Learning.' The Quiet Father's footsteps faded into the night.

Rabakak rolled his huge body around until he was lying on his back and looking into the sky. As nice as that moon was after the events of the day, he found it a bit bright for sleep. Now if only he had a toothsome cat at hand. Or four.

Down the hill, on the other side of Shari's bridge, the four priests greeted the six children with an almost choreographed bow. 'Welcome, Kings and Queens of the Black Kot,' Bhante called out excitedly. 'We gree—oh my, what is that?!'

The yellow-throated marten had gone bounding ahead, the sinuous hopping glide on something that large rather startling. 'Galahad!' Iti called sternly. 'Come here!' The marten pulled up short and plodded obediently to the girl. Shari trotted ahead to explain Galahad to the four priests who huddled in terror.

'Are we going to have to rebuild the bridge?' Safir asked

nervously as they stepped onto Devagarh. 'What are people going to say when they see this?'

'Nothing,' Mademoiselle affirmed. 'I'm going to suggest to the villagers that the bridge has always been like this, and they won't think twice about it.'

'*Suggest?*' Tal said curiously. 'Like…in their minds?'

'I don't like doing it,' the lady said. 'But the alternative is to tell them that the magician Mister Mer almost destroyed the village and all of Kumaon by opening a Gate to Mount Meru after defeating me, a secret deva queen, and Rabakak, a giant rakshas who lives on the next hill. Then that you six young yakshas and a rakshasi jumped in to stop him. And finally a son of Shiva arrived in the nick of time to save everything.' She raised an inquisitive eyebrow. 'What do you think?'

Trikaya waved her hand and stated dismissively, 'Suggest, suggest.'

The sound of music coming from the village caught Shari's attention. 'Are they celebrating the Barbarika Festival?'

'They don't remember anything,' Mademoiselle assured them. 'Not from the moment that Mer jumped in. I also cleared the villagers of his manipulating spell, no need to have that floating around.'

'But what about the statue, and all the shops that were smashed?' Safir asked.

'Magic,' the pâtissière said, winking. 'All back the way it was.'

They all began to walk from the bridge to town. Safir had wrestled out the packet of pains au chocolat and distributed them freely. They munched on the delectable treats as the Lodge came up on their left, and there the six children and Kariba stopped for a minute, while the adults talked quietly at a little distance.

'Now, Galahad,' Iti instructed the yellow-throated marten. 'The priests are concerned about your size. I know you hunt deer and bears and things, and that's fine. But you can't hunt people, all right?' The yellow-throated marten stood on his hind paws, staring at her rapt. 'Do you understand?' she said. 'No people.'

Galahad blinked a couple times, looking a little vexed, but eventually bobbed his head around.

'All right, that's a promise,' Iti said, sighed, and then smiled. 'You've been brilliant, Galahad.' He perked up, eyes bright. She took out one of their slingshots and touched it to his right shoulder. The marten sniffed at the weapon curiously. 'For your service in the defence of Devagarh, Yakshagarh, and the Black Kot,' she began, moving the slingshot to touch his left shoulder, 'I, Iti the Midnight Queen, grant you the title of Knight and Protector of the Secret. Rise, Sir Galahad, and hey!' she cried as the marten scampered off into the grass.

The yellow-throated marten stopped and stood at the top of a little knoll. They could see his sleek and beautiful silhouette, his jaws and breast a white streak brilliant in the darkness. For a moment more he stared at them, outlined in moonlight...

Then Sir Galahad turned, slipped over the knoll, and vanished into the night.

'That was nice,' Trikaya told her sister, and called out, 'Good night, Sir Galahad!'

The whole group ambled up the road to town. They could hear Kumaoni music, its flutes and hard drums drifting into the night sky and out across the valley over the lake. The lights of the Festival twinkled and cast a general golden glow out into the night, warm and welcoming.

Kariba left them at the edge of Devagarh. 'We have our own Barbarika Festival,' she told her friends. 'They'll all be waiting for me. And I have to tell the Quiet Father what happened. I'll see you in a couple days, when I get some time!' The rakshasi skipped away back to Yakshagarh, waving over her shoulder.

They walked eagerly around the corner...and there was all of Devagarh, milling around excitedly, drinking chais and coffees, eating sweets and snacks, playing games, watching the performers. Rising above them all was the large colourful statue of a deva (they now knew) in a warrior's pose with the same huge mace and shield.

It was Mr Pillai who stumbled across them first, with Mrs Pillai and Jyoti walking arm in arm after. He had a paper hat on, and blew a big red party horn out when he saw them. 'There you are!' he exclaimed. 'They're here!' he called over the crowd, then nodded at the adults with them. 'Mademoiselle, and mister...?'

'Charles, Robert Charles,' Geoffrey Gordon introduced cheerily, shooting a meaningful glance at the children.

The other parents soon gathered, all of them in high spirits. Except, of course, Mr Idris. He stood over Safir and said, 'I saw you today, hotfooting it into town. Didn't I tell you explicitly that you were to stay at home?'

Isaac saw Trikaya's hands gather into frustrated fists, and the others tense up. It was Safir himself, however, who responded very simply, 'I had to go. Even though you told me. It was *that* important.'

The Brigadier stared at his son, startled. And then... shrugged. 'Well, I guess if it was that important, then you had to go.' He bent down and smiled into Safir's surprised face. 'I have to admire that kind of bravery in a man.' He leaned back up and eyed his son appraisingly. 'Are you taller than this afternoon?'

'What have you done with Safdar?' Mr Kandhari

demanded, grabbing the Brigadier by the collar. 'Who is this gentle giant you have replaced him with?'

'Speak, you freakishly good person!' Mr Pillai ordered, threatening Mr Idris with a jalebi.

Jyoti directed the bewildered Safir away from the jovial belligerents. 'Coffee and jalebis in excess,' she explained to the children. 'They do things to an adult's mind.'

Mademoiselle excused herself and slipped away, taking Mr Gordon with her, but the children hardly noticed. With the mothers there it was time for indulgence, and they soon had their hands full with premium treats from Bintu's.

They sat in a row on a low wall, sharing snacks off each other's plates. Dr Negi passed by and fiddled with all their throats and foreheads a moment, still stunned that they were up and about after such a bout of night fever. 'Never seen anything like it,' he muttered as he wandered off, medical bag in hand.

They saw Mrs Dangwal stroll through the crowd, Kumar Fourteen cradled in her arms. The children called out to him, Trikaya offering some of her snacks and singing, 'Milky-moo!' but the cat just frowned at them disdainfully.

When a howling began from the village, barely staying in rhythm with the sentimental instrumental music it accompanied, the children exchanged knowing grins and announced, 'Dobal.' The Constable had set up his karaoke and was pouring his soul out into song.

They hopped down from the low wall and began to make their way through the crowd, when Shari shot out an arm in warning.

Rudra, Ruma and Reva blocked their way, paper plates and cups in hand. The leader looked uncomfortable, but clearly wanted to say something to them. 'Hey,' he croaked. Reva nudged him, and he cleared his throat. 'I wanted to apologize. We don't know what happened, none of us were in control of what we were doing. It was like I was watching myself do these things from some other place. So…I'm sorry.'

'We're offering a truce,' Ruma said in a dull monotone, obviously a rehearsed speech. 'And I'm sorry too.'

Reva stepped forward and put out her hand. 'Truce?'

Iti was closest, so she took Reva's hand and shook it for them. 'Truce. How's your leg?'

The girl laughed awkwardly. 'It's fine, thanks. We all had a bit of fever this afternoon, after…' Ruma tugged at her elbow peevishly, and Reva sobered up. 'Okay, bye.'

R2R watched the six younger children walk away looking rather confounded by this most unexpected of interactions. 'Happy now?' Rudra growled at Reva. He rolled a wad of saliva onto his tongue and thwacked his spit out on the low wall in disgust.

'Apologizing to those little slugs…' Ruma sniffed, then shuffled close to the wall, frowning. 'Eww! Why's your spit green?'

The three youngsters bent down where that nasty glob of Rudra's spit hissed and popped. It *was* green, and grossly glutinous. A stinking acid smoke curled up as they watched it gnaw right through the solid stone in seconds, boring holes into the wall and making it look like Swiss cheese.

Reva and Ruma turned wide eyes to Rudra, whose mystified expression turned malicious. 'Cool…' he drawled. 'Let's go see what it does to other stuff.'

Away from their nemesis R2R, the six children gathered together, a little dazed. 'Well, that happened,' Safir announced.

'Should we take care of them?' Trikaya wondered. 'I'm sure Galahad wouldn't mind having another go at them.'

Tal put an arm around the girl's shoulder. 'They asked for a truce, Tri. We all need a little peace now anyway.'

'The piece I need right now is big, chocolate and chunky,' Shari growled.

Isaac stood on tiptoes, craning his neck to look over the crowd. 'Looks like we're going to get more peace than you can handle, Shari.'

The crowd seemed to be getting more and more excited, until everyone was clapping rhythmically. 'What's going on?' Shari asked anxiously, ready for Mister Mer, ghosts, or anything else.

Trikaya had clambered straight up onto a plastic table to peep over the heads of the crowd. 'It's Mademoiselle!' she yelled, and then roared, 'It's *cake!*'

There were four carts in a row coming from Dharm Square into Bazaar Round, drawn by beautiful bullocks that stepped along with graceful intelligence. Mademoiselle sat perched on the foremost one, waving and smiling broadly at everyone. The carts were brightly decorated, festooned with red ribbons and brass bells that rang merrily. And on each cart was a thick bowl of solid chocolate a metre wide, filled to the brim with rich chocolate cake, chocolate mousse, strawberry compote, and crunchy nougat.

The sound from the crowd was reaching a height of frenzy as Mademoiselle nimbly sprang off the water buffalo and cut the first slice. 'In honour of Barbarika and his father Ghatotkacha, I present to you...Gateau-tkacha!' The crowd cheered, and Mademoiselle began serving with the help of her assistants and Mr Gordon.

The Englishman soon came to find the children, carrying a covered tray. 'Special order from the Wolf Queen.' He pulled back the pink cloth to reveal personal servings of Gateau-tkacha: six traditional-looking pots with a wide body and a narrow mouth, made entirely out of carved chocolate.

Six pairs of hands reached out impatiently to grab the pots. 'I almost don't want to eat it,' Trikaya murmured, eyeing the exquisitely crafted cake, and hastily emphasized, 'Almost!'

Mr Gordon left the yaksha Kings and Queens to their just desserts and went back to help Mademoiselle. The children wandered in a single file through the raucous crowd, looking for a quiet place to eat. They made their way around the corner of Bintu's and sat together just off the road out of Devagarh.

Before them the hill sloped away along the path to the Lodge and towards Shari's bridge, and thence to Yakshagarh, the haunted village, and the Black Kot. As they settled down on the grass, Isaac looked at his new friends. He hadn't known any of them yesterday, and now they were closer to him than anyone he had ever met. They were like family, he thought. No, he amended after a moment, they *were* family. Safir had revealed how all of them were tied back to Devagarh. Isaac was actually related to Iti and Trikaya, like distant cousins several times removed. And going even further back, they were all linked. Family... Isaac basked in that feeling for long seconds, that warm, fulfilling feeling of not being alone anymore.

'Not hungry?' Tal asked Isaac, breaking his dreaming.

He fiddled with his pot awkwardly. 'No, I am, just...just some random thoughts.'

They all got into their Gateau-tkacha, and for many minutes the air resounded with the noise of lips smacking, moans of delight, and grateful benedictions pronounced for the existence of Mademoiselle Fulara and her baking hand.

'The question I still have in my mind,' Tal declared once they were all sitting back, 'is: shouldn't the KSS get paid for this job?' Protesting groans came up. Why would she bring up this subject again, right now? 'I'm just saying, are there any honorariums involved in saving Devagarh and Yakshagarh?'

Everyone looked back and forth from her to Shari. Lying on his back with his knees up, he shrugged and said, 'I guess… maybe…we could ask for an increase in our allowance?'

'Allowance?' Tal cried, flapping the knees of her crossed legs in exasperation. 'We're the Midnight King! We stopped Mister Mer! Maybe there should be, I don't know, a yaksha hero tax or something?'

Iti yanked Tal by her sleeve and back onto the grass to shut her up. They rolled over, giggling, and everyone wriggled around until all six of them were lying side by side.

'So are we back together?' Trikaya called out the question on everyone's mind. 'The True and the Real KSS?'

'Yes sir,' Shari said immediately, putting his hand out.

'Yes ma'am!' Tal countered, grabbing and shaking his hand firmly.

'Finally!' Trikaya hollered, and leaped to slap her hand on top.

Iti and Safir pounced up to grab the hand pile. The five paused, waiting, and then turned to their newest member.

Isaac grinned and smacked his hand on top of theirs.

Tal announced, 'Look out Devagarh, we are re-formed!'

And they raised their six voices to echo to the hills: 'The Kumaon Secret Society!'